Sweet Scripts
Book I

NIBURU CHILD

Musings of a Creative Expressionist

A Collection of Short Stories and Sweet Scripts

By
Michael Yaeger

authorHOUSE™

1663 Liberty Drive, Suite 200
Bloomington, Indiana 47403
(800) 839-8640
www.AuthorHouse.com

First published by AuthorHouse 11/30/04

ISBN: 1-4184-9158-6 (sc)

Printed in the United States of America
Bloomington, Indiana

This book is printed on acid-free paper.

Previous books by the author:
Squim – the Untold Story
The Dahlia Connection
An Insider's Tour of the Pike Place Market
Things from the North Arcade

This book is dedicated
to the memory of
Brian Dunn
a friend, confidant, scholar
and, above all, a gentleman

(6/24/46 – 6/8/03)

Contents

Introduction

My writing has been called visual (and descriptive) and rightfully so, because much of it was written for possible screen and TV projects.

I studied writing in college and began with poems (see EPILOGUE) – but actually I came to my writing style through my acting career. Funny, my most "influential" performance was a stint at acting out American slang for English language students at an international language school in Rome in the very early 1970s. I came full circle back to writing through this experience. (There is no way to explain slang other than by acting. Slang like "Hit the road, Jack" or "Let's run it up the flagpole and see which way the wind blows.")

My expertise proved timely because film production was shifting back to Hollywood and thus, within just a few years, I became a story editor in London specializing in Americanizing European screenplays.

Joe Janni, the London producer I worked for, was moving his base of operations to Los Angeles and I was to work with him there. But poor Joe had a heart attack and had to retire. (He had produced many famous films: *Darling, Far from the Madding Crowd, Poor Cow, Alfie*, and a slew of others.)

In preparation, I had moved to Seattle to raise my family with the intention of commuting south to help Joe shape his film projects. By then, I was deep into writing and quickly understood how big TV was becoming, so I hunkered down to learn to write teleplays. I wrote several on spec for "Laverne and Shirley," "Murder, She Wrote," and two series of my own: a live action kids TV show called "Pioneer Kids," and "Great Expectations," a talking heads situation comedy set in Seattle's Pike Place Market. (Several episodes of "Great Expectations" aired on Seattle's Public Access channel. (See "A Hydro Racer Cages His Morning Coffee.")

In the near future, several of these works will be published in my "Sweet Scripts" series.

Writing for TV was a hell of a learning curve: "Pioneer Kids" came the closest to becoming a mainline TV show with several studios interested in it. The project was shot down, however, when actor Vic Morrow and two child actors were killed on location while making a film. No more live action kid projects in the States. Even so, "Pioneer Kids" was considered with "Danger Bay" at Disney. "Danger Bay" got the nod because it was set outside the U.S. (in the Vancouver, B.C. area), and was partially financed by the Canadian government.

The writing bug deepened through the years. I wrote for newspapers and magazines. Short stories and political commentary and many "Sweet Scripts" as possible film productions. I use the term "sweet script," because again, my writing is visual. I wanted a first draft of a screenplay I was submitting to be read like a story, thinking someone was more likely to read it in that form. (See "Mio Campo.")

This book is a sampling from well over a hundred rarely read stories. Enjoy.

Once upon a time…

I
The Power of Rust
(Of Zen and old Ferryboats)

Socially, the 1920s and '30s bohemia world influenced the 1950s beatniks who, in turn, had a profound effect on the hippies of the '60s. From hippie to yippie to today's mainstream society, this social chain is commonly accepted as a major U.S. cultural movement. Where this chain was fused, link by link, was aboard the retired ferryboat "Vallejo."

Since the turn of the century, Richardson's Bay, in Marin County, California, just across the Golden Gate Bridge, has been a haven for floating homes of all sorts. At the end of World War II, when the Marin shipyard was abandoned, a dynamic new era of houseboat living began. The Yard, built over what was Waldo Point just west of Sausalito, was left filled with wartime surplus including a flotilla of obsolete metal barges that used to anchor anti-air attack balloons of the type we see clustered over harbors in old war flicks. The balloons were secured by cables to the voluminous metal barges, which had to be quite sturdy to withstand the fickle elements.

In the late '40s and early '50s, touristic Sausalito, which somewhat resembled an Amalfi coastal town, supported a small underground artist/ political movement that started to grow; first, because the mudflats of the abandoned shipyard offered refuge to the prototype "new bohemian." And, secondly, because the cheap and plentiful balloon barges made a perfect platform from whence to build houseboats. Soon, a fantastic jazzlike community rose like a Jackson Pollock painting where every type of floating object was put into service to create catwalks, studios, and living quarters. Walking through the "town" was like being inside a Charlie Parker improve, a kaleidoscope of color and rhythm formed by resurrected landing ships, wheezy old tugs, barges and the odd Chris Craft. Three retired ferries were brought in and nudged into the sludge to become recycled cathedrals in honor of the individual (or maybe Count Bomarzo – because the huge edifices only floated at high tide, while at low tide they rested in the sludge and the decks were often at such angles that one felt tipsy just walking on them).

The West Coast workingman's houseboat communities from Lake Union and the Duwamish in Seattle, to the Willamette River in Portland, and just below Long Beach harbor down south, watched their sister community on Richardson's Bay radically transform into a sophisticated social experiment, fueled not by the traditional idealistic working class comrades but by their spiritual sons and daughters, contemporary utopians, cut from the same mold but with new visions to explore. An interesting magnetic fix was the name Waldo Point, which suggested the idealism of another era popularized by the experiments at Walden Pond by Thoreau, Ralph Waldo Emerson's young charge. (Ironically, Walden Pond still exists, while the actual Waldo Point was dredged out of existence around 1914 to make way for the construction of the shipyard.)

Meanwhile, flamboyant artist Jean Varda, a celebrated member of the bohemian world centered in Paris, followed his close friend Henry Miller to Big Sur. (It was said that the prodigious Varda was the only artist who had painted more pictures than Pablo Picasso – another one of his close friends.) The colorful Varda or "Yanko" (Uncle), as he was called, moved up to Sausalito where he, artist Gordon Onslow Ford and architect Forest Wright, went looking for suitable digs. Their search led them to a scrapyard on Sausalito's waterfront, where Gordon purchased the ferryboat Vallejo.

At the scrapyard, several dilapidated ferries were tied to the quay, brought there for dismantling. They had serviced the military bases on islands in upper San Francisco Bay and San Pablo Bay but now were considered surplus scrap. According to her documents, the Vallejo had a wooden hull, thus was dirt cheap – in other words, the right price – so the deal was struck and the trio went down to the dock to accept their purchase. Berthed next to the Vallejo was the more costly, metal-hulled "City of Seattle." It was well understood at Sausalito that metal hulls, like the balloon barges, were far better suited for settling into the muck at Waldo Point. Legend has it that the trio switched nameplates with the City of Seattle and had their prize quickly undertow. She was berthed by the old West Gate or east end of the shipyard. Shortly, the car deck was transformed into three apartments and with the trio thus ensconced, the "Vallejo" quickly became the pulsating heart of the colorful floating home community.

The "legend" can be disputed because the Vallejo actually had a metal hull that was covered in wood. But the switching of the nameplates was revealed to me by people who should know. The original documents of the Vallejo don't match up with the actual vessel. They match the configuration of the ferry now called the City of Seattle. This is verifiable because the City of Seattle (or the old Vallejo) was saved from the scrapyard as well, and is presently docked at the "elegant" west end of the Waldo Point community. More on this later.

In the late '50s, Varda became the unofficial patriarch of Waldo Point, not so much because he was older than his associates and neighbors and harked from the earlier bohemian era, but rather because of his colorful paintings, his entourage of beautiful women, and especially for his bacchanalian parties frequented by every type of social cast and outcast. Such luminaries as Allen Ginsberg and Jack Kerouac were frequent guests and eager listeners of Yanko's stories of his bohemian past.

After a few years, Gordon Onslow Ford moved onshore and the celebrated Zen philosopher Alan Watts moved into the apartment next to Varda's. Alan was a wild esthetic, a spiritual hedonist, so to speak. A kind of spiritual soul mate – a contrast to the earthy, celebratory Varda. Alan's study and practice of Zen and of exploring the universal spirituality had a profound influence on many people. He died in 1973, but his legacy is alive in his numerous essays and books. (The Alan Watts Society owned the Vallejo for a while.)

I attended a couple of Varda's parties in the early '60s and vividly remember the joyful madness. Over twenty years later, in 1986, I retraced my brief moments aboard the Vallejo. Peter Kraemer, the present tenant of the Varda pad, led me aboard at the Watts apartment. I hadn't known that Alan Watts had lived there and was completely baffled because the place was so plain and elegantly simple (befitting a man of Zen). Peter told me about Alan as he led me to a little trap door that entered into Varda's kitchen. He revealed that years ago the door didn't exist, but another secret door existed between the two apartments. It opened into Varda's bedroom -- once there, the world of Varda as I remembered it exploded through my senses. The joy and gaiety are still there, for in honor of Varda very little has been changed. The earlier trap door, as with the existing one, was a link between two totally different realities. As I think Alan Watts would have agreed, this was an example of a Zen yin/yang situation. (His apartment, like Varda's, is preserved and looks like it did when he lived there.)

During the '50s, as Peter Kraemer was growing up, he would accompany his artist mother aboard the Vallejo and for several years was exposed to her heady world filled with fantastic personalities of the beatnik era. Later, in the early '60s, he entered the University of San Francisco, in the Haight-Ashbury section of the city, and quickly got involved in the new ideas that were being discussed on and off the campus. He took up the guitar as well as experimented with prototype light shows. With his rich knowledge of art, poetry, jazz, drugs, and access to the underground movers and shakers of the period, he quickly became a leader. Shortly, he formed one of the first "psychedelic" rock groups, the "Sopwith Camel," originally at Virginia City, Nevada. The "Camel" was the prototype acid rock group that defined the style around which the identity of the hippie generation of Haight-Ashbury evolved. The hippies, in turn, influenced and changed the Beatles puppy love shleppy first offerings into a deeper musical experience, starting with the *Rubber Soul* and *Revolver* albums. This "new" sound reverberated with the bohemian spirit that was absorbed by Peter aboard the Vallejo and passed on to a whole generation that has matured and is now a major part of mainstream culture today. The Vallejo provided the environment for this to happen. Not bad for a spent derelict just barely saved from the scrap heap.

Today she is in worse shape than ever, with her once-sturdy metal hull rusting through just above the water line in enough places to cast a glimmer of daylight over the thoroughly rusted Pittman engine. Her decks and gunnels are in need of very major repair. To the east and north, below her shabby but still graceful contours bob sterile plastic sailboats moored in straight arrow lines that seem to pen the old ferry in. To the west floats the stalwart houseboat community, now with formal docking, electricity and sewerage.

Atop the Vallejo this colorful world can be fully appreciated with the fantastic Christopher Roberts-designed houseboats looming over the others. (Unfortunately, his masterpiece, the massive Madonna and Child creation, burned down.)

Looking west over the community, one can barely see the tall smokestack of the City of Seattle, perhaps the real Vallejo bobbing ungainly on her barge – her wooden hull having rotted away long ago. She is very well kept up, prim and proper, in contrast to the forgotten Vallejo. It's been suggested that the torch has been passed to her, and that she is now the flagship of the future. West of her a new style of houseboat grouping has been built. Ones that reflect her primness; in other words, designer-built.

There's nothing out of place over there; the owners make sure it's that way by keeping their walkways locked! That's not the spirit of Waldo Point. What do they fear? Fear was never a part of this community! (Another sad development affects the live-aboards who went out in Richardson's Bay to anchor and live a peaceful life. They are now threatened by proposed legislation that would force them out of the Bay completely.)

Sadly, the community's spirit seems to have gotten a bit diffused of purpose after Varda died in 1971. Back in the '60s, he was crowned the King of the community and on New Year's Eve he would embark from the Vallejo and lead a flotilla of some of the most wildly decorated craft ever seen around the Bay. The spirit appears to be just a memory. Oh, the community has honored Varda all right, calling the mud where the Vallejo is berthed "Varda Landing," but they ignore the mother lode, the old ferry. She is the one they should honor. Varda was just one of her offspring!

Today, Sausalito has more than prospered. Richardson's Bay has attracted a whole new generation of successful people nurtured and schooled by concepts of freedom and celebration acted out on her decks. (Literally, for Marian Saltman also lived for a while aboard her; she was a prime innovator of adult games that have also had a profound effect on our culture.) These new Sausalitans should understand and appreciate the contributions of this old ferryboat, the Vallejo/City of Seattle, and preserve her.

Peter and some of the concerned people who have lived through these epochal times discuss ways to restore her. They revealed the switched nameplate caper to me and showed me the ships' documents because they had the impression that Seattle people preserve their ferryboat heritage. In other words, to their way of thinking, if the people of Seattle realized that the Vallejo was actually the City of Seattle, then maybe Puget Sounders would help pay for her restoration and upkeep. (I was amazed – they should see the condition of our stately San Mateo ferry that was in Lake Union and was spirited away by Canadians at night. Or comprehend the exile of our beloved Kalakala! Not to mention the struggle live-aboards are having across from the city in Eagle Harbor to maintain their lifestyle!)

Still, I would love to be totally convinced that the Vallejo, the mothership of our contemporary society and a core icon of the wild, celebratory, bawdy San Francisco Bay area, is in reality the City of Seattle (named after the neat and prim Scandinavian-souled Queen City of the Northwest!). Because, yet again, this is another example of the yin/yang principle of Zen harmony that Alan Watts searched for. Perhaps he knew of the switched nameplate, and understood the significance of the many ironies of this wonderful ferryboat. For her real secret is she is a living example that the power of opposites, existing in harmony with each other, can influence and literally transform whole cultures.

UPDATE: 2003

I just visited the Vallejo and learned that Peter Kraemer returned to Virginia City, and that the Vallejo is now a condo. Varda's and Watts's apartments are gone. Richardson's Bay will never be the same.

Once upon a time…

II
Birds of a Feather
(Venezia present-day)

First: Some history

Between 350 and 550 A.D., Aquileia, the elegant Roman provincial capital of Veneto, was repeatedly sacked by barbarians from the north. The survivors moved to islands deep in the Venetian Lagoon centered at Torcello. Torcello swelled to a population of twenty thousand and was the main city of the area until Venice was created less than ten kilometers south. The rest, as they say, is history.

A powerful link to this bygone era is the time-softened throne of Attila the Hun squatting in a courtyard filled with statues and sculpture remnants as time-worn as the throne itself.

Torcello, with a present population of less than twenty, is wrapped in a compelling solitude that is in sharp contrast to nearby Venice. Through the years, this solitude has been broken by "new barbarians," spiritual sons of Attila, who come in small groups to pay homage to his throne. These men are mostly in their forties and fifties, successful in their fields, and with families. But, when they come to Torcello, they raise a little innocent, old-fashioned Cain, and wear helmets with horns, just like those worn by the Huns, their spiritual ancestors.

Present-Day Venice

Giulietta Pond, thirty-three, lost her dance career when she severely twisted her ankle while shopping along the San Barnabas canal in Dorsoduro. Slated to perform at La Fenice – her big break – she instead had to spend three years rehabilitating her ankle. Though she now walks, she does so with a limp and pain if she has to stand for any length of time. She met Fernando Beckman during rehabilitation and she and the tall, remote Anglo-Italian industrialist quickly became lovers.

Fernando and a group of his "lodge associates" come to Venice once a year to "honor" Attila the Hun by visiting his throne at Torcello. Giulietta affectionately calls them "Huns," because they all claim descent, either actual or spiritual, from Attila and his times. For the last two years, Giulietta, in her new career as tour organizer, has been arranging this annual gathering for Fernando. Mr. Beckman has chosen to attend this latest reunion by arriving on his private yacht, the *MV Riga*. Giulietta is directing the gathering from the Riga, docked at Burano. Maria, her able assistant, is arranging the details from Giulietta's elegant office apartment complex in Cannaregio.

Fernando has invited and paid for eighty-seven guests, by far the largest group that Giulietta has had to deal with on such a personal level. To make matters worse, she is finding herself further distracted by Fernando's having asked for her hand in marriage. The worldly Giulietta, although intrigued, wrestles with his offer. "Why at this time?" Doubt permeates her personal and professional life. She must focus doubly hard to pull off the event: "Me? Raised on the streets of Trestavere to be the wife of Fernando? Birds of a feather?" She recalls that Fernando's mother, Mia, was a Ligurian chambermaid and his father, "King Fred," was the king of all the dart rooms in all the English pubs in San Remo. "Birds of a feather." She laughs as she remembers Fernando explaining that his father was an Anglicized Pole who bragged that his lineage could be traced to King Attila himself. She recalls the anger in Fernando's eyes when he mentioned his father's "political" disappearance when he was ten.

Recently, Giulietta had gained the derisive title of "Queen of Mass Tourism," because she was accused of opening up the Serenissima to large-scale package tour groups. The real reason for this ridicule was her success as a woman in a male-dominated industry. (The controversy was inflamed by rumors that pointed the finger at her for pushing mass tourism beyond San Marco and San Polo to the other Sestieri.)

The small groups of "Huns" she brings to Venice three or four times a year are a different matter. They are welcomed by Venetians, who love their playfulness, their convoluted sense of history and, of course, as has been the case throughout the centuries, their money.

For this gathering, she has arranged everything first-class: "It must have cost Fernando a fortune." She has contracted the services of the "Marco Polo," a large, fast "motoscafo" to transport the group from the airport to their hotels and to Torcello. They stay at the most expensive hotels, centered near Piazza San Marco. The most sought-after rooms are at the Bauer Grunwald, followed by The Danielle, and their multistar kin. This time, however, six of the group have complicated her planning by specifically choosing a little-known three-star hotel called the Bisanzio, located further along the Riva Dei Schiavoni.

Giulietta is perplexed by this request until Fernando blandly explains to her that the hotel is dear to them because it is named after Byzantium, the city that became Constantinople, and which was recaptured by Crusaders outfitted by Venetians early in the Middle Ages – Crusaders who, for the most part, came from the north. In this way, the six were honoring this historical event.

Giulietta notices that the six are very close to Fernando, even though they are professional men easily ten years younger than he and decidedly middle-class. Included are Lars Schmidt, a doctor; brothers Peter and Joachim Burt, both lawyers; John Thompson, a chef; and two administrators, one in government (Gregory Aimes), and Nico Brahms, an official at Citroën Austria. Again, Giulietta perceives their close association with the Mayfair-based Fernando, a sleek billionaire industrialist, as odd.

The main event for this gathering is a picnic she has arranged in the "piazza" at Torcello, where Attila's throne sits. She has hired the staff of the "Restaurant of Attila," a popular trattoria on Torcello, to cater the picnic. The event is being held under a huge, ornate, Bedouin-style tent provided by Fernando. The expensive foods and wines being served were brought to Torcello from the cargo holds of the Riga, docked at the island of Burano, five hundred meters away.

As our story unfolds, Giulietta becomes aware that this gathering is somehow different, but she is too busy overseeing the event to think it through. It doesn't help that Fernando spends a lot of time at the Bisanzio. Aboard the Riga, she notices that a Burano fishing boat, the *Nina*, has taken the place of the *Rigalita I*, one of the two sleek launches that act as tenders to the Riga. The sturdy craft, which has been revamped and fitted with a radio and tall antenna, looks oddly out of place on its cradle next to the *Rigalita II.*

During an inventory check, she notices a small forklift strapped down in the hold. Her inquiring mind compels her to read the papers attached to it which state that it was picked up in Trieste a week earlier. That evening, she asks Fernando about the Nina, and Fernando laughingly tells her that he wants to use it in the future when he returns to Torcello. "Why don't you use it this time?" she asks. He scoffs: "My dear Giulietta, my Roman love. What is this, another inquisition? I saw the Nina and fell in love with her last year. That's all." She blurts out in a laugh: "And the forklift from Trieste, plopped so voluptuously among the cases of champagne and proseccio and Parma hams and the expensive gull eggs, you fell in love with that too, eh? (She punches him playfully.) In Trieste, just before arriving? Darling Fernando, I know you're a lover, but I'm jealous now of the Nina and what's her name?" Fernando is confused: "Who?" She laughs: "What is the name of the forklift?" She gives him a big kiss. They go to bed.

On Torcello, the morning of the feast, Giulietta is once again puzzled as she observes Fernando joining the Bisanzio group, which had arrived in a water taxi before the others. They exchange pleasantries with Giulietta; then Fernando leads them on a tour of the tiny town. Later, as she waits for the Marco Polo to arrive, she notices them walking through what appears to be a set pattern – like a rehearsal, she thinks. She tries to listen in, but they are speaking some Eastern European language that she doesn't understand. The Marco Polo arrives and the other eighty "Huns" disembark, each carrying a large day bag.

Fernando takes his place sitting at the head of the picnic tables, next to Attila's throne. When all are seated, he rises and states: "Gentlemen, shall we begin."

In unison, all eighty-six pull from their bags heavy metal-horned helmets, the same as their spiritual ancestors wore fifteen hundred years ago. As they solemnly put on their helmets, the mood of the gathering shifts. It's as if mental chains were broken. The group becomes more animated and expansive in their gestures and speech. The feast is an instant success, with the men taking turns having their pictures taken seated on the throne.

Fernando is offered a toast by Lars: "Dear Fernando, a toast for keeping the spirit of Attila alive. And for making it possible that we could all attend and honor our forebears in such rustic elegance. (He grasps his goblet and moves his outstretched arm in an arc around the tent. He stops at the church.) To you, sublime church, the link to the ancients. To your revealing frescoes, to your respository of history and timelessness. For that is where we live, gentlemen, in timelessness. (He turns to the throne.)

To you, dear Attila. To your eternity. To all of us. Salute! And to you again, Fernando, we salute you!"

The group salutes by chanting: "To you, Fernando; to you, Attila; to you, Fernando; to you, Attila!" Fernando walks slowly to the throne and sits down. Giulietta notices the deep, satisfied gleam rise up in Fernando's eyes. She smiles openly at his "triumph." A huge cheer rises from the group.

Lars is exuberant as he continues: "And, to this glorious day. Will the future turn to the past glory? We shall see. That I guarantee you, friends. (He pulls a sheet of paper out of his pocket and reads.) We are from all over the world. The spiritual heirs of Attila. From Austria [a contingent of Austrians claps]; from England [more isolated clapping]; from the U.S.A. [more claps]; from Russia, Latvia, Poland, Japan [two Japanese nationals stand up and are cheered]; and from Germany, Switzerland, Spain, Lombardy, and even Roma herself." Several men rise and hold their helmets aloft. The group stands in unison and starts chanting, "Hail, Attila! Hail, Attila!"

Lars, even more exuberant, continues where he left off: "We are a nucleus for a world movement, and I guarantee you, friends, after tomorrow…" (The microphone is grabbed by Fernando, who deftly derails Lars' atavistic euphoria.) "Tomorrow. Tomorrow belongs to you, my lads. Tomorrow we will return to our homelands recharged, refreshed, bathed in this moment. Enjoy yourself and have good cheer." He hands the mike to the more sober Peter, who leads the group in a series of "For He's a Jolly Good Fellow," directed at Fernando.

The party continues deep into the evening. Giulietta notices that more champagne is needed, nods to her assistant, Maria, and the job is done.

At the end of the festivities, the well-lubricated group boards the Marco Polo. Giulietta does a head count and finds six are missing. She finds Fernando and tells him. Fernando edgily assures her that they had left earlier by water taxi since they had early flights to their homes. As the Marco Polo leaves, Giulietta scans the group and realizes the six are Lars and the others who are staying at the Bisanzio. Though about to go aboard as planned, she decides to stay. She waves to Maria: "You take it from here. I have things to work out." The boat leaves, swallowed by the embracing fog.

As the fog thickens, the tender Rigalita II enters the channel leading to the center of Torcello. Several boat lengths behind her chugs the Nina with the forklift and the Bisanzio group aboard. Before entering the channel, the Nina backs off, as planned, and stays hidden in the thickening fog behind the log pilings. On board, Lars looks at his watch. They wait.

The Rigalita II docks. Fernando is talking with the caterers and has just given them a huge tip. All are grateful. Fernando sees the enveloping fog and says, "Best get back to the boat quickly." He is about to get in when Giulietta appears out of the fog. Fernando masks his anger by putting on a stern demeanor. He stumbles over his thoughts. "My guests... some of them have drunk too much. They need you."

"Maria can handle them," she answers.

"Well, we'd best get back," Fernando curtly states. They climb aboard the tender and head for the Riga. Fernando notices that Giulietta is worried and deftly reassures her: "It is no problem. Remember, the Riga is just five hundred meters away."

Giulietta looks back at where Torcello has disappeared in the fog as the skillful deckhands follow the beeping of the radio from the Riga. They pass close by several of the upright log booms lashed tightly together by iron straps. The log booms act as channel guides, but impish Giulietta bursts out with a bitter laugh as they pass a particularly suggestive coupling, "Looks more like a bunch of phalli to me." Fernando smirks and throws his shoulders back: "Like a bond, like a brotherhood."

She quips: "Like a bunch of Huns hung up on each other." He ignores her bitterness as the massive bulk of the Riga takes shape in the fog.

Back at the channel, the six from Bisanzio silently pole their way up the channel in the Nina. The fog is now thick and their arrival is not noticed. They move past where the Marco Polo had docked to another small private landing close by.

Back at the MV Riga, Giulietta is restless. Her Roman mind is working overtime trying to weave the loose strands of coincidence into a reality. Her efforts crystallize when she walks aft and discovers that the Nina is not on board. She goes below decks and sees that the forklift is also gone. Then it dawns on her: Fernando and the six who are staying at the Bisanzio are attempting to steal the throne of Attila.

She rushes back to the cabin she has been sharing with Fernando. He's not there. After a brief, frantic search, she finds him in the radio room and confronts him. He laughs, denies everything, and adds that it's not such a bad idea: "At least it would be in a proper setting – back where Attila came from. Protected from the elements. Yes, Giulietta. Maybe not such a bad idea at all. One thing, though, that perplexes me about your idea. Why does one steal when one can just take?"

She looks at him, speechless. She understands what he is saying – and asking – of her: Is she with him or not? It is up to her. Her silence forces Fernando to demand that she return to their cabin. He explains that something important has come up that he must attend to. She leaves, but quickly returns, demanding to be told the truth. Even though she has guessed it, she wants to hear it from him. Fernando insists that she return to her cabin and think, "…to be logical, like a good Roman." She refuses to leave. The chief mate escorts her back to her cabin and locks her in.

On Torcello, the townspeople have retired for the night. The ornate tent billows ominously in the slight wind. Under it sits the throne of Attila.

Through the fence bordering the piazza, we see Lars peering in and giving a hand signal behind himself to Peter, who in turn repeats it to his brother, Joachim. The process is repeated until all have the signal to move forward. At the Nina, Gregory activates the silent electric-powered forklift and drives it up the ramp and down the path, which is lined with ancient, time-worn statues that glint palely in the shrouding fog.

Shortly, the forklift emerges from the gate that Lars has opened. The six circle the throne, wearing their helmets and shouldering long wrecking bars.

After a moment of silence, they go to work, wedging their bars under the throne and prying it up from the rear, creating just enough space for the forklift to work its tines under its mass. They grunt and groan as they slowly work the throne onto the forklift. Once it's on, they attempt to lift it, but find that the throne is heavier than the forklift. They are in a quandary until Lars figures it out. All six of the "Huns" then clamber aboard the forklift and the weight of the throne is counterbalanced. Slowly, through the fog, the throne, with a halo of helmeted Huns, makes its way down the long, statue-bordered path to the canal and the waiting Nina.

Aboard the Riga Giulietta is furious at her treatment and tries to get out of her cabin. Failing in that attempt, she pulls out her cell phone and calls 112. After several rings, the sleepy voice of Antonio, on duty at the Burano police station, answers: "Pronto?"

Giulietta tries to explain that the Huns are stealing Attila's throne. She only manages to confuse Antonio, who assumes she is drunk. She has an idea and tells Antonio they have already killed six people who were staying at the Hotel Bisanzio. "It's late. Check the hotel and see if they are there."

Upon hearing of killings, Antonio decides to call the Questura at Venice. A sleepy Raphaelo answers and becomes just as confused when Antonio gives his convoluted report. Raphaelo calls the Bisanzio and finds that indeed the men are not in their rooms. He notices on his duty roster the name of Fernando Beckman and realizes he is a very important person whose well-being is assigned to Commandante Vero himself, so he decides to bite the bullet and calls Vero at his Lido home.

The sleeping Vero irritably answers. When Raphaelo explains the situation, Vero scratches his bristled face and mutters to himself: "What is this?" Rosa, his wife, is awake and asks: "What's wrong?" Vero answers questioningly: "Someone at Burano called in and said six people were killed trying to steal the throne of Attila." Rosa snorts: "Get back to bed. Somebody is having fun with you." Vero mumbles to himself: "Can this possibly be?" He tells Raphaelo that he will deal with this personally. He hangs up and checks his phone book and finds Fernando's phone number on the Riga and prepares to dial. Rosa stops him: "Be sensible. No one would want to steal the throne of Attila, much less die for it. It's not a Tintoretto." Frustrated, Vero explains: "But… but Mr. Beckman is a close friend of mine. He… he's a lover of Venice and has helped in many restorations. Who would spread a rumor like that?" Rosa snorts sarcastically: "Well, if you're really such a good friend of his, then call him. It's only three in the morning." Vero, half-dressed, silently agrees: "If he is in any danger on my watch…" He gets on the cell phone to Antonio at Burano and tells him: "I'll handle this myself. I'll be at the Riga in ten minutes by helicopter. Stay out of it." He rushes out into the night, sees the fog, and swears. He jumps into the cockpit of his chopper, the Andiamo, and starts the turbines.

At Burano, Antonio sits at his desk, frustrated, then has an idea. He will check it out for himself. He races down to the canal, jumps into his small outboard, fires it up and heads for Torcello.

Aboard the Riga, Fernando and "Sparks," his radioman, are deep in concentration, listening to the signal from the Nina confirming that the throne is on its way to the Riga.

The Nina is dangerously overloaded as they move cautiously through the dense fog and down the silted channel, making sure that they stay in the center. The Nina plows through the water, with only an inch or two of freeboard.

At the other end of the canal, after a lifetime of fishing the waters with his father, Antonio enters by instinct. He hears the throb of the Nina's engine but can't see her because of the fog. As the sound gets closer, he turns on the powerful spotlight he would normally use for fishing. The Nina emerges out of the fog like an apparition from hell. The six "Huns" are still wearing their helmets. They instinctively raise their forearms to shield their eyes from the spotlight's glare.

In an instant, the heavy Nina plows into the outboard, forcing it against the wall and hurling Antonio into the water. It is so silted he doesn't go under, but sinks deeply in the muck. He flops around as the silt's suction on his legs causes him to lose his balance. He pulls out his service revolver and blindly fires several shots into the gloom in the direction of the Nina.

On board the Nina, one of Antonio's bullets hits Joachim in the back. He slumps over the throne, his blood spilling over the while marble. Lars attends to him while John monitors the radio signals. The Riga is barely two hundred meters in front of them.

Fernando hears the loud buzz of the helicopter so, as planned in case of an emergency, they stop the beeps – the signal for the Nina to shut down and wait. Vero lands the helicopter, shuts off the rotor, steps down, stiffens his posture, and heads smartly up the gangway.

On board, Fernando sees the helicopter and quickly directs the chief mate to free Giulietta from the cabin. Fernando and Giulietta meet the Commandante, who nods curtly to Giulietta but directs his interest to Fernando. Fernando wears a disarming smile: "Perhaps the good Commandante will come into the warmth and comfort of my cabin and explain why he has honored us with his visit. Giulietta, please join us."

Inside the cabin, Fernando introduces Giulietta: "Commandante, this is Giulietta Pond..." Vero realizes that this is the person who made the accusations to Antonio: "I understand you're the queen of the mass tourism that's overwhelming Venice. Pond is your last name, right? You're not Italian, are you? Where are the six men who are staying at the Bisanzio?"

She ignores Vero's arrogance and mentally prepares to deal with him on her own terms, and repair the consequences of her impulsiveness in calling 112.

Vero continues: "I received a call that six men have been killed." Fernando intervenes, laughing: "The men you speak of are out drinking. They left by boat. They are as close to me as you are, Commandante Vero. (He looks sardonically at Giulietta) Giulietta has worked very hard organizing our event. She is very tired, Commandante. Besides which, I have complicated her life. Commandante, you are the first to know, I have asked Giulietta to be my wife." Giulietta is silent.

Vero stammers: "I... I didn't know. This is indeed an honor. I'm sorry I said... I... I didn't know."

Fernando confides: "Don't worry about what you said about her, but be forewarned: she is pure Trastevere. She can be a tiger. My proposal is to be kept a secret. So please, Commandante, keep it to yourself until the official announcement. And if the good Commandante would be so kind as to give my bride-to-be a lift home to Cannaregio, I will pay the cost of the inconvenience. And Commandante, the idea of someone stealing Attila's throne. Come on! Perhaps someone should take the throne and clean and store it. Now that is not such a bad idea, no?"

Again Vero stammers: "'Ah… yes… yes… you are right, the throne should be treated more honorably." Fernando looks deeply into the Commandante's eyes: "You will give this a first priority, will you not? I will pay all expenses." The Commandante salutes Fernando. Giulietta doesn't say a thing. Fernando gives her hand to the heel-clicking Commandante. Vero says: "This is indeed a great honor." He leads her to his helicopter.

As the Andiamo is fired up, Fernando hurries back up to the radio room to join Sparks and resume the beeps directing the Nina back to the Riga.

Meanwhile, with the motor turned off, the Nina had drifted out of the channel, passing a set of pilings dimly illuminated by the frail beam of their lone flashlight. When John starts the engine and attempts to get back into the channel, he misjudges the distance to the pilings and brushes against them. The Nina wobbles, water splashes inside, but the craft moves forward. They are not so lucky with the next set of pilings, hitting it squarely and wedging the prow deep into the three cabled-together pilings. The crash jars Joachim, who is still alive and being attended to by Lars.

On board the Riga, Fernando and Sparks listen to John explain what happened and tell them that the pilings are marked "Number Three." A map of the area is laid out and Fernando pinpoints their location barely one hundred meters away. The Rigalita II is lowered to the water to help rescue the Nina.

Hovering above in the Andiamo, Vero turns toward Venice. Giulietta, sitting next to him, is aware that the Commandante reeks with self-importance. She takes charge by opening her legs just two inches, turns, and stares directly into his eyes. "Commandante, fly low over Torcello and turn your spotlight on the piazza so I can say goodbye to Attila's throne."

The Commandante is bewildered by her body language and her request. He jerkily shifts his craft over to Torcello and turns on his powerful searchlight. The beam fights its way downward through the fog. She deliberately does not tell him of the tent and the turbulence of the chopper's blades makes the huge Bedouin tent whip wildly about, like some gigantic angry bird. It is only through Vero's skill that they don't crash. They move away.

The Commandante is shaken to his very core and wide-eyed with horror at the close call. Giulietta, on the other hand, is in total control. She calmly opens her purse, takes out her mirror, gazes into it, and flicks at her hair. She turns to Vero and smiles: "Like birds of a feather, Commandante.

16

Take me back to the Riga. Andiamo." The bewildered Commandante obeys.

~ ~ ~

Once upon a time…

III
Stockton During the Recount

Early morning Stockton, California

Julie was restless. She kept popping her head through the back window of our pickup. I knew that she was as snug as a bug in the cabover because I sealed it from the wind and rain. I also had fitted a thick piece of foam mattress on the floorboard. Over the mattress laid an exquisite piece of rug we had found in a curbside rummage sale in Burbank. With three sleeping bags and a big soft pillow, she had to be comfortable. Her long hair was frazzled from tossing and turning. When I slid open the window, the air turbulence created by the gap between the cabin and the cabover flicked at the ends of her hair, creating a fuzzy aura effect as seen through the rearview mirror. My tee shirt hung loosely on her shoulders revealing her ample breasts. Why she insisted on wearing my clothes I'll never know. I'm a big bulging guy. Julie and her two sisters could fit in the shirt with room for a serious pillow fight between them. I had this goofy thought that the rest of her body could pass through an opening if her fabulous breasts could much like cat's whiskers.

We had met in the Merchant Seamen's War Memorial on the Palos Verdes peninsula. Having been a sailor in my twenties and based at San Pedro just a few miles south, I've often come to this beautiful place situated on the cliffs with the Pacific Ocean as a backdrop. San Pedro was just one of the union hiring halls back then in the 1960s. I was a member of the Marine Cooks and Stewards Union, a subunion to the Sailors Union of the Pacific, and I have been hired out of most of the West Coast ports. When I left sailing the big ships, I never stopped my lifelong ritual of traveling up and down the Pacific Coast, from British Columbia to Mexico, only now it's with my trusty Toyota Tacoma.

We live in Jefferson County, at the base of the Olympic Mountains, down the road where *The Egg and I* story was created. Julie always mentioned this because of her love of the nostalgic. Our neighbors, who were born easily twenty years after the story was written, parrot a common negative that the story was false. The irony is they run a country store down the road with their main customers being folks attracted to their store because the name of the street is "The Egg and I."

We met two years ago. Julie had revealed that a year earlier she had lost her husband, Captain Josef, in an auto accident in Bishop. She explained that he was driving up to meet a buddy to go fishing when he got hit head-on by a kid who had been drinking too much. He had captained several of the coastal freighters for years. When he died, she made a promise to his memory that she would visit the Seamen's Memorial each year as they had done in the past.

We fell in love, moved north, and found ourselves driving down to the Seamen's Memorial these two years since. It's ironic that Julie has never learned how to drive, chiefly because she had been on the ships since she married at seventeen. I didn't mind, because I love to drive but now, after Stockton, I'm making sure that Julie learns.

She had explained to me that her intimate world aboard the freighters suited her and Josef to a tea. She had plenty of time to work out her magical watercolors. Being a writer and loner myself, we hit it off from our first meeting.

Regardless of losing the one she loved deeply, time and tenderness has served her well. On this, our second journey to Palos Verdes, her rich radiance filled the truck with love and warmth. My goal in life had been to write The Book "to send them all reading." Thankfully, the agent liked the final draft. It has a chance to be published and her tiny, intricate illustrations will complement the novel perfectly. An adult children's book is all the rage in this era of uncompromising politicians counting and recounting Floridian ballots in the face of what is good, fair and reasonable for the country. I yawned and was about to continue my moralizing to no one, but my head bobbed in a sleep daze for a hair-trigger second. I squeezed my eyes and slapped my face awake. Time to pull over – the fatigue was creeping up on me. Julie wanted me to turn off at the next rest stop so we could get a little shut-eye. I had agreed and she ducked back into the cab and shut the sliding window. I watched her maneuver deep under the sleeping bags so I decided to skip the rest stop and pull in at the next one twenty-five or so miles farther down the road.

The drive down I-5 had been filled with signs of irritability and unstableness. In Olympia, Washington State's capital, a BMW suddenly took off weaving through traffic at high speed. At the Corvallis turnoff, the Oregon State Patrol had stopped supercharged University of Oregon rooters who had just watched their team get beat by Oregon State. Later in the night, at Redding, California, a massive truck turned over, spilling its load of Christmas trees. Things were smooth from then on, but I-5 was busy even at this early hour. Speeds were in the high eighties. Perhaps the Highway Patrol was letting people speed home because of the upcoming Thanksgiving weekend.

I was running low on fuel so turned off at the last Stockton turnoff. The rest stop was another ten or so miles down the pike. I was tired as well. I had been driving nonstop for about seven hundred miles in fifteen or sixteen hours. I didn't want to stop even now because I was afraid of crashing. Not the car. Me. I filled the tank using my credit card and decided to get a coffee in the 24-hour café next door. It was called the Lions Café and had stylized lions as a motif. The only relief in the harsh red walls was the graffiti scrawled on the wall next to the entrance. The lions stood out from its scarred walls like bleak guardians of what lay within.

I called into the cab and asked Julie if she wanted a coffee. She murmured that she was finally falling asleep so I started the Toyota and moved it into one of the café's parking spots. I chose one of the parking spaces far off in the dark so the lights from the restaurant wouldn't bother her. I got out and peeked into the cab again. It looked so inviting. I hesitated, thinking I should crawl in and wrap myself around her warm body.

M-m-m, my Julie looked snug, snug as a bug. I sighed and walked stiffly to the café. Along the pathway I noticed more graffiti, kind of faded lines drawn around prostrate bodies. Like in a murder mystery where a body had been found. These looked more like a college prank. I laughed at the thought of a bunch of initiating freshmen having to take turns lying down and chalk-marking their torsos. The lot was full of patrol cars. In my own vagabond college days, my alarm bells would have gone off like it was a four-alarm fire, but with age and respectability – not to mention fatigue – they were muted.

With barely a sense of trepidation, I opened the door and entered. Inside, I found myself the only civilian in the place. The joint was filled with uniformed cops of every stripe. A sizable contingent of California

Highway Patrol took up two tables. Next to them were four huge sheriffs who looked for all the world like pigs in uniform. There was a large group of black-dressed cops at the other tables that I saw were Stockton city policemen. You could feel an uneasy tension between the forces. Their focus was only on their buddies, while they seemed to ignore the other groups. They all, in unison, stopped talking and turned and stared at me when I walked into the place. Every uniform was so crisp and shiny and creases so sharp you could smell singed air. My rumpled T-shirt, flopping sandals, and baggy shorts had me fighting back a nasty case of guilt fueled by so many pairs of riveting eyes.

I should have back-pedaled in hopes my persona would register as an apparition occurring between the odd wink. But I had entered, so, as a man, I followed through and moved stiffly to the counter to sit and order a coffee. My sitting down helped my audience refocus on more important things like the Florida voting fiasco. I overheard intense arguing how Gore had stopped the absentee military voters. They registered their feelings by nervously rubbing gun butts and snapping holster buttons. The drumming fingers over tabletops sent marching rhythms vibrating in the air. This was as unnerving as their constant jerky glances. I looked at myself in the mirrored wall behind the counter and realized I must have looked like I was covered with Gore buttons, the second coming of an aging hippie straight out of a voting booth. I laughed to myself, 'Shit,' I thought, 'if they saw my car with my Nader sticker they would be shaking my hand.' I looked back in the mirror. Hm-m, lots of stubble. I smiled, feeling much safer without my beard of thirty years. I looked more like a drifter than a hippie. Like I'm a gored ne'er-do-well rather than a left-wing Gore hugger.

"I voted for Bush," I wanted to scream out. And I did, sort of, with my Nader vote. I'm a lifelong Democrat but I am sure no lover of the people who have gained control of the Democratic Party. You can have the Clintons and the Gores and the Larry Flynts. This crowd is creating the divided country in their power-mad obsessions. I looked at the sheriff staring at me in the mirror. I smiled and gave a short, friendly nod. He just stared back with unblinking fish eyes.

A chill went up my spine as a thought rose from the primordial soup kitchen churning in my mind. Julie. I'll never see her again. This thought exploded instantly through my tired mind. With rising fear I reassured myself that she was sleeping soundly. I kept my outward cool. It was stupid of me to feel threatened by the cops. The fear will pass. The fear will pass.

The pleasantly plump waitress refilled my cup while arranging her smile, then asked if I wanted to order anything to eat. With my stomach in a knot, I shook my head no but as she turned to leave I called out for some oatmeal. It will settle my stomach, I assured myself. I tucked into a discarded newspaper and after a brief moment the steaming bowl arrived. I plopped the raisins on, then the nuts and brown sugar, and shoved a glob of butter deep into the mush, sniffed the dubious milk and poured it on. I waited a second or two wondering… what was it? A foreboding premonition of what? Then dug in. I ate with relish. I hadn't realized how hungry I was. I smirked to myself, 'for a last meal this was heaven.' I blinked myself out of my unconscious negatives – Why in hell was I thinking such thoughts?

The rumble of the crowd stopped again as the door opened and in walked a very short officer. He had to have been under five feet tall, actually because his brutally shiny boots had high heels that must have barely taken him to regulation. His uniform was more tailored than the others. It was crisper, the creases sharper. His bearing was that of a Mussolini. He was definitely the cock of this group. A bantam cock, or should I say, cop. The twenty or so officers paid their respects with a deferential silence. On his arm was a young woman of about thirty, about six feet tall. She was beautiful in that Scandinavian way. She wore tailored Levis, a thick blue sweater, and a brown leather vest. Her hair was as made up as his was greased down. She was stunning in every way even in her look of disdain when she spotted me at the counter. The couple sat down and again the grumbling and rumbling rose as the crowd of cops sank deeper into their coffee and newspapers. I scratched my stubble and yawned. Maybe she was the mayor of Stockton coming out to service the fellas. I blinked, is it mayoress of Stockton? I blinked again, Boy was I tired!

With their entry as a diversion, I thought it was the best time to escape (make my departure, dammit!), so I grabbed the bowl with two hands and drained it with purpose, got up and stretched again. As if on cue, the heavy silence rippled through the room. I got up purposefully and moved through it to the cashier. It didn't help that I had to pay with coins, but the waitress' grimace turned into a wide smile when she spied the five quarters that were her tip. Before leaving, my stomach gave a slight spasm, sending a cold shiver up my spine. My mind flashed. Damn! – the milk! I wanted to visit the bathroom but thought it more expedient to get the hell out of there fast. I turned to leave and my eyes naturally fell on the tall blonde who stared back, then cast her mean eyes down and looked at her bantam rooster mate.

I made it out the door but halfway down the walkway I had another stab of pain in the gut that triggered hallucinations that the door was swung open behind me by the bantam copy yelling, "Just a minute, son." I stopped, confused, trying to get my bearings. I tried to turn to face my fantasy but couldn't. My pride demanded I confront myself. This rude young man, half my age, is not real! So no one said anything.

I fought a massive hold over my psyche. "Move, move," I commanded myself. "Get to the car now!" My weird reality answered the phantom bantam and I said to nobody but the grave, "'Are you referring to me?" "Yes you, son." It was a hollow echo as hollow as a hollow shelled bullet piercing my reality, forcing me forward through the illogical restraints holding me back. Forward! To the car! GO! I trudged on, bent in agony, as he struts over. In my mind the other cops merged behind him. Behind them, towering over all, stood the smirking blonde, waiting for her little man to perform his duty. She done her job baiting her pint-sized man into action. Out of the corner of my eye I saw my Toyota Tacoma resting just ten feet away. A game of inches. That's what they call it in football, dammit! I reached out to hold on to something as my mind screamed at me to move forward, but I stood frozen in an abyss of indecision wrapped in paranoia. I didn't want the cops – real or imagined – to know of the truck and that Julie was in it. I prayed she would stay asleep till daybreak. I wanted to run away into Stockton like a bum, leading the cops away from Julie. I giggled to myself sternly as I dry-heaved, acting like a stray dog. Voices from ? "Where you headed?" "South." "South – meaning, where are you headed south?" "Palos Verdes. I'm a sailor and need to get to San Pedro. I hit some bad times up north, got to catch a ship." "Got a driver's license?" "Certainly." I bent down in the hope that the momentum would force me forward towards the car. I imagined I pulled out my wallet from the lower pocket of my campstyle shorts. I rose, clinging to the door handle of the truck only to rise up into the barrel of his service revolver. "Keep your hand movements smooth and easy, young man, and hand it over." I opened the door carefully and was about to get in when my stomach started bucking. As I did, another cop came up. He was in the same uniform as the bantam cop. The Stockton police. Over his shoulder was another cop, but he was pure CHP – California Highway Patrol. The good guys. Hooray, I belched. I looked between them and saw the four sheriffs arrive. The bad guys. The bantam cop followed my gaze and jammed his gun into my ribs. "Where is it?" "Where is what?" "Your dope stash. Where?" The vomit was rising. The acid taste preceding was beginning to ignite the pending eruption.

A whirr of internal voices from my pathetic imagination trapped by the morning snapped through my mind. "Look, I don't use the stuff." "Where's your bag, your clothes?" "All I have is this bag; I tell you, I ran out of luck up north." "Where?" "Tacoma, I was in Tacoma having drinks when I got into a poker game. I lost... everything." He looked at his sidekick and both of them got a grotesque look on their face. I started to sweat and realized my guts were aching. My Nader sticker! My Nader bumper sticker, see? See? The phantom bantam cock grabbed my sweater and pulled me to him, sending me off-balance, and my hands automatically came forward on him to stabilize myself. I felt his gun go off deep inside my stomach. I sunk to the ground and wretched beside the truck. I struggled to right myself and saw that the bantam copy had neatly side-stepped my heave.

Holding my guts, I saw the grinning waitress' face flicker across my mind. I rose, thinking about what the hell was in the mush the grinning waitress served me. Spiritually, I was fully aware of my body there at his feet half on the curb and half in the street. The bantam cop turned to his partner who had also drawn his gun. He spoke first. "You were fast, man. I thought he was going to vomit all over you." The bantam was coughing and arranging his perfectly cut uniform, brushing away where I had touched him. The other cops crowded around and began arguing among themselves as I clambered into the truck and slumped down in the driver's seat in a daze.

In my mind, the drama kept unfolding, fueled by the thick drumming of my heartbeat as a CHP pulled out his report and some chalk. The Stockton cops yelled, "What the hell are you doing? This is city business." The CHP retorts: "He landed in the street. This officially is a California highway." The bantam cop and his sidekick bend down and grab my carcass and flop it on the sidewalk, taking out some chalk and rapidly starting to draw a white line around my body. The CHP officers, the good guys, grab my hulk and try to place it back the way I fell. Their pink chalk comes out and they try to outline me. The four huge sheriff guys lumber over and get into the middle of the argument. The biggest sheriff bellows: "Look here, you can't keep moving the body. I saw it land half in the street and half on the sidewalk. So we're assuming responsibility since you airheads are tampering with the evidence." The bantam cop guiltily yells, pointing at the vomit, "Evidence? There is your evidence. He tried to vomit all over me when I was questioning him. I had to shoot him." "I ain't arguing you on that score. But we have got to file a report. Hell, I seen it." He turns to the others and they all nod. "Hell, we all seen him go for you but a report has got to be filed." "'Damn straight and it happened on city property so

<u>we</u> make out the report. Not you. Not the CHP." The bantam cop bends down to pull my carcass back to the sidewalk. The CHP officer backhands him and pulls my carcass back. Then the bantam cop's partner grabs the hands of my carcass as the CHP holds onto the legs and a tug-of-war ensues. The other Stockton city officers help the bantam cop pull towards the sidewalk and the other CHP cops pull towards the street. The sheriff draws his gun and shoots in the air, stopping the tug-of-war. I blinked and turned at the sharp crack Julie made when she opened the rear window. She looked at me with growing fear. I started the car and moved out of the parking lot. I looked over at the entrance of the café. The door was wide open and the phantom bantam cop was there looking at my truck move away. Behind him, just as my mind had depicted, the other cops emerged behind him. I turned, found first, and moved on to the disputed roadway. The freeway entrance was just a few hundred feet away. I would make it out of there and into the streaming Thanksgiving traffic and be gone from Stockton with a full tank of gas.

Julie asked if we were going to stop at the next rest stop. I wanted to tell her about my incident but how could I? It was mainly mental fueled by the milk and the vote... the lousy Florida vote triggering an end to what we love about America. On one side hysteria and mob rule stocked by a power-mad Gore. On the other, by the to-the-letter-of-the-law Bush.

I pinched myself. Yes, I was here. I told Julie to come up front now. "Tonight, I'm beginning to teach you how to drive." She squiggled through, arousing me at absolutely the wrong time. "Shit!"

"What's wrong, baby?"

"Nothing. Nothing. Everything will be fine as soon as you learn how to drive."

~ ~ ~

Once upon a time…

IV
The Cloud Tenders

Ten miles above the Atlantic Ocean floats Cumulus, comprised of platforms suspended by an intricate lacing of support cables, girders and guy wires; a three-dimensional spider web effect leading up to the maze of multicolored balloons above. The balloons are purposely brightly colored to stand as a beacon of hope to whomever is still alive on earth's surface.

The very highest platform is called Capital Platform or, in jargon, "The Deck." Here, Dogon, Jenny, his stepdaughter, and Creely, his aide, stand with high-powered binoculars searching the turbulent clouds below. A loudspeaker from above announces: "Approaching, London 419." Jenny is the first to spot the approaching balloon and points to it. Dogon yells into a phone, "De-shield, 419, West quarter! 2000 yards out!" After embarkation, the force field is reactivated and 419 continues to Station A. The deradiation process begins. 419 slowly moves along a conveyor that "washes it." At the end of the conveyor, its radiation count is measured. 419 passes muster and continues on the conveyor from Station A to City Platform deep below "The Deck." Dogon, Jenny and Creely enter a "shoot" (vacuum-propelled elevator) that sends them down to City Platform, the official entrance to Cumulus.

At City Platform's main docking station, 419's hatch opens and crusty Captain Seth-Smith and handsome new recruit Peter Ward emerge. Peter is a "refugee" from New New York, where he had served as a navigator. Dogon and Seth-Smith are old friends, but Peter is introduced to the city officials for the first time. Jenny is concerned because Peter appears to be under heavy stress. Dogon questions him briefly. Peter tells him truthfully where he came from (Warsaw), about his family (all dead). Dogon and Seth-Smith move on to a private room. Creely attends to the balloon 419's paperwork. Jenny and Peter exchange a shy conversation. Behind them, several cartons are removed from 419's cargo hold.

Inside the private room, Seth-Smith tells Dogon of the terrible conditions at London, and asks that he be allowed to stay on Cumulus. Dogon hedges: "We are not yet totally self-sufficient." Seth-Smith pleads: "The charade is basically over because the only plant life not radioactive are the deep seaweeds, and we are losing our ability to harvest them. Each new explosion intensifies the radioactivity on land and extends it deeper into the seas." Dogon asserts: We have to give the siblings the impression that the seaweed sustains us. We also need the nodules." Seth-Smith reluctantly agrees to continue the shipments.

Later, in a floating restaurant dangling 200 feet below the main part of town, Dogon and company sit down to dinner. The meal is served and the conversation shifts immediately to "The War of the Petulants."

"They say they want to end the war, but every time a treaty is announced it's broken in a matter of days.".… "It's a game with them.".… "They don't live in the real world.".… "They believe in the bullshit they transmit over their TV networks.".… "Their world, the one that motivates them, is simply not real."… "Why aren't they stopped?" Dogon breaks in bitterly, "They will destroy themselves." Jenny comments off-hand: "We could destroy them instantly, but we're pacifists." Creely mutters: "His trying to protect his siblings is destroying the world."

A small tableside TV is turned on and switched to a New New York-controlled station. The image projects a rosy world, completely staged and artificial. Clear blue skies without a cloud in sight. Through the window, the party gazes down at the grey turbulent gloom of reality. On the monitor, the president, Tre, is reclined on a lounge. He's gaunt, with just about every bit of his anatomy pierced. He talks about peace and prosperity for all. In the bottom right of the screen is a box where viewers can push a button to register their vote on the latest faddish question. "Is the President wearing a pierced ring in his scrotum! Press once for yes and twice for no." Dogon changes the station to an ABC broadcast from Paris. The broadcast is of their president, Sue. She too is dressed like a punk rock star. She has a goatee that she strokes while conveying that "Productivity in the district of Egypt is up 20 percent…"

Jenny switches the channel selector and surprises Peter. "I thought there were only two channels." As Jenny adjusts the focus, she explains: "These are self-contained mini video cameras that monitor the real world. We smuggled them down to Earth about five months ago. They are activated when they sense human vibrations like voice, movement and heartbeat. We have about fifty set up around the world." She shifts the dial. Johannesburg. No movement; no transmission. She presses a button activating the camera. All the camera picks up is a grey fog. She fiddles with a joystick, turning the camera left, then right, then up, then down. On the ground in front of the camera lies a heap of corpses. Large cockroaches crawl over them. Jenny hurriedly turns the dial, switching to Stockholm. Humans are beating themselves; they have succumbed to a "Blood Mania" condition. It's a self-destruction disease — a symptom of radiation poisoning. She switches to other locations: Boston, Barcelona, Rio... It's apparent that life is terminating in these cities.

Jenny switches back to the Androgenen station and a cooking show is starting. Peter cringes. He mentions that the restaurant food is delicious but that he isn't used to it and feels sick. "I haven't had meat or such sweet vegetables like these in years. Where on earth do they come from?" Jenny kids him that the balloons have been bringing the seaweed up for a long time. Peter chokes: "This is seaweed?" Jenny laughs: "Well, you're not on Earth anymore. You got to eat what the natives eat." Jenny and Peter have shared a closeness, and she hopes that Peter survives the supply runs. She soothes him; "Relax, Peter, you're among friends."

In the darkness of the night, 419 departs, with Peter as navigator, and disappears into the thick clouds below.

Later, at London, 419 descends through the huge cavity where the dome of Saint Paul's Cathedral once was.

Under London, Seth-Smith and Peter shake hands and go to their respective quarters. Seth-Smith takes the long subway escalator down to the depths of London to arrive at a briefing room. Through a thick plate glass window he peers into the Thames where a submarine named Camille is held fast next to an underwater docking station. Seth-Smith checks the captain's video log. The ship's last mission was gathering seaweed. Next, he goes through a doorway into the off-loading area. A watertight linkup with the sub allows for efficient off-loading of the seaweed. He sees a pile of valuable alloy nodules that were found lying on the bottom of the Pacific Ocean. These are especially needed at Cumulus for repairing the balloon cable rigging. Seth-Smith takes out a piece of blue chalk and marks the best nodules. Weight is a problem with delivery, so only so many can be delivered per balloon.

Up higher, but still below London, Peter switches on the TV and slips in a video of the cooking show he had glimpsed at on Cumulus. The host appears and looks directly in the camera and Peter instantly goes into a hypnotic trance. Deep under, he relates what he learned on his first trip to Cumulus.

At Paris, on Sue's TV screen, a miniature blip expands. Peter's face fills the monitor. He mechanically speaks in a rapid fire delivery, so fast that Sue must read from a printout: "…No life in Barcelona, Boston, Johannesburg…" then she gasps and angrily says to herself: "Serving meat to my agents! This is treachery. Dogon must be destroyed! He is making a mockery of me, perverting you, poor Peter, with rich food. How low!… Do you still love me, little snookums?" Peter nods dully on the monitor. "When's the next shipment of nutrition from London being sent up, Peter?" Peter answers, slurring, "five p.m. tonight." "Are you on the flight, Peter dear?" "No." "Good, now go to sleep, handsome. Think deeply of me."

At 5:05, balloon 420 is hit by a missile and blows up just as it rises above the shell of St. Paul's. Immediately after the explosion, Tre, in Seattle, appears on TV. "Who blew up 420? London is New New York territory!" Sue coos, "Why the alarm, brother? Both our stated policies are to blow up supply runs to the hated sky city when we catch them. After all, we both want to rid ourselves of the dark shadow in our sky, don't we?" Sue baits her brother again by asking him for his hand in marriage. Tre, enraged, declares that if Sue does not apologize immediately, the bombing of Paris will begin the next morning.

Later, Tre, still miffed, orders an attack on Cumulus "to see if we can catch them with their pants down." Cumulus defense barriers easily ward off the missiles. Frustrated, Tre fixes his sights on London (his own territory). "To hell with the goddamn treaty. That balloon rose from London. I'll wipe out their supply lines down below. Fire!"

At Capital Platform high in Cumulus, Dogon and Creely witness the attack. Creely yells to Dogon to stop them. "My beloved London! London is finished. My home, my home." Dogon rebuffs him, "Let this epoch end itself."

Meanwhile, at Paris, Sue slams her diamond-encrusted glove on the table, and pleads with her brother: "Please, stop, or we won't have any link to Cumulus."

Above London, missiles explode, creating wild turbulence. Among the smoke and flame rises balloon 419. Sue shouts, "Leave the balloon alone, Brother, I beseech you!" The attack stops.

At Capital Platform, Jenny looks for balloon 420 through her binoculars. To her surprise, 419 appears. She's happy that she will see Peter again. Creely initiates the docking procedures. 419 docks as before but takes much longer to go through the deradiation process.

Inside the Deck, Seth-Smith briefs Dogon on the destruction of London. "How we got through I just don't know." Later, Creely comes in, reading a computer report, which shows the state of life on the planet. Behind him is a large political map of the earth. On it, green flags note where human life is reputed to be. He slowly takes down the flag at London. Large green areas around Paris and Seattle are shown. These are the last inhabited land masses on Earth. As he speaks, Creely shades out some of Seattle's green. "Radiation has shrunken New New York's border to just this area around their capital. Perhaps 2000 square kilometers. About 400,000 souls. Both capitals have registered just a few pregnancies, and no live births for two years. All stillborns. Life expectancy on Earth at today's radiation levels is now below six years... Of course, if they stop the bombing..."

The next day, Peter is attending orientation sessions when he meets up with Jenny. He looks exhausted. Jenny goes with him and helps him get comfortable in his new environment. "Please learn to relax, Peter. You're among friends now."

On Deck, Dogon tries to scan London via his TV monitors and gets nothing – ditto at Boston. But at Stockholm, the monitor tracks down a long, empty cave. The camera sensors have picked up a heartbeat. The camera moves in. A human form appears faintly on the screen. At closeup, we see a face scarred by radiation. The face has no eyes in its sockets. The body flails about wildly. Dogon changes channels as Creely removes Stockholm's green flag from the map.

Peter is at an indoctrination class being taught the Principles of Pacifism, upon which Cumulus was founded. He is a copious note taker, eager to learn.

Later, Jenny, dressed in tight black leotards, takes Peter down to the lower storage platforms. Behind a warehouse, he sees a brewbird for the first time. It is clumsily eating a piece of lichen-like material. Peter reacts to its ugliness. It looks like a cross between a miniature bulldog and an anteater. He curtly asks what it is. Jenny is embarrassed, explaining that he isn't supposed to know it exists. She gathers up the docile beast by its long neck, opens the warehouse door, and plunks it in. Peter peers over her shoulder and sees that the warehouse is actually a kennel for brewbirds. Jenny is very nervous now because a security rule has been breached. Peter was not to know about the birds.

"Peter, please don't mention that you have seen this animal alive." Peter agrees, but matter-of-factly asks where it came from. She blurts out that it is what he has been eating with his vegetables all along. Peter bites into the lichen plant. "No, no!" Jenny laughs. "Not those plants! That's a hybrid meant to feed the birds with." Peter spits out the bitter lichen and asks, "Where do the sweet veggies come from?" Jenny coyly steers the conversation away. "You'll find out soon enough the way you're studying. Hey, do you want to try some cloud sport?"

They move to the edge of the platform. They peer over at the series of platforms floating around the bottom of the city. Suddenly Jenny leaps out and free falls gracefully down to a taut net stretched a hundred feet below. The center of the net is held fast to the girders that support the restaurant another hundred feet below the net.

Jenny lands in the net spread-eagled, rebounds to another net, then to another and another, completing a circle that takes her back to Peter. Other members of the Bounce Club arrive and take off. Jenny grabs Peter's hand and coaxes him to jump. He does, holding her hand, and they complete the circle. Then he enthusiastically jumps and completes the circle by himself. He does another as the two start to really enjoy each other's company. Suddenly, Peter turns serious and looks as his watch, shows concern and excuses himself. Jenny wonders what is wrong but passes it off as a delayed reaction to his London escape. (Peter will find release in his new sport and will continue it with dedication.)

Later, in the privacy of his quarters, Peters turns on the Androgenan cooking show and lapses into a trance once again. On the program, Sue's image blips out and she purrs that she is happy that Peter is alive on Cumulus. Still in a trance, Peter gives his report in a rapid-fire monotone, but Sue cuts him off quickly: "A sending blip has been detected. Send your report down by parachute immediately." Sue's image disappears.

At the Deck, Creely tells Dogon that Security has just picked up a minute sending blip from the TV station beaming up from Paris. He suggests that it's probably a simple malfunction. Concerned, Dogon tells him to dissect the blip. Creely explains that it will take a while but he will do it.

Strolling along City Platform, Peter and Jenny look up to view the many layers of platforms capped by the Capital platform. Peter asks if he can go up there. Jenny answers, "No, only community members with higher security clearances may go up there."

"How do people get the clearances?" asks Peter.

"First, by absorbing the Principles of Pacifism, then by working hard at a position that helps the community."

Peter blurts out that he wants to be a cook. Jenny laughs. "You're a trained navigator with wartime experience. As soon as you learn the Principles, you will automatically rise in our hierarchy." Peter is insistent; he wants to contribute to the society immediately. Jenny replies, "Okay. We'll see."

Through Jenny, Peter gets a job as an apprentice cook and dishwasher. Since he is just starting, he is assigned to odd hours, which helps him in his unconscious spy duty. He learns more about the brewbirds and the recycling of Cumulus' waste matter. But he still does not understand where the life-sustaining vegetables come from. He puts off sending in his report until he understands more.

Peter and Jenny make love for the first time, and through a slip of the tongue by Jenny, Peter discovers the existence of the cloud farms. Later that night, when Jenny leaves, Peter completes his report in Androgenine code. Even though he still doesn't understand the brewbird, he now understands the food chain.

Peter tears up his notes, sends them down the recycling chute, then finds plastic bags to fashion a pouch and a parachute. He puts his report in the bag and conceals his parachute. Dressed in leotards, he then descends in a chute to the lower platform where the brewbird kennel is located. He enters, grabs a docile brewbird, and stuffs it into his bag. He secures the bag, moves to the edge of the platform, and takes off. On the rebound, over a section of the jump where there is no net, he lets go the bag. It drifts down, and within a few seconds disappears into a cloud.

By chance, the bag lands in Wisconsin, where it is picked up by a roving patrol and sent to Seattle. The Androgenine code proves undecipherable. Tre calls his sister Sue via a TV phone and tells her about his find. Tre refuses to tell her what he has found; just that they should discuss the contents together in person. They agree to meet in Rome. Tre tells Sue that he will provide the food. He is afraid that their conversations will be picked up by Dogon . (He's right.)

At Capital Platform, Creely briefs Dogon on the phone conversations between the siblings. "They're meeting at Rome." Creely adjusts a TV monitor and Tre and Sue come into focus. They are sitting in a sealed clear plastic dome in the Roman Forum. "The visuals are perfect but I can't pick up the audio – it's jammed." On the TV, a roasted brewbird is being served. The siblings rip at the beast, slobbering and slavering like pigs. Dogon yells, "What? That's a brewbird! How did it get down there?"

At Rome, Tre tries to get his sister to decipher Peter's report. She refuses, but consoles Tre by suggesting they collaborate to destroy Cumulus "...and father;... but not before we find out about his delicious pets, the brewbirds."

"Is this another pact between us?" asks Tre, warily.

"Let's shake on it, Brother; trust me. I'm your older sis." They shake hands and Tre hands over Peter's report.

Back at Cumulus, Peter's mental condition is worsening. He now believes deeply in the community. He cannot grasp the control Sue has upon him. Jenny is at his side helping him through his fever. She notices that his thick notebook is missing and asks him where it is. He tells her he has thrown it in the recycler. "It forces me to remember things," he explains.

He looks at his watch. It's time for the cooking show. He rudely asks Jenny to leave, then turns on the show. The subliminal message dictates a formula containing minute metal filings that Peter is to pour into Cumulus' recycling system, and which will eventually enter the cloud farms as a part of the nutrient mix. This will expose the cloud farms to radar. Almost instantly after receiving the order, Peter screams: "Why?" Jenny rushes in to find Peter in what appears to be a nightmare.

At Capital Platform, Creely tells Dogon that a second sending blip from Cumulus was intercepted. It was filled with the word "Why." Dogon asks: "Why?"

In Peter's room, Jenny is rubbing his shoulders. He explains: "I must have had a nightmare."

*

Back at Capital Platform, Creely is briefing Dogon, reading a printout of the latest live human count on the Earth's surface. "Seattle's borders have expanded to 2500 square kilometers; Paris to 4000. Both areas' populations are holding. Seattle has recorded 30 pregnancies so far this month. Still no live births. Ten stillborns. Paris has 60 women in pregnancy. No live births in six months...."

Creely looks up from his readout: "We haven't had a live birth up here either. But if the siblings stop their attacks, the radiation will cool. Then perhaps. It's hard to tell. It looks like we're all sterilized now. I just don't know." Dogon irritably breaks in on Creely's negative report: "Once things are stable for just three months, our radiation absorption systems will kick in. If we switched them on now they would become rapidly overloaded. (He turns and looks into his TV monitor at the fog-enshrouded landscape, switching between several locations.) "Things are too quiet down there. It's not like my beloved children. Get Seth-Smith."

Seth-Smith arrives and Dogon questions him about Peter. How long had he known him? What did Peter do before he became a navigator? Then he sends for Peter and asks him if he ever was in Paris. Where his family lived.

"I told you before, sir; they're all dead." Peter is very nervous but answers convincingly. At one point in the interrogation, a question about sports led to Peter's love of net diving, which almost unmasked Sue's manipulation of Peter's unconscious state. Peter leaves The Deck, nervous and confused.

Later, in his room, Jenny asks him about the meeting with Dogon. Peter rages at her that it is none of her business. Then he breaks down, sobbing.

Still later, at work, he prepares the metallic formula (ground Brillo pads) and pours it into the recycling bin. In a sort of a stupor, he checks out, saying he is sick. Jenny finds him wandering in a daze, close to the edge of a storage platform, dragging an empty case with the name "Brillo pads" on it. He is so horrified by his inability to control or understand what is happening to him that he appears to Jenny to be on the verge of jumping. Jenny ignores the empty case and helps him back to his quarters.

Jenny reports Peter's condition to Dogon, telling him about Peter's trancelike states, his depression, and what looked like an attempt to take his own life. Dogon orders Creely to have Peter taken to the hospital.

After a thorough checkup, it is determined that Peter is in good physical health. Next, they interrogate Peter again, with far more pointed questions. He responds by regressing deeper within himself. The doctors almost force an opening into the vicelike hold Sue has over Peter. But each time they get close, Peter's condition worsens. At one point, he is near death. Dogon understands now that Peter has been brainwashed and that if they 'cure' Peter, he will die. Dogon fears the worst, that an attack of some kind is inevitable. He sends out orders: "Place all laser platforms on red alert! Lock on Seattle and Paris and on all their bases. Prepare for their attack.

The metallic formula has reached the cloud farms. One by one, the floating farms are exposed to the siblings' radar. Both at Paris and Seattle, the farms take shape on the radar screens. Their vague massiveness frightens the controllers, but Sue explains what is happening to her officers. At Seattle, confusion reigns because Tre has no clue what is going on or how he should respond. Sue delays her attack hoping that more cloud farms will become visible. She orders her missiles at the ready.

At the hospital, Jenny tries to console Peter as he screams: "We've got to stop them!" Dogon, Creely and Seth-Smith arrive. Peter sees them and in a blind panic leaps out of bed and runs out of the hospital towards the edge of the platform. His path is blocked by guards. He turns and runs up into a laser platform, slamming into the gunner and knocking him unconscious. He takes charge of the gun and swings it wildly around in an arc. Its fire-control radar picks up a now metallicized farm, which automatically locks on the laser and fires it at the target. The cloud farm is destroyed. Dogon, Creely and Jenny are dumbfounded. Seth-Smith blurts out, "But the farms are invisible to radar!"

At Paris, Sue accuses Tre of shooting first. Tre accuses his sister of holding out on him. The pact! Is broken. They both take aim at the exposed cloud farms.

On the Deck, Dogon and company watch in dismay as still another cloud farm is destroyed. They cannot raise a protective barrier against incoming missiles like they can at Cumulus. Peter slumps out of the gun platform and Dogon enters, giving the order to destroy Paris and Seattle.

Peter looks up and they watch as Dogon destroys his siblings. The attack lasts for less than a minute; then Dogon grimly announces, "The deed is done. Let the new epoch begin." He slumps dejectedly out of the gun platform and slowly walks to his quarters.

Later, on the Deck, Dogon pins on Peter's navigator wings. (Behind the ceremony, the Cumulus' 30-piece orchestra plays the city's anthem. Their instruments are the taut cables that hold the city platforms under the balloons. They sound like high-pitched massive cellos and violins.)

Still later, at Capital Platform, Creely reads off the effects of the final battle, which ended the War of the Petulants. Dogon, Jenny, Seth-Smith and Peter sit deep in thought. Peter is now wearing his Cumulus navigator's uniform. He has passed his tests. On the world map behind Creely, there are no green flags. Creely says: "Now, no area is free of radiation. A first possible landing appears to be in four months, perhaps in the Rocky Mountains. Then we can put in place a radiation-absorbing unit and start the process of clearing the earth of radiation. Our city units are almost at overload stage, but they are keeping our air pure. Good news is that four cloud farms are still in operation. With rationing, we will survive. No pregnancies have been recorded in two months at Cumulus. That's a sad, sad portent for the future of our species."

Jenny interrupts, turns to Peter, then back to Creely and Dogon, and says, "I'd like to report my pregnancy."

~ ~ ~

V

Riding Shotgun

Last Wednesday, the Fantastic Kobbleman and I left Bainbridge Island by ferry and headed out of Seattle for San Francisco in his 1970 Citroën DS 19. It was filled with Deux Chevaux 2 CV parts; three engines, cowling, tires and tools. The stop in Seattle to charge the battery of a running 2 CV (one of 12 he owns) was a premonition that this trip was going to be unique, a trip far removed from Plato's theater where the action is logical. To Plato, our trip would have made no sense at all in sum or in parts.

Fantastic put the 2 CV "experience" in perspective by explaining that it is one of the world's favorite cars. Citroën started 2 CV production in 1948. It was affectionately dubbed the "ugly duckling" by the populace. Even though it is still more advanced than today's cars, it never caught on in the U.S. as a mass-market car. It has enjoyed a cult following, however. Fantastic is a devout member.

While passing the port area of Tacoma, he explains that his mission is to reclaim the remaining three (of six) unwanted 2 CV's he had previously sold to the retail outfit that was going to use them as decoration in their mall stores.

Further south, in Portland, he reveals that, as per the contract, he had gutted the cars but now has a tentative deal with an L.A. filmmaker – a 2 CV plus cash for the man's mechanically suspect DS 19. Thus, one of the cars had to be refitted with an engine. (Fantastic's logic was that bringing three engines down would ensure a working one.)

It was explained to me that the L.A. guy wanted to drive the little car to Florida. Perhaps, Fantastic speculated with a gleam in his eye, his inspiration was the celebrated trip from Ashland to Madison, Wisconsin, that Chris Beebe and a friend had made with his 2 CV that was recorded in "Road and Track" magazine (October 1988). We were just passing Ashland, Oregon, as he spoke.

Throughout the journey south, we tested each other as men do: How far to take a joke. How well one took a putdown. At the time, I didn't realize that he was preparing me for his world. Softening me for spontaneous surprises; creating an atmosphere where he could operate unfettered.

Allow me to sum up Fantastic in my personalized interpretation of Zen opposites: The physical expression of his yang seems to be his love of getting old Citroëns to run again. An unabashed love with a vengeance.

His yin: He is a professional magician highly trained in the world of illusion. He bills himself as "The Fantastic Kobbleman."

The curious crucible is his hands. Hands are the magician's most valuable tool. They must be smooth as silk, as mesmerizing as fine art. Hands are also extremely important to a mechanic. Hard, strong, callused hands to withstand the hard knocks of dealing with metal and grease. The mechanic, like the magician, is judged by his hands. Fantastic gestures with his hands in the round, fluid, graceful movements of a polished, professional magician, but they are oil-stained, gritty and dirty.

As you must have gathered by now, Fantastic is a "natural" man, a charmer when necessary, a critic at times. Well-read and bred, he assures me. I counter by ribbing him that I think he is a man of the moment obsessed with the action of the moment. I add quickly, "…like a good lover."

As with every "surprise" stop, Fantastic instantly became the center of attention. Such is the force of his personality, his guile, and his world. Fantastic always had a gift for his hosts. Usually it was a poster. A fine reproduction of a movie announcement done in 1920s style. The caption read: "Metropolis."

He was my master for the six-day trip. I was his shotgun partner ready to do his bidding. His energy and drive and mind speed left me out of breath at times. I obliquely apologized on several occasions by alluding that at forty-four he was four years my junior but had the faculties of a person half his age. He beamed and speeded up to 75. I hastily suggested that a person with this kind of gift had to be careful because his mind speed was infinitely faster than posted speed limits. I mentioned that in Europe several countries have no speed limit. He told me that's where he learned to drive – on autobahns in Germany. He launched into 220 kph Porsche tales. He had lived in Europe for four years. I told him I had lived there twelve. He cruised at 75.

As we talked, I solemnly revealed that I felt I was going through a sort of mid-life crisis – "...most men go through it," Fantastic interrupts. He starts needling me: "You lost direction, thus purpose, right? ...No goals no go... bet you place yourself in the position of being the scapegoat in a negative situation, right?" He kept hitting nails directly on their heads. I became aware of his hammering on a coffin I had been unwittingly preparing for my ego. "...What you believe in is dead or dying... your world is maternalizing, right? In the past you fought to make sure your position as a male was woven into your family and social life... You thought you were socially relevant, right? ... Today you don't care anymore." More nails, bang, thump, slam. "...Kids call you fat. Right? A fat authority figure ... AUTHORITY FIGURE BECOMES REDUNDANT YEAH YEAH YEAH... READ ALL ABOUT IT! ...Back off, Shipman. Hibernate... Relax... Take trips... like this one. He he he..."

I think to myself, 'like this one?' This was turning out to be torture, or, was it a form of guidance? I knew then I was being selfish with Fantastic because these were my "dog days." He had every right to ride me. I vowed to myself that I wouldn't get in his way. I'm riding shotgun. An historic position of honor.

Fantastic attacked me unmercifully. I had little hope of any dignity riding with this guy... unless I fought back with my own sense of biting humor. I meekly counterattacked. I said he was full of bull and that he lied about the nature of the trip. He accused me of having a hard time getting it up. "Oh, did your wife tell you that I was built for comfort and not for speed?" I woodenly asked. (Being totally unoriginal, I was quoting a Willie Dixon blues song – but actually, how did he know???) He ignored my dig but answered my thoughts? "...Part of the package, son." "Kobbleman, you are a presumptuous rutabaga!" (I felt my counterattacks were still a bit one-dimensional but getting stronger.) Fantastic started humming the Willie Dixon tune.

Riding shotgun for The Fantastic Kobbleman was a totally off-the-wall decision on my part. We weren't really friends. Our relationship was of a business nature. The Kobblemans bought one of my wife's pictures and she featured their DS 19 in another watercolor – the same car we traveled to California in.

Before we left, Cory, Fantastic's wife, expressed some concern about the trip. She was interested in preserving the ambience of Seattle's old Pike Place Market as I was. That and a party we attended at their house were our only social links.

Brenda, my wife, was worried too. I admitted I was as well, but for selfish reasons. I'm very difficult to get along with. I want to dominate situations – feel in control. Here I was telling myself in no uncertain terms to follow and help a mechanic/magician I knew little about. Many times during the course of the trip I wanted to grab a jet north and abandon Fantastic. The impulse came often because Plato's stage completely disappeared and our shared reality became as loose and free as a Charlie Parker riff. Brenda asked me, "Why do you, a successful and responsible businessman, allow yourself to ride shotgun with a magic man, or is he a mechanic?" I simply could not give her an answer.

We arrived in the Portola district after the run down I-5 with a motel stop at Winters just before the Bay Area bypass road. We also made a quick stop at Dennis' Citroën shop behind Jack London Square along the Oakland waterfront. Dennis specializes in 2 CVs.

Dennis seemed a bit unsure of himself. He was very thin, about five eleven. He mumbled as he spoke. (Later, Fantastic pointed out that he had just cut his very long red hair and that he had problems with his teeth. He thought that maybe Dennis was going through in his way what I was going through. He quickly added that Dennis was doing what he wanted to do, and that I wasn't. He pointed out that there was more hope for Dennis' getting his act together than me. 'Humph!' was my only response.)

Dennis tells me that his shop is in a group of World War II bungalows situated on an old torpedo boat fabricating plant. Dennis' neighbors are artists and craftspeople both dealing with the maritime world and the mainstream culture. A huge, forty-foot metal sculpture of a tooth sits among these sagging WWII buildings. The main shed is over a hundred feet long and is now used for contemporary machine work; like props for rock concerts and film special effects units. Presently, a ninety-foot sailboat is being welded together in the shed. Dennis was the source of two of the retail outlet's 2 CVs – he sold them to Fantastic. Fantastic, in turn, made a businessman's profit in the deal. Dennis, a throwback to the laid-back '60s, didn't seem to mind. He looked at me quizzically but I hastily assured him that I was only along for the ride.

I mentioned to Fantastic that I had lived in the Portola district of San Francisco in 1959 and '60 about a half mile from the Checker loading dock where his three bashed-in Deux Chevauxs were sitting. As we arrive at the dock, he waves to ex-cop Chuck, the yard foreman, and Russ, his East Bay roughneck helper, as they come up on the dock. Chuck heaps good-natured scorn on Fantastic and his obsession with his cars. Russ goes over and makes out like he's peeing on the green one. Then, he acts like he is zipping up as they both turn and gaze at me with silent interest while fondling their earrings. I quickly introduced myself and assured them that I was only along for the ride. Fantastic accuses Russ of taking out his frustration on his cars. Russ, with a twinkle in his eye, slaps Fantastic on the back and asks in his American twang: "Now why in hail would I want to mess with your little ol' Frenchy cars anyway…?" The two go back to work in the warehouse.

I tell Fantastic that in the early '60s Portola was a neat, trim working-class neighborhood. I was a merchant seaman paid well and loved jazz. He mentions that he used to see Dave Brubeck and other west coast jazzmen who played at the Blackhawk in the Tenderloin a few miles deeper in the city. He tells me he was under age and had to sit behind the fenced-in area. I remembered the Hawk and the Jazz Workshop up on Broadway, in North Beach. That's where east coast musicians like Miles and Cannonball played. I mention that Barbara Dane opened her folk bar just down the street. He laughs about Carol Doda who wiggled her silicone titties on the corner of Broadway and Columbus. Across the street was my longtime hangout, Mike's Pool Hall. Best subs in town. Now a Carl Jr.'s fast food joint is on the corner. Behind, down Columbus, squats the Transamerican Pyramid, the symbol of a new alien city. We both agree that Zippy the Pinhead could get elected Mayor today. Because of all the voters with MBAs.

I told Fantastic that I remembered San Francisco as a multicultural beehive of activity. I used to go over to Sausalito and party among the maze of houseboats and old ferries. We both agreed that today the city is polarized culturally, economically, sexually, and racially. It smells. The air is bad and the streets are dirty. Reminds me of Tacoma. Not to put down the fair city of Tacoma – because Tacoma is on the upswing. Frisco is just passing on her downswing. The city is violent. A few days before our arrival, Portola was the scene of a drive-by shooting. Rival gangs gunned down an innocent bystander. Residents are sullen. Perhaps it is dangerous there all day long. Across town, the old sign above the door at Vesuvio's in North Beach reminds partygoers that they are not in Portland, Oregon. They're not in San Francisco anymore either.

Fantastic roots around his three bashed-in cars with wild-eyed obsessiveness. The putdowns by the incumbents Chuck and Russ passed over him like rain on a duck's ass. He shut them up by offering to sell them a Deux Chevaux each. They hightailed it out of there real quick. They knew how persuasive Fantastic could be.

He decided on the car he was going to prepare for the L.A. filmmaker and immediately took the three engines out of the DS 19. Our agreement was that I could use the DS while he worked. But, uncontrollably, I rolled up my sleeves and proceeded to help Fantastic with his work. Bashed-in doors had to be removed. Broken windows replaced with parts from the other cars. We worked feverishly into dusk. The first engine wouldn't start. The second one did. Chuck and Russ ran up in disbelief. Fantastic stood there proud, giving all three of us the finger. He knew I wasn't a true believer. Our Deux Chevaux was assembled but looked like a clown because it was red, green, and orange – the colors of the different cars. So it had to be painted. I again took the doors and other panels off the chassis. An easy process because they interlock like kids' Legos. Then I sanded and stripped while Fantastic went to the hardware store and bought out their supply of cans of lemon yellow spray paint. (Nobody wanted that color so it was on special.)

About nine p.m., I gave up. I thought the car was too far gone. I tried to rib Fantastic out of his obsession but to no avail. So I rented us a motel room just up on busy Bayshore Highway, and promptly fell asleep. Fantastic came in several hours later smelling like rustoleum.

The next morning over breakfast at the corner diner I continued trying to convince Fantastic that an L.A. filmmaker wouldn't possibly want the old Deux Chevaux.. But he would not listen. I reluctantly rolled up my sleeves and went with him back to the loading dock. I'm the kind of guy who will work diligently if I believe in a project. But when I saw the results of last night's efforts I threw up my hands. He had hand-painted by brush the interior ceiling, walls and floor a thick rustoleum black. It looked good, but trouble was, shards of safety glass from the shattered windows were stuck to the floorboards and invisible because of the black paint. It was like a wartime type of booby trap the North Vietnamese pulled on their transgressors – run your hand across the floorboard and it would be painfully shredded. He was angry at himself. He explained that he had worked in the dark! Then, he yelled that if I hadn't given up, it would've never happened. I was flabbergasted. He yells, "…your hands, they don't have any calluses, you would've felt the shards if you were painting like you were supposed to." I shook my head. Chuck and Russ, our cheering section, reappeared, chewing gum to look at me as if the whole episode was my fault. It took us hours to dig out the shards.

It was late afternoon when the light bulb switched on above Fantastic's exhausted head. He remembered that the L.A. filmmaker had suggested that his DS 19 was having mechanical difficulties. Fantastic called down south to check. Sure enough, the filmmaker's car was broken down and it would be impossible for him to drive up to meet him as was the plan. Fantastic announced that the deal was off. Our new orders were to tow the Deux Chevaux we were working on back to Bainbridge Island the next morning.

Fantastic actually looked relieved. Chuck and Russ high-fived at being proven right. Their workday was over and they cracked a six-pack and offered him a beer. Fantastic doesn't drink so declined with a grunt. I admit I was relieved by the turn of events as well. Old Chuck starts to tell us his life story carwise, what cars he has owned through the years. This conversation turns into bitterness as he compares an ex-wife to a Chevy he once owned that gave him all sorts of mechanical problems. However, his new wife is A-OK but she doesn't allow him to ride his 750 Honda bike anymore. All he can do is shine it now and then. Russ interjects, talking about the latest Budweiser commercials. Soon they depart for their suburban homes and Fantastic invites me to dinner.

As we start up, he suggests that we eat at Fisherman's Wharf – "…only life left in the city…." I suggest we go over to Sausalito to visit my esoteric friend Peter, who lives aboard the old ferryboat Vallejo. We glide over the Golden Gate and proceed to Varda Landing. Fantastic hadn't been to the hamlet in years. When he sees the old ferry his jaw drops. The Vallejo, like Fantastic, is a survivor, an icon from the past. A huge, esoteric, rusting hulk larger than contemporary life.

I explained to him that in the '50s and '60s the ferry was at the epicenter of the bohemia/beatnik/hippie movement. She is famous for the wild, colorful parties Jean "Yanko" Varda hosted. He was the "king of the houseboat community." His waterborne New Year's parades were world-famous. Alan Watts, the Zen mystic, lived aboard as did Marion Saltman, the adult games innovator. All three have passed away. The present tenant, our host, Peter Kraemer, is considered by many to be the first "hippie." His artist mother was a constant guest of Varda, so the son was raised on Yanko's knee. As a young adult, Peter formed the Sopwith Camel rock group that was the prototype acid rock group. The hippie movement changed our culture for better or worse depending on one's point of view.

At the rickety gangway we meet Peter and I introduce Fantastic as Fantastic. Peter humbly shakes his hand. Fantastic bows. Peter turns to me and I assure him I am only along for the ride. Peter nods solemnly and ushers us aboard. Peter has not changed much from the last time I saw him last summer. He has the look of a person who has done it all – from sugar to shucks to shit and back to sugar, as the late, great writer Chester Himes put it. He is tall and handsome with many girlfriends. He says he doesn't go out much, what with AIDS and violence. He prefers to work on his abstract art. The colors he uses are stark and contrast each other on his canvases. I particularly liked one of them. He gave it to me, just like that. I was a bit at a loss – no one has given me something so unique in a long while.

Peter was about to deliver cargo to a couple of houseboaters who lived in the bay. He asked us to come along. To get to his boat we had to climb out his bedroom window. It was tied to the brooding ferry. He explains that his little fishing boat is filled with history itself. It participated in the only successful escape from Alcatraz. We hoisted up the anchor and putt-putted through the maze of houseboats anchored in the bay to arrive at "Ale's" boat. He earned his nickname because of his love for the Green Death (Rainier Ale). He also made a fine home brew that we wanted to try, but he wasn't home.

Since Fantastic was buying dinner, I suggested we eat over at Tiburon around Belvedere Island. It was dark and we had no running lights, but we were halfway there so Peter agreed. We arrived at a bawdy waterfront dive a short time later. The joint featured loud blues. The clientele was even louder. The fish dinner proved to be good, however. Afterwards, we strolled the town's one main street.

Peter explained to us that Tiburon's bacchanalian past was well documented. Dashiell Hammett wrote about it in his early detective novels. At a curio shop we saw a poster done by the late caricaturist Sketcho, or Mr. Zip. He drew the popular poster of the town in the late '60s. Mr. Zip was well known in the Pike Place Market up north where he worked in the summer months. He migrated to the Vieux Carre for winter. In springtime, he moved on to Greenwich Village, where he eventually died.

While Peter and Fantastic checked out another bar, I, as usual, was tired, so I went back to the boat to snooze. But I was kept awake because the pier filled up with expensive sailing boats and yachts. Well-scrubbed sailor types sniggered at Peter's old boat as they swished from ship to shore. However, one guy recognized the stylized eye Peter had painted on the bow. It was the eye that Yanko was famous for using. The sailors didn't know I was lying below decks within earshot.

The trip back exposed us to a gentle, but cold wind from the Golden Gate. The old boat had no cabin so Peter opened Ale's cargo. A bottle of rum. In darkness we chugged past the ruins of several WWII dry docks that still floated. They were anchored in mid-harbor off Sausalito. Many live-aboard boats were tied to the platforms. With the aid of a powerful flashlight we saw a chicken coop as well as what looked like a vegetable garden on the platform. The famous butterfly houseboat that almost sank a few years ago was lashed to the docks. Its "helmet" or wings were half-submerged. The whole conglomeration created weird imagery by flashlight.

Ale was asleep when we arrived so we left the half-empty bottle on his poop deck with a note of explanation under it and headed back to the Vallejo.

We spent the night aboard her. I slept out on deck. The night sky was a deep purple tinged with gray clouds. Fantastic crashed on the guest bed inside.

The next morning, as was my habit – before entropy entered my life – I rose early and walked for miles around the quaint town. I had coffee at the Lighthouse Café. A place I have known for years. It's been modernized a bit but still has the same folksy charm that only a harbor café can exude.

I returned to make breakfast from what I bought at a supermarket along the way. At breakfast, Peter claims the Vallejo ferryboat is really the "City of Seattle" and that Varda switched nameplates at the scrapyard when he first bought the boat. He explains the logic for the switch; it was simply that the 'Seattle' had a metal hull and would last longer. He was right. The 'bogus' City of Seattle's hull had rotted out long ago. Then her superstructure was fitted to a barge. Today, she's a prim floating home docked at the other end of the houseboat community about a quarter of a mile away. (The City of Seattle plied the waters from Alki to downtown Seattle around the turn of the century.)

Through all this nostalgia, Fantastic was downright respectful. No cutting asides, no smirks, no farts. Nothing uncouth or derisive. I couldn't believe it. However, when the snout of the DS 19 nudged out of the muddy Varda Landing, he was back in his element: "...great time even though the fish was tough... Peter's just an old hippie... boat'll sink in a month, betcha... That helmet scared me, it should be sunk...."

As we are about to enter the freeway to head back to the city, Fantastic spies a flea market getting started. Obsession takes over as an invisible umbilical cord straight to his psyche tugs him into the flea market. At the first booth his cunning switches on: "how much? ...too much. I'll give you $5 for it... what the hell, look, look, see the crack?"

We were in the flea market two hours. I spent the last hour in the car waiting for him to negotiate the purchase price of an old spanner. He got his offer and proudly announces that it is worth five times what he paid for it. He paid two dollars. I finally talked him into leaving. Our plan was to pick up the 2 CV and head out of town. But that too would change as the light bulb switches on over his head. He suggests we visit his friend in Carmel and spend the night. Whoosh – we were off before I could interject. We roll down Highway 1 passing the spot where another drive-by shooting had just occurred.

At the city's edge, we whisk around the graceful curve that leads down to the Pacific Ocean. The DS 19 is a dream car for taking long trips in. It has an oil/nitrogen type suspension system that cushions the ride. It's as sensual in seating and style as only the French can design. The front end looks like a cross between a smiling snake and a phallus. The car is an ode to Hermes' and Aphrodite's son because the rest of it is as curvaceous as a Parisian prostitute. Heads turned everywhere we drove. Our DS was a bit crumpled though. Things like trees and curbs and other inanimate objects had a way of getting in Fantastic's way.

We drove in silence for about twenty minutes; then his light bulb flickers on again. He turns to look at me and states matter-of-factly that Channing Pollock had the greatest pair of hands in the world. I didn't know who or what a Channing Pollock was and had the effrontery to say so. "He is the greatest modern magician.... What a pair of hands!" To emphasize his point, Fantastic shows me both of his oil-stained hands at once. We freewheel around a slight curve and are about to hit the curb. At the last moment, Fantastic grabs the wheel again. I try to shrug my tense shoulders while I again tell him evenly that I never really heard of him. Fantastic explodes. "He appeared on TV many times, Ed Sullivan Show and so on... everybody has heard or seen Channing at your age.... He was going to be Errol Flynn's replacement in the swashbuckling films.... He has *savoir faire*, you know, personality..." Now, being somewhat of a film buff, I take umbrage to this last bit of info and bluntly repeat that I never heard of the bum.

Exasperated, with hands flailing like he is doing some sort of magical incantation at 65 mph, Fantastic yells, "Shipman, EVERYBODY knows Channing Pollock... it's your brains, they're rotting... you're rotting from entropy... wake up, Shipman, wake up!" I bristle but politely ask him to please keep both hands on the wheel while I'm in the car. I added another 'please.' He continued to claim I was brain dead. A low-blood sugar type. "...My hands leave the steering wheel because my passenger is so numbed I have to emphasize my points." I yelled out that maybe I <u>had</u> heard of him just to shut him up.

Fantastic turned emphatic. "It's his hands, he has perfect hands... you gotta remember the hands. He perfected the illusion of doves appearing from nowhere... hell, he raised it to an art form... perfection! It was his hands; they're so smooth.... He mesmerized the audience who followed his hands. Exactly like the Istanbul belly dancer I once knew. His hands were like her belly button... she could strip her marks of watches, wallets, rings and other things before the spell was broken... Magic, Shipman, magic.... The doves. The doves appeared from nowhere. The audience followed the hands..." As he was talking, his hands flitted about the car, fingers snapped to emphasize a point. I had to needle him about the condition of his hands by pointing out the oil stains, the grit under his nails, the clumps of grease between his fingers, and the calluses. Fantastic simply stated that he soaks them in expensive oils a whole day before a performance.

"Are you a magician or a mechanic?" I asked matter-of-factly. "Both... I, well, I'm not a real mechanic. I'm a parts changer type.... I know my Citroën parts and how to change them." He wasn't biting. I mumbled that it was pretty obvious that he was a parts changer type. He retorted that if he was required to work on a Chevy he wouldn't guarantee the results. But if it was a Citroën he would perform magic. I grimaced.

We drive along in silence until almost to Half Moon Bay Fantastic spots a yard sale sign at the next left. Varoom! He races down the street like a dog in heat. By now it is Sunday afternoon and most of the goodies would be gone. I point out this bit of logic but to no avail. Sure enough, the sale has been stripped of its deals and finer things and we are left with old magazines and *National Geographic* (every one from January 1987 to mid-1988). I bought an NBA sport magazine and got into a conversation with the guy running the sale about who had the best chance of winning the Western championship. Fantastic threw up his hands and waited for me in the car. The guy liked the Lakers but thought the Sonics had a chance. I disagreed because I liked Sacramento. He commented on Gary Payton and how the Sonics screwed up by trading him. Our conversation was rudely interrupted by bleatings from the DS's car horn.

We depart with Fantastic revealing that he can't stand sports figures and their cheerleaders. Sure, he likes the cheerleaders' bottoms but they were cheering on bums. Bums that make too much money. They use too much dope. They bend the economy, or something like that. I couldn't understand the logic but then understanding his logic wasn't my chief concern at the moment. We were trying to cross Highway 1 and it was proving impossible, especially with his mind speed set on explaining his dislike for sports figures. A couple of cars behind us simply pulled out and went on their way.

It seemed we were at the intersection for another ten minutes. It was here that I broke my oath to myself and started telling him how to drive – how to get across the highway. I put myself in the position that if the roles were reversed, I would be angry. Fantastic just gave me a quizzical look, turned back somewhat calmed, and quickly maneuvered across the roadway. I was angry at myself for interceding and vowed to watch it in the future.

We rode along in relative silence for Fantastic was humming the Willie Dixon tune, "Built for Comfort and Not for Speed." At Moss Bay, his old effervescence returned and he whooshed up to a pay phone. He jumped out and yelled back with a gleam and a wild laugh worthy of the Joker of Batman fame: "I'll prove it... It's all in the hands." After a minute or two, he hung up and announced that we were going to meet Channing Pollock.

I told myself, 'of course we are. I mean, I should have known, right? I mean, well, I don't know what I mean.'

We tooled down a long private drive and stopped in front of this classic weather-beaten beach villa. At the portico stood a lean, tall, ageless figure. Strikingly handsome with a close-cropped beard that made his powerful eyes seem almost other worldly. It was Channing Pollock. His aura glowed as if he were some sort of saint. He led us inside and to a vast table set in front of huge windows overlooking the Pacific Ocean. Far below, the afternoon sun bounced off the rolling surf. Little wetsuit-clad scuba divers waddled around the rocks like deformed seals. High above the riff-raff, we entered into conversation with a mythical figure in magic. A cult figure in film. Channing was indeed a classic example of the "typifying statement." Film jargon for the type of person that others think they know instantly. Why the minute I saw him I knew him. At least I thought I did. When I was told he starred in Franju's cult films... hell, I knew it. Or I thought I knew it. I mean, maybe I wanted to know it. With Fantastic, at any moment, reality was up for grabs. As I was struggling with the fact of did I or didn't I know who Channing Pollock was, he turned and looked at me in a clear, direct way. I sort of apologized and told him that I really was along only for the ride.

As we talked, Effi, Channing's strikingly beautiful wife of oriental extraction, hovered about behind us. Our conversation was formal. It was obvious that Channing was happy to see Fantastic. He was also concerned for Cory. It was explained that on the last visit, Cory was quite sick with asthma aggravated by springtime pollen. As Fantastic was talking he used his hands. They were still covered in grease and oil. Fantastic paused and explained why they were so dirty. That struck me. Why did he explain at all? Well, I thought, I was going to tease him about this later.

Channing's subtle hands were quietly folded in front of him. They were indeed profound. The fingers were very long and smooth. He noticed me looking at them and raised his right index finger ever so slightly. The sensation the movement created in me startled me. I gently asked Channing if he still performed. He answered that he hadn't performed in twenty years. What happened? Why the suspended state of animation? He was seventy-plus but one would never know it. Even close up he looked half his age. Effi moved out of earshot. The conversation between him and Fantastic shifted. They talked about Channing's wild European past. The conversation turned positively ribald, as they talked about the filming of Petomane the Frenchman who could keep a tune with his flatulations. Wild, unrestrained laughter brought Effi quickly back. She hovered just behind us cleaning a shelf, looking every bit like Yoko Ono's mother.

The conversation deteriorated to talking about Luis Fechner, the French movie producer who created the illusion of levitating over a barstool.

Too quickly our visit was over. We got into the DS and Fantastic started it up. One cannot just go after starting a DS because the fluid suspension must raise the car to its driving level. It gave me a brief moment to look over the scene one more time. The lonely villa high on a bluff. Even though the sun was bright, foliage kept the entryway in shadows. The surf deadened sound. In the doorway stood this beautiful specimen of a human. Indeed his hands were a gift from the gods. I wished he would use them again.

As we glided down the coast, I got to thinking that Carmel was quite far. We wanted to get an early start in the morning. I mentioned my observation to Fantastic, who laughed, "You have a chance to spend the night in a classic Carmel home and you don't take it? Wow, Shipman, you are jaded. Tell you what... I'll spring for dinner at the Hog's Breath. You know, Clint's joint. Got bad reviews, but what the hell!"

"What the hell is right," I laughed, and said go for it.

A short while later we approached the old hippie watering holes of Davenport. A town about ten miles out of Santa Cruz. It's famous for the seedy critters who frequented the town bar. Last time I was there was years ago. Today, over a hundred Harley choppers were lined up side by side down Main Street. We slowed but didn't stop.

We arrive in Santa Cruz around four-thirty. The light bulb over Fantastic's head flickers on. He stops and makes two calls, then returns to announce that I was right – Carmel is too far away. Did I mind a change of plans? "We're heading for Jacques' Citroën Garage... a pit stop." He points at his bent-up engine hood. "Got to change hoods." I shrug my shoulders as I look at several golden California girls swishing by.

On the way across town, I ask Fantastic if this is the first time he called Eric. He looks impishly at me and counters, "Well, the old mind is losing a bit of flab." I ask him again. He admits: "...OK. So what? He's got guests up for the Laguna Seca motorcycle races... I know you don't like grease so why bother them? Besides, they're L.A. rich... they scent their grease...."

At the garage entrance, we meet Jacques who directs us into a tiny fenced-in yard. Jacques has the bearing of an officer in the French Foreign Legion, graying but in very good shape. He could be called short if he wasn't so well-proportioned. Before he spoke to Fantastic he flattened his already flat stomach. His smile was not directly on his face. He wore it kind of suspended to one side. It wasn't disarming and it wasn't empty. It was sort of just there. It was like he wasn't focusing on your face when he spoke. Maybe he just needed stronger glasses. He hands were well-manicured. It appeared he hadn't picked up a wrench for years. He was the brains of the outfit.

The little yard was filled with rare Maserati-powered Citroën SM sedans that were made briefly in the '70s. I gawk at all the luxury gathering dust. Jacques looks hopefully at me. I smile tight-lipped and tell him that I don't want one. I mention that a friend of mine had an SM in Spain but it didn't look at all like his. Jacques explains in careful English that the European versions had different cowlings and headlight configurations.

Headlights were to play a major role this warm full-moon evening on romantic Monterey Bay. The Frenchman introduces us to his mechanic, Thor. A quiet, purposeful Scandinavian who is indeed the brawn side of the operation. He is a big man who doesn't crack a smile the whole time we are in the yard. It seems Jacques and Fantastic had struck a deal over the phone. A second-hand hood for a hundred bucks and Fantastic's DS 19 turning headlamps. The headlamps would be replaced by less-expensive fixed-direction lamps. Thor, with Fantastic's help, would do the actual work. To do the job properly, the DS's fenders had to be removed, so the airducts had to be disassembled, wiring unplugged. On top of this operation, the hoods had to be switched... and on and on into the balmy romantic night.

At the two-hour mark, I was fed up. The tease of Carmel seemed a smokescreen to get us to Santa Cruz. No Hog's Breath. No sandy beaches. Just grease and more grease. Jacques, the brains, was going to leave in a few minutes. This alarmed me to no end, so I hastily asked him for a lift to the airport bus at the Greyhound station. He agreed, exaggerating his smile and flattening his stomach in the process. I told him that it was ok because I was only along for the ride. He nodded knowingly. However, five minutes later, when Jacques was ready to go, I had second thoughts. I was giving up. I wasn't following through on my objective. Entropy was winning out. So I thanked Jacques and went back to riding shotgun for Fantastic.

Three hours later, the DS is reassembled and the new hood is slammed down. It doesn't fit. The stoic Thor had not bothered to test it when he put it on four hours before. It had hung there in the balmy evening, wide open, like a giant alligator's mouth waiting to trap a dodo bird. It trapped us instead. Fantastic dives in to help, but after at least twenty adjustments even Thor's patience is wearing thin. I watch Thor's knuckles get whiter and whiter as he opens the hood, does some adjusting, then closes it trying to get it to fit. In our sixth hour, the sweating Thor finally has it lined up properly. Fantastic mumbles to me that it's important to have it lined up because they fly open at speed destroying the windshield and the hood. This is what happened to Fantastic's last hood. Incidentally, I lashed the old hood to the top of the DS in a gesture of solidarity to Fantastic. He inspected it and said I did a fantastic job.

Fantastic thanked Thor profusely. Thor didn't bat an eye as he watched us swoosh out into the Monterey Bay night. Fantastic was furious at Jacques – yelling that Jacques had taken advantage of him. He swore that Jacques must have known that the hood was warped when he bought it. "…Gotta stop payment on that check!" he roars.

In the darkness, he drove like a swooshing cushioned banshee down the twisting freeway. The harder he pushed the 30-year-old DS, the better it performed. The dent-filled crusty old warrior seemed to want to be set free. To return to France to conquer tortuous switchbacks in mountain roads that lead down to pristine Mediterranean beaches. I felt the full glory of the engineering of this fantastic automobile. I also felt that regardless how fast Fantastic drove he had mastered this machine. I relaxed and tried to enjoy the experience. But Fantastic was screaming for Highway 101.

I assured him that that was where we were heading. The longer we drove, the worse his sarcasm. He kept insisting: "You're guilty, Shipman… that's it, you're guilty!" I wouldn't bite. After all, I was only along for the ride, and trying to enjoy it.

Finally, the Los Gatos city limits sign appeared which proved that we were heading in the right direction but were miles from Highway 101. He yells: "You see, you're guilty…" I yell back, "Guilty of what?"

"You're guilty of going in the wrong direction…your type always are… 101 is in the opposite direction. Hah, Hah, Hah! Take your entropy and shove it, Shipman…." Another road sign appeared announcing 'SAN FRANCISCO 50 MILES.' The freeway straightened out and Fantastic speeded up.

Soon, I recognized that this was the freeway (280) that ran atop the hills from San Jose to the city. I had always thought it rivaled the Autostrado del Sol in Italy in scenic beauty. It's the freeway connecting Milano and Firenze that runs along the crest of a small mountain range as well. I mentioned it to Fantastic, who only grunted. We passed Foothill College.

Its architecture was somewhat influenced by Aztec or Inca cultures. I attended classes there in the early '60s. I mentioned this to Fantastic and he grunted again. He drove the distance transfixed. Must have been averaging way over 80 mph. We whooshed through the darkness in silence. There was very little traffic and the road was straight. Soon the airport turnoff appeared and we veered right, en route to the Bayshore highway. At Santa Cruz, I had thought seriously of asking him to let me off at the airport when we passed it. But as we glided by the huge complex, I kept my thoughts to myself.

We didn't get back to the motel without another minor test of wills. I told him that it was the Third Street exit he wanted. He drove right by it and took the next exit. It made our trip two miles longer, but I kept my mouth shut.

The motel was the same one we stopped in before. Same room, in fact. The next morning I got up early again but decided not to walk to the Portola district. I felt it unsafe. I went to the coffee shop that was part of the motel complex and sat for an hour waiting for Fantastic to wake up. The bar was shaped like a diner. The cook had very little room to work in. His back was always towards me. He was a black man with sloping shoulders and a big butt. Fantastic arrived and we took a booth. When I left, I told the cook I knew half of him well, his back half. He laughed and bade us a good trip. The cash register girl was a petite Pago Pagoan. She gave me a warm smile. I started feeling pretty good about myself.

We slid back to the loading dock. Hooked up the 2 CV and were ready to depart. It was then the old bulb again went on over Fantastic's head. He decided to load all the doors, hoods, seats and other pieces of auto he deemed worth something. I rolled up my sleeves again and in an hour the two cars were jammed with junk. As we worked, Fantastic started singing, "Built for Comfort and Not for Speed" again. We left about an hour later after twenty run-throughs of the song. Good riddance, Portola!

A short distance later on the Oakland Bay Bridge, Fantastic speeded up and several objects fell off our load. Small objects because we didn't see anything, just heard their rattle and clunks. It was good riddance, San Francisco.

We drove up the Sacramento bypass road. Halfway up and we have a flat tire. The Citroën is easy to fix a flat in because of the liquid suspension system. (Don't ask me how or why!) The flat was changed in one-tenth the time a normal car would take. I'm starting to suggest the DS is abnormal? I'm getting Fantasticized!

The flat was caused by a piece of the fender that got bent while being worked on at Santa Cruz. When the day heated up, the tire expanded and touched the metal, causing friction.

We drove without incident all the way to Ashland, Oregon. I dozed most of the way. At Ashland, Fantastic takes the off ramp and heads directly to a phone booth. He makes a call, then returns to announce that Jason Beebe will see us. He gets in and we speed off. In afterthought, he tells me that Jason has a Citroën Mahari he wants to give to Fantastic for free. I groan, for I believed that if anybody wanted to give a car away it must be in pretty bad shape. But this was Fantastic's trip, not mine.

Shortly, we arrived in Ashland proper. In the past, on my many trips down south, I bypassed the place. I wasn't prepared for this delightful, sophisticated town. The place evolved and grew around its annual Shakespeare festival. The women were beautiful and the cars sleek and clean. The whole place had a tidiness about it. In other words, our ensemble stood out like a dandelion bouquet in a rose parade. Sure enough, we were stopped by a trooper for failing to stop at a railroad crossing. The cop asked all sorts of questions about the DS because he had never seen one before. He was friendly enough. Fantastic demonstrated the suspension system that raised and lowered the car. All the while, the trooper was making out his ticket. He handed it to Fantastic and told him: "Now you shore have a nice visit to our town... you hear?" Fantastic was out-Fantasticized.

In a kind of daze, we arrive at the Beebe spread. It is classic Oregon. Swards of veggies and flowers being cultivated. Little kids and dogs cavorting. A rustic old house and a huge workshop. We find Jason in the workshop. He is a stout man whose wide suspenders wrap around his shoulders with authority. He has clear Oregonian eyes that burn with an intensity somewhat like Channing's. Where Channing's eyes glowed, Jason's burned like lasers. His thumb was hooked to an unused belt loop in his Levis. His hands looked average for a man who is considered one of the finest woodsmiths in the country. In the shed stands his main project, the restoration of a coach built in the '30s that rested on a Rolls Royce chassis. His work was faultless. The curved wood frame he had hand-hewn was just about ready for the aluminum skin to be bolted on. It rested in the loft above. I commented that the car must be worth at least a hundred thousand dollars. He corrects me and says the starting price will be closer to eight hundred thousand dollars. Just outside the door sits another one of his projects. Two fifteen-thousand-dollar luxury 2CVs. He covers the car interiors with teak paneling, adds leather seats, then details the car to perfection. He started the green one. It was as silent as a Rolls. The concept of turning something so inexpensive into a fine jewel excited me. Fantastic comments: "This is like the one Chris used." Was I missing something or what? I ask, "Chris who?" Jason explains, "Chris took my old 2 CV to Wisconsin. 'Road and Track' wrote about the trip." I look at Fantastic who looks back innocently. Of course I wasn't missing anything. Fantastic had told me all about it. I hadn't listened... I guess.

Trinka, Jason's Chinese wife, their kids, Brandon and Mi Lan, and her eighty-year-old father, are waiting in her car in front. They're late for dinner and have to hurry. Another family is meeting them at a Chinese restaurant. Jason invites us to join later. He points to a junk pile by the roadway and gets in and tools off with his family. Fantastic and I go to the pile and start digging. At the bottom is the crumpled and thoroughly broken Mahari. Wheels are missing. So is the engine's manifold. Fantastic makes the right decision by putting the junk back. We silently depart for the restaurant.

On the way, we stop at a motel to get a room. About ten minutes later, we find the restaurant, go inside, and join the families at a long table. At the head of the table sits the grandfather. We are introduced to him. He's visiting from California. It's obvious he loves being with his grandkids.

We take chairs at the far end of the table next to Brandon and Jason. Brandon is, at twelve, Jason's oldest kid. Fantastic gave him a present – a thick book explaining magic and illusions. Brandon loved magic and it was obvious that he looked forward to the visits by Fantastic.

Jason and I got into a conversation about the cars from the mid-'50s through to the mid-'60s. He explains that a friend of his races a 1965 Lotus "Super 7" against the modern sports cars and wins hands-down. At every race, the 7's legality is challenged. This means that the tedious task of dismantling the little car's Cosworth Ford engine had to be done to see that it's stock. The modern sports cars are factory backed and their managers hate to see a "vintage" car beat theirs. So this was their way of trying to force his friend to race his car in the "vintage" races.

I tell him that my all-time favorite car is the Austin Healy. I had a 1954 100-4 model. Quite rare. It was akin to the one that was involved in an accident with the Mercedes at Le Mans that is the worst accident in car racing history. Well over one hundred spectators were killed. Jason remembers the incident and states that Mercedes stopped sponsoring a car race after that tragedy. He asked me what happened to the car. I had to explain that I destroyed the 100-4 in a single-car crackup on Sunset Boulevard at Beverly Glen in West L.A. coming back from classes in the valley. I knew the roadway and its curves intimately but it was late at night and a road crew had torn up the street to resurface it. I hit the curb at over 90 mph, turning the aluminum body into silly putty and moving the engine back four inches. The machine still drove though and I made it back to Malibu. He tells me the car is worth twenty thousand today depending on its condition. I said I sold mine for parts for one hundred dollars.

The dinner was over and their other guests departed. Jason invited us to his house for the remainder of the evening. As usual, I was tired. But also I felt that they had a lot to talk about among themselves. So I was dropped off at the motel. Fantastic was more or less a one-on-one person. I got the feeling Jason was the same.

The next morning, Fantastic said how great his evening went. Jason is an avid jazz buff. So am I. Damn, I wish I had gone along.

We had a small breakfast at an upscale bakery in downtown Ashland. It was as together as anything in Seattle. At the table I smiled a lot. Something I hadn't done in many months. I felt more relaxed than I had in a year. I flirted with our waitress a bit. She could be my daughter but certainly didn't see me as a papa type. Fantastic had a smirk on his face as we left. "Shipman, I thought you told me you couldn't get it up anymore," he laughs. He slaps me on the back as the DS rises to drive level. We depart Ashland, a jewel of a burg.

It was a short ride to Fantastic's next stop, Medford. An old magician friend has opened a magic shop in the Rouge River Mall next to the freeway. His specialty is card tricks. While we talked, he demonstrated several. He was quite good. But I was a bit bored with illusionists. I walked around the mall as they talked. Other than the name, it was nothing special. One shop stood out: the Made in Oregon shop. It featured only made in Oregon products. The state must be filled with artists and artisans that are almost of Jason's caliber.

On the road again and without incident. We both sensed that the trip was just about over. We were kind of irritable. We passed the city of Eugene. Fantastic said he liked the town. I sort of nodded. Soon we passed Salem. Then Aurora, a town founded by a religious group in the 1860s. There are many white buildings with corrugated roofs from the period still standing. I mention this to Fantastic and he grunts.

Somehow our banter evolves into a ribald conversation about Peter runs. A bunch of guys compare the length of their peters. I assure Fantastic that a peter run with him involved would be no contest. Now a brain test would be a different matter; he probably would come in last. "That quart of blood hanging down your pant leg would be more helpful to you if it was residing in your head when you're not making love."

He laughs at my attempts at a putdown. He is about to answer with his greasy hand poised in mid-air when the car starts a lurching motion. He yells that we're out of gas.

Now this was occurring on the long bridge over the wide Columbia River that separates Oregon and the State of Washington. It was a hot, hazy day. Majestic Mount Hood was looming to our right. The stunted, brooding Mount Saint Helens rose in front of us. To the left, Portland glittered in the distance. Fantastic kept the gas pedal to the floor and both cars lurched violently as the DS gasped for fuel. Here is where I violate our relationship. I tell him to ease up on the gas. Then I buddy punch him several times on the shoulder to try to get him to do it. We lurch across the river with the 2 CV in tow looking like a vaudeville partner slightly out of step. I yell as I point to an off ramp. Fantastic wants to continue up the freeway even though it is on an incline. I demand that we leave the freeway. He turns off and we find ourselves on a long, lonely spur of road that meanders along the river's edge. There is no gas station or turnoff in sight. Worse, Fantastic spots a police car behind us, which he is sure is going to stop us. Our relationship is at a simmering, all-time low. The cop just passes us without a look. Fantastic waves as he goes by. At the next turnoff, we completely run out of gas – and glide to a stop in front of a distribution yard. Fantastic is as furious at me as I am. He had every right to be. He should have stayed on the freeway to the next gas stop. I didn't know the tolerances of the DS. It ran for another five miles before it was completely out of gas. The lurching occurred because we were on a slight incline. I saved myself by suggesting that the company we stopped in front of would have gas for their trucks. I point to one pulling out from their loading dock. Fantastic would hear none of this and insisted that he would walk to the next gas station with his gas can. I run into the yard and ask the first person I see, who says for sure we may have some gas for free. Fantastic walks with him to the pump as I slink back to my post of riding shotgun.

Later, at the gas station, the silent Fantastic looks at me and says, "you were lucky... just plain lucky."

I thought to myself that this was a hell of a note on which to end our six-day journey. I was completely in the wrong. But I couldn't get myself to apologize to Fantastic. I did allude that perhaps he was right – we should have stayed on the freeway.

The ice broke when Fantastic asked me why I hadn't read the gas gauge for him. Why I let the car run out of gas? It was doubly my fault because I was interrupting him by talking about ribald things. Then he asked me for the first time if I wanted to drive. I felt I had passed some sort of test. But I said no.

Fantastic laughed and called me chicken. He suggested that the DS was too much of a car for me. I countered, pointing out that the 2 CV in tow was never fitted with proper rear lights and I didn't want to risk getting a ticket. He had no answer to that. We drove on towards Puget Sound in silence.

We were trying to get back to Bainbridge Island before dusk, before we had to use the lights. When he asked what route we should take I suggested Highway 101 up the Olympic Peninsula. He said he had his fill of Highway 101. My next suggestion was nixed as well – going to Seattle and taking the ferry across like we did when we left. He said it would take too much time. So he did what he wanted to all along – the most direct route via Tacoma and through the town of Poulsbo. At the bridge over to Bainbridge Island, we both heaved a huge sigh of relief. At my place he asked if I wanted the 2 CV? I laughed and told him "no... no thanks."

~ ~ ~

VI
Alex

Some history

ALEXANDER CONLIN – THE MAN WHO KNOWS
(6/30/1880 – 8/5/1954)

Alexander was a star performer on the Pantages circuit specializing in elaborate magic and illusion with his assistants, the Nartell Twins. He was very successful, both financially and socially, in the Hollywood of the '20s and '30s. Other stars of the era, such as Clara Bow and Harold Lloyd, were close friends and spent summers at the Conlin Villa at La Push, Washington.

Alexander's influence not only lives on in fact and legend, but also as place names on maps. He perfected lavish scale magic performances that are still popular in today's Vegas. He knew many people who went on to fame and great fortune, such as his early friends Alexander Pantages, and the legendary Seattle political mover and shaker (and Prohibition bar owner) Mr. James.

The "factual" history of the historical Alexander will be told chiefly through the dream sequences of the story. The legends surrounding Alexander paint a far different picture.

Today, La Push locals tell a legend about a Wizard who lived in the "Wizard's Castle," and who brought famous people up to his castle. As another legend has it, the Wizard brought 'evil' and that's why the Wizard's Castle was burned down.

The fictionalized side of my story is based on these legends, and our young Alex soon discovers that legends die hard.

Once upon a time...

On a foggy morning in Seattle's Pioneer Square

In a dark flat sits Alex; a tall, stooped, balefaced man, 30 years old. He is sitting in front of a wood framed mirror. Tacked on the walls around him are frayed posters of operas, magicians, and a bullfight announcement. On tables and shelves sit piles of dolls, cheap busts of famous men, artifacts from fairs and exhibitions. A plastic Space Needle stands next to an Eiffel Tower and a miniature totem pole. A 1950ish brass cowboy/horse clock shows 8 a.m. – if it's accurate. Alex is listening to The *Phantom of the Opera*. He is staring at himself as if he is trying to decide what to do next. He cocks his ear, then turns off the music. A faint thumping is heard. He pushes a woman's makeup tray towards the mirror and gets up.

In an adjoining room, a frail hand is hitting the wall. It is connected to a very thin, geriatric figure – a very old, bald person with unblinking oriental eyes, staring straight ahead. The figure lies in bed, unmoving, save for the thump-thumping of the hand. On the walls are many 1920's magician-type posters announcing a performance by

MINSA MAHATMA, THE SELECTED ONE.

The posters depict a beautiful oriental face. A subheading reads: "From the mystic Orient flies Minsa Mahatma – seer of the Himalayas." The only light in the room is from a little bedside lamp.

The door opens and Alex enters. He walks to the bed and plants a kiss on Minsa's cheek, then picks up a wig and places it on her head. It's slightly askew so he works it until he gets it right. Minsa appears to be smiling from his efforts. He gently stops her closed hand from beating on the wall, then talks to her about the news of the morning, He looks at her and, as if he is reading her mind, rearranges a pillow on her right side. Again a faint smile on her face. He then lights a pipe and holds it for her. She takes a slight puff, then two more. Alex winces at the smoke. Next, he places the pipe back in its holder and prepares to change her diapers. As he works, we explore the room and the posters. It is obvious from them that she is Minsa, a former marquee vaudevillian who worked the Pantages circuit.

Alex looks at his watch, wants to leave, but is compelled to stay. He stares at Minsa, then turns in a trance and opens a drawer and lifts out a crystal ball. He turns back, holding it awkwardly and says, "thank you." A faint smile is registered on Minsa's face. Alex gives her a kiss and tells her he must prepare for work, and leaves.

Back in his room, Alex holds the crystal ball up and gazes into it, then places it on a cushion. He turns, sits and busies himself with the makeup tray. He starts to darken his eyebrows but stops. He stares at his face, smiles, and puts down his brush. (This is the first time memory that he doesn't wear makeup.) He rises and moves to his closet and selects a turn-of-the-century outfit, complete with vest, suspenders, and top hat. Once dressed, he tosses the top hat back into the closet and picks up a gray dishcloth and wraps it around his head as if it were a turban. He has difficulty with the folds but finally manages. He looks at himself and smiles. The makeshift turban keeps unraveling a bit but in costume he gains courage. *(The metaphor of a clown being sad out of costume clearly applies to Alex at this moment.)*

Later, outside, on the brick-lined street, Alex passes a somber Native American totem pole. He stops and studies the intricate designs, then moves on and climbs aboard a trolley. He bows deeply to the conductor who breaks out in a deep smile and pats Alex on the back. The trolley clangs on down the street.

At the main entrance of the City Market, people wave as the tall Alex strides in. He bows and waves back as if on stage as he makes his way past vegetable stalls and walks down the narrow hallway to the lower levels. On the wall behind him is a reproduction of a huge poster of the magician ALEXANDER, THE MAN WHO KNOWS. The magician is holding a crystal ball.

As Alex enters the Magic Shop, the harried owner, Daniel, yells to Alex to hurry because he's late. Daniel looks at Alex's getup and shakes his head in exasperation. He's busy with a large load of books that has just arrived. Alex slides through to the other side of the counter and proceeds to help/entertain a mother and her son. He does one magic trick and then another. Daniel nervously snaps his finger and points to the cash register and mouths "hustle… hustle buddy." Alex continues his routine until the kid makes up his mind and buys a magic trick. Daniel notices and relaxes – the day has begun.

Later, during a slow period, Daniel takes a break and Alex goes over to a shelf of books on great magicians. He spies a stack of the new book Daniel has just brought in. It's a profile/tribute of the magician Alexander. He rearranges his sloppy turban as he opens one of the books and flips through the pages, stopping at the image of the poster he passed in the hallway. He looks up, fumbling with his turban and sees, reflected in the mirror in front of him, another poster depicting Alexander in a turban shaped like a question mark. His own turban, with its unfolded 'tail,' looks just like it. He looks at his reflection and realizes just how close he resembles the original Alexander. He nervously jerks the makeshift turban off his head.

Slowly, Alex turns more pages of the book. He becomes transfixed with himself in the mirror. His baleful concentration fuses himself with Alexander. He slowly closes the book. Daniel re-enters and grabs the book, admonishing Alex that... "this book costs a hundred and fifty bucks so it's not to be touched!" As he puts it back, he assures Alex, in a mock, condescending way, that it is one he could never afford. Later in the day, when Daniel has closed up the shop, Alex again lets his eyes fall upon the book, then grabs if off the shelf and takes it home.

That night, he reads to Minsa from the book: how Alexander, The Man Who Knows, got started, his Klondike Goldrush days, the Nartell Twins, his shows, and the Pantages circuit.

Minsa's eyes shimmer with tears and brightness from the memories Alex's reading bring. Alex holds her pipe for her. Later, he slowly takes off her wig, gives her a kiss, and leaves. The light burns on in her sad, staring eyes.

Alex arrives for work the next morning in the same outfit he wore the day before. Daniel sneers at him as he counts his new books on display. He's missing one book. He swears he knew exactly how many he had put out. One was stolen! He turns and accuses Alex of stealing the book. Alex says he's innocent, but Daniel smirks and asks him why he is wearing the same outfit as he did yesterday. Alex blushes. Daniel tells Alex that even if he didn't steal it, it was stolen on his watch so he's going to dock his pay one hundred and fifty bucks. Alex accepts the rebuke by ventriloquizing, "fuck you." Daniel whirls around, then turns back to Alex, scratching his chin, "not bad, boy... not bad."

That night, Alex once again reads from the book to Minsa. He becomes thoroughly engrossed and reads for a long while. He covers Alexander's Hollywood days leading into his life at La Push and how he named Rialto Beach. About his Prohibition friend Mr. James. He reads that James and Alexander Island were named after the two men.

The bedside clock shows that it is past two a.m. At one point, Minsa had grasped Alex's arm tightly, then released it. Alex was startled but continued reading to the staring lady. He lights up her pipe and tries to give her a puff and discovers that she has died. He tries to shut her eyelids but they will not move. He gives her a final kiss, then slowly draws the sheet up to cover her staring eyes. The sheet slips down, exposing her eyes. Alex stares at them for a bit, then looks down at the book and on the page is a picture of Rialto Beach. This was the home of Alexander during his heyday in the 1920s.

The next day, Alex tells Daniel that he wants a hiatus from his magic shop job. Alex explains that he wants to work professionally and must practice his magic acts. Daniel asks how he is going to pay his rent? Alex explains that he is leaving his apartment. Daniel understands, goes over to the cash register, and takes out Alex's pay plus a $100 bonus. Alex pulls out Minsa's crystal ball and asks Daniel to take care of it for him. Daniel agrees and gives Alex a friendly pat and tells him he has a job anytime he wants to come back, and to forget about the lost book. Under his gruff exterior, Daniel has a heart of gold.

Back at Pioneer Square, Alex opens the door to Minsa's apartment. It is bare. Nothing remains. No furniture, no posters, nothing. He gently closes the door and enters his own apartment. He dresses in a turn-of-the-century outfit much like the one he has been wearing to work, lifts up his lightly filled suitcase, and leaves. *(The persona of the original Alexander is blending with Alex.)* He takes the trolley to the Bainbridge Island ferry. At Bainbridge Island, he takes the bus to Port Townsend. On the bus, he opens to the last half of the Alexander book, to the section that describes the magic tricks of "Doctor Q."

Shortly, the bus arrives at Port Townsend. Alex admires the place for it is filled with early twentieth-century buildings. Downtown, the bus stops and picks up more passengers and heads for La Push and Rialto Beach, three hours away on the Pacific Ocean. On the bus, he entertains a group of kids with his 'different size rope' tricks.

By late afternoon, they arrive at the tiny Indian town of La Push. The settlement is on a cove nestled under James Island. He enters a wooden beach office, festooned with northwest Indian motifs, to rent a little beach hut. The office staff are Native Americans. The woman who helps Alex starts humming in a sonorous tone. Another woman looks up at Alex and joins in the humming. A third starts up. The humming is done unselfconsciously. A man peers out a doorway to look at Alex. When Alex leaves, they all stare after him. Alex tries to appear to take no notice as he leaves. He settles in his hut. *(The spirit of Alexander seems to be taking over Alex's body. His mannerisms begin to change. He becomes increasingly nervous, yet falls deeper into the role of Alexander.)*

In the morning, it is stormy but Alex strides to Rialto Beach to start his search. (Through the years, the waves have tossed up a huge berm of gray sand deep into the forest. The saltwater from the sand has killed the trees, casting a long swath of beachfront in a monochromatic hue of gray.) Halfway down the beach, he is stopped by a man wearing a gray Macintosh. He had stepped out of the dead, leafless forest and walked stiffly towards Alex because he is being buffeted by the wind. His slate gray eyes are framed in a somewhat mad smile. He greets Alex: "Hi… you know, I was driving down from Port Townsend last night and picked up this tipsy Indian girl… this morning she introduced me to the oldest Indian I ever saw… Fantastic… I'm from Detroit…" Alex is completely baffled and blurts out, "I'm looking for a tall chimney; have you seen one sticking out of the forest?" He pulls Daniel's book out from under his raincoat and shows the young man the picture of the ruin. The man looks at the book, then up at Alex and laughs. "Look, I'm from Detroit… I don't know this neck of the woods…. Well, gotta go."

He looks over Alex's shoulder, up Rialto Beach, wipes his wet face with the length of his forearm. He backs away, holding his arms wide to support himself from the force of the wind. Alex turns and looks up the beach and notices that the tide has taken the man's footprints away. He turns back and the man has disappeared amongst the groaning, swaying dead branches. He continues his search for another fifty feet before turning back. The wind hitting the lifeless limbs creates images that make Alex's hair stand on end. Today, the actual beach is a far cry from the colorful picture in the book. In the late afternoon, he stumbles across a line of unusual trees that form a wall. At the end of the "wall," he finds the ruin. He takes his bearings and returns to his cabin as the storm has worsened dramatically. That night, he has dreams of aspects of Alexander's life.

This dream sequence should be filled with distorted monochromatic glimpses of what he read that happened in Alexander's past. The Nartell Twins dancing in the storm, levitation from one of his magic shows, the home, the guards, the smuggling, etc.

The effect here is that the rosy "reality" depicted in Daniel's book is giving way to the results of this isolated community living with the living negative legends surrounding Alexander's stay at La Push. This is the crux of our story.

At night, lying in bed, Alex is particularly vulnerable to anxiety attacks. On the third day of his stay, he finds himself at the tree-lined walkway that leads to Alexander's old property. A young girl of deep olive skin walks up to him and stops and stares. She says, "You're the Wizard." Alex is frozen in fear as she continues, "My grandmother told me all about you... you are him, aren't you?... you are him."

Alex tells her that he is not. The girl continues, "You're walking next to the Wizard's Wall up to the Wizard's Castle... you are him, the wizard Alexander." Alex, in a panic, stumbles past the girl. She yells out, "Don't be afraid..." and follows him. Alex starts running. His long legs put distance between them. He crosses the little bridge over the river and makes for his cabin. That night his nightmares continue.

He has flashes of activity at Alexander's house in the past, the watchtower, Chinese girls on opium, parties, images of friend Harold Lloyd, and on and on.

He develops a fever and spends the next day in bed. He inhales steam with a towel over his head to try to clear his nasal passages. He looks into the mirror through the steam at his baleful eyes.

That night, the girl arrives with a dog-eared scrapbook about Alexander. Alex has been playing a tape of the *Phantom of the Opera* over and over. At the door, they stare at each other as she enters. She announces, "My name is Clara." They both act as if in a trance and undress and make love to the "phantom" music as if it was preordained. In the middle of the night, the lovebirds hear shouting. Clara fearfully says, "It must be Father. He drinks a lot... He's looking for me, I expect. I stole his Alexander book." She points to the scrapbook. "He's obsessed with you... I mean with Alexander."

Hastily, Alex gets dressed. Clara tells Alex to hide in her boyfriend's boat on the docks. "It's called the 'Illahee.'" The shouts get nearer as her father searches the vacant beach huts. Alex sneaks out the back door as Clara's father enters through the front. He finds Clara and spies his scrapbook. The huge, red-faced Caucasian is stunned by a thought revelation, whirls around and switches on the overhead porch light. It's a powerful bulb meant to light up the beach at night. Crouched in the center of its bright beam is Alex. In his drunkenness and surprise, the father instantly recognizes him as Alexander. He yells at him. "What the hell?... the Wizard!... the fucking Wizard." He looks back at Clara and then down at his scrapbook. He is drunk and very confused. "... a... the smuggler... opium... you enslave our little girls..."

Alex feebly answers, "I'm not Alexander... he died years ago... I'm Alex... I'm..." He sees the father take aim with his shotgun and runs off in the direction of the docks. The father fires and misses. He backhands his daughter and throws her out of the hut and kicks over the wood burning stove, setting fire to the beach hut, then gives chase.

Clara screams, "...He ain't Alexander, Pa...he can't be!" Clara turns and runs back into the hut, gathering Alex's belongings and throwing them out in the sand. Then, she tries to stop the fire but it is spreading up the wall. The hut quickly creates a huge blaze illuminating the docks, as her father lurches down looking for Alex. He doesn't find him and moves on down the beach continuing his search. He rages drunkenly, "...You killer bastard... I'll find you." He shoots wildly into the sky.

The next morning, Clara's boyfriend, James, climbs aboard his boat and discovers Alex asleep. He takes him for a drifter who has spent the night on his boat. He pulls out his gun from a cabinet, then kicks him awake. He is holding the gun on him as Clara arrives and tells James about Alexander and that Alex must be related to him. She opens her father's scrapbook and points to Alexander's photograph and then at Alex. James knows the legend of Alexander's drug smuggling well and gets a mental picture that Alex may be able to help get him back into drug smuggling. James begins to plot. He has a "backer" in Port Townsend he could introduce Alex to. Alex tries to explain that Alexander's drug smuggling was only hinted at in Daniel's book. James tells him to "shut up," and that he will turn Alex over to Clara's revenge-minded pop if he doesn't cooperate. They tie his hands behind his back, then James goes up to the grocery store to call Port Townsend. Clara stays and guards him. She flicks his hair playfully. "You just might be our meal ticket," she says.

While James is gone she brings out her father's scrapbook and shows Alex a picture of Alexander's boat. It's called the Illahee, just like James's boat. She explains that James's father had found this boat washed ashore on Rialto Beach in the fifties and claimed her as a derelict and restored her. "... Just before he passed away, he gave it to James."

Alex shrugs and mumbles that it is just a coincidence about the name. Clara says that she heard that the Wizard named Rialto Beach and that he also named Alexander Island. She points out in the bay. "Boy, last night was weird...they said that the Wizard had a powerful light on his castle that lit up the night. That is how his fleet of smugglers found his dock... spooky, huh? Local folks burned down his house because they thought he seduced young girls just like you did last night.'

Alex is perplexed. "I didn't seduce you, you seduced me.' Clara eagerly corrects him, "Up here, the guys seduce the girls."

James returns elated. "...the deal's on!" James has to wait for the fuel dock to open but explains that it is best that Clara clear out with Alex while Clara's pop is sleeping it off.

James gives instructions to Clara, "Meet you at Ted's Café tomorrow afternoon." They shove Alex into Clara's truck with his hands still tied behind his back. James gets in his face and threatens, "You be cool because the locals are looking for you to pay for the hut, OK?" Clara revs up and departs, stopping at the burned-out shack. She finds some of Alex's belongings that she had thrown out of the burning hut. They drive out of the village undetected.

On the way, several miles from La Push, Alex calmly pulls his hand forward and puts his Beethoven tape in. Clara freaks out. "You're supposed to be tied up!"

Alex laughs, "I'm a magician." She winces and grabs her tape of old 50s tunes, removes the Beethoven and shoves in her tape – the tune "SUZY Q" blasts out. Alex grits his teeth at the ditty and orders her to "just get me to Port Townsend."

Alex searches the pockets of his soggy clothes and finds no money. Clara, smirking, pipes up, "Injuns in the night took your wallet and money. If they find you they are going to make you pay for the damages. Those shacks cost some bucks to build. Cops probably already have a APB out on you. You better stick with us."

Alex looks at her in a bemused sort of way. "Your old man burnt it up."

"The injuns see it differently. Alex looks at her openly. "Maybe I'll just ride shotgun a spell."

Clara is a little nervous. "What's that supposed to mean?"

"Well, you know, find out what I can about the old man... Alexander, I don't think he was as bad as you people are making him out to be. What does James really do?"

"Oh, he's just a carpenter today (she boasts) but he used to supply the entire Olympic Peninsula with dope before he was busted on an assault charge." She laughs. "...it was a nothing thing, but the big boys didn't want to deal with him because of it. He just drinks too much...like my pop...like all the guys up here. They all go bananas when they drink. But now, with you, it will be like old times. Did I tell you my pop named me after Clara Bow, the movie star? Pop says she stayed here with Alexander."

Clara starts singing and twitching to the ditty, "Oh Suzy Q, my Suzy Q..." After a bit she squeals, "Ain't these old songs great... that's the name of my truck,, my Suzy Q!"

On the way they pass Lake Crescent and Clara comments "Isn't this where you, I mean your great-grandfather met the President?... there down at the lodge.

Alex answers as if he is related to Alexander, grunting, "That's what it says in the book."

Clara then reveals to Alex that she thinks Alexander was her mother's true father; "...least I hope he was," she gushes. "That's why I have olive skin because he was from Alexandria, Egypt... or they named the town after him, something like that." She again explains that that is why his house was burned down. The locals hated him for bringing what they call 'evil' to La Push.

"I'm not evil."

She continues, flippantly, telling him that he was just different – is all. "Rumor has it that he brought all sorts of movie stars out here, not just Clara Bow...It must be true; what does your book say about it?"

Alex grunts that it mentions that. Alex tells her that the book says he was born in the Dakotas. She admonishes, "You can't always believe what you read in a book.

"Was your grandfather famous in Hollywood?"

Must have been, says Alex, "...because the book says so."

Clara says she would love to go to Hollywood. Her tape ends and Alex quickly shoves in the Beethoven and they ride on. Alex asks how her pop knew where she was last night. Clara tells him that that is the only place in town where strangers can get a room.

"I've met a lot of guys there. I guess my pop gets a little pissed, maybe I tease him sometimes, egg him on... you're lucky; most of my boyfriends get real beat up."

Alex grimaces. She looks over out of the corner of her eyes and questions him, "You thinking of high tailing out as soon as we get to P.T."

"P.T.?"

"Not that, silly. Port Townsend."

Alex laughs. "May'be... like I say... may'be I'll ride shotgun for a bit... learn about Alexander. The Wizard as you call him." He holds up a discarded beer can he found on the floorboard and gazes into it as if it's a crystal ball. Clara watches him impishly.

"What do you see?"

Alex stares intently at the bent up can. "I see a cop in the rear view mirror."

She looks up and sees the flashing red lights and pulls over. The cop explains that she was going too fast and gives her a warning after running a make on her driver's license. The cop had looked over at Alex several times but didn't ask him for his I.D.

At Port Townsend, Clara rents them separate rooms at the Palace Hotel and they bed down for the night. (Alex stays upstairs as Clara rummages around her bag to find Alex's wallet and takes out the money needed to pay for the rooms.) Later, Clara sneaks over to his room and Alex half-heartedly fights off her advances, and they spend the night together. Alex asks, "What about James?" Clara snickers that she is a modern woman and anyway, "…what he doesn't know won't hurt him."

"But," Alex argues, "we're supposed to be related."

"That's a long time ago," she retorts, "and besides, what was good for my grandmother is good enough for me."

The next morning, Alex gets up early and goes to the town library with Clara's scrapbook and compares it with Alexander's book. It is made up of faded photographs and newspaper clippings. The reporting was basically slanted against the presence of Alexander, suggesting that he was involved in smuggling liquor and opium, plus the importation of Chinese illegals. There were some letters written in the 20s that gossiped about the stars visiting the wizard on the hill and about how he was 'after' the young girls of the area. But again no proof, just gossip. He closes the scrapbook and tries to look up old files on Alexander. He scans old newspapers and finds nothing that interests him. Alex sees a history book on Victoria and flips the page stopping at the chapter on smuggling. Next to it is a display of a hometown magician named Virgil. Centered in the display is a sad used 'boule' ball that is supposed to represent a crystal ball. As he is about to leave the library, he sees an Old World globe set in an antique wood stand. He looks down at it from a straight back posture and puts his finger out and spins it and stops it at Alexandria, Egypt. Then he spins it to the Dakotas and finds the town of Alexandria, the birthplace of Alexander. As he looks down, his eyes look up and into his reflection, then slowly back down to the globe. He looks up at the wall clock. It is ten thirty a.m. He realizes that the Magic Shop is open, so he goes to a pay phone outside and places a collect call to Daniel. Daniel, after expressing great anguish, accepts the call and agrees after further reluctance to send Alex half of what he asked for. Fifty dollars will be waiting for him at Western Union sometime in the afternoon. When he hangs up, Alex looks back at the library and then takes the 'boule' ball out of his sweatshirt, holds it up and gazes into it.

Later that day, Alex and Clara are waiting at Ted's Café beside the city docks. Alex is entertaining the café's clients with the different length rope trick. (The ropes are of uniform length and when finished are of different lengths.) He has been hoping that he could get to the Western Union office before James arrives. But, he is unaware that the Illahee has arrived early and James has tied up and is walking up to the café. Clara sees him approaching and tells Alex who then rushes out the back door in the hope of getting to the Western Union office. Ted gives chase, yelling down to James who joins Ted. The chase takes us through the alleys and back ways of Port Townsend. They corner Alex and they fight. Alex is knocked out. Ted goes back to get Clara and they place the groggy Alex into her truck and go back to the dock and board the Illahee. They pass the Western Union office on the way. James tells Clara to guard Alex because he must stop and call his Backer. Alex wakes up and stares woefully at Clara. Clara tells him to heed his own advice and "just ride shotgun a while."

James returns angry because the Backer only wants to meet Alex before any deal is done. He angrily explains, "...I never even met the guy and now, just like that, he wants to meet you!!" He grabs Alex. "I told them you were an asshole. From this point on, buddy, you're playing with the big boys... don't fuck up."

As directed, Alex walks up past the café and turns onto a long street lined with old houses. A Mercedes stops and picks him up. He looks back and sees James and Ted standing at the corner watching them. The car, driven by a well-dressed oriental man, takes them to a huge old Victorian home where Alex is introduced to a suave older man who studies him intently. With the silent oriental standing behind Alex, the easy-going Backer bursts into a smile and announces that Alex is a chip off the old block. He explains that he knew Alexander, "...well, when Alexander was retired in Los Angeles... or Alex as we called him... always seemed to be able to have the right stuff... just at the right time... you understand... quite a remarkable fellow he was... now you keep James out of the bottle, you hear?" He winks, then opens a map and gives Alex instructions. Later, at the café, Alex is let out of the car.

The car waits as Alex returns to the boat, then pulls away. James's hurt pride is buried in his elation to be back in business. In his focus, he doesn't notice that Clara's affections are shifting towards Alex. Alex becomes more at ease with himself. Later, the three sit down in the boat's cabin and Alex tries to explain the plan but James grabs the map and takes over. They will take the boat east, then up the inside passage past LaConner, then through the San Juans to Roche Harbor, about twenty miles from Victoria.

The trip up the inside passage goes without a hitch. Alex searches for his Beethoven tape but can't find it. Clara says absently, "Must've lost it when you guys were fighting back in P.T."

The three become somewhat friendly but James notices that Clara enjoys Alex's company. At Roche Harbor, they have to wait. At one point, while James is sleeping, Alex and Clara take a walk through the abandoned limestone quarries and find a beautiful pond deep at the base of one of the quarries. Alex looks high up to the ridge of the quarry and sees the oriental driver looking out to sea. Clara doesn't see him as they make love deep in the quarry. Shortly, they return to the sleeping James.

The following night James gets a call and it's off to Victoria. They enter the harbor and go through customs and are cleared for entry. It's early so James acts as a guide and leads them to the old opium marketplace. It's a tourist trap, modernized and filled with franchises. He checks the time and they go to the tea room of the elegant Empress Hotel, enter, and sit rather self-consciously as they are in dungarees. At tea, a waiter comes up with a card for Mr. Alexander. James is jealous; he thought he would be the one summoned. Alex follows the waiter to a private phone booth and picks up the receiver, taking directions on how to get to the contact's abode. He goes back to the table and, full of self-importance, explains that he must go alone to the contact. James is now really angry at being relegated to second place, but he has no choice in the matter. (Alex, in his fascination with the unfolding events, has unwittingly become a willing participant in the smuggling.) Outside, a dark-windowed Bentley takes him to an elegant home high on an Oak Bay hill. They enter a garage – inside, a butler receives Alex. He is taken up to the main house via a tunnel and an elevator. At the house, he is presented to a quite elderly man who looks him up and down as the Backer had done in Port Townsend. This Victorian gentleman is much, much older. He beams and puts out his hand. "Garland McPherson at your service... I knew your great-grandfather... what was your mother's name?... or your grandmother's... the time... where does it go?"

Alex has become somewhat embarrassed, but before he can utter a word Garland tells him that it didn't matter. "...Alexander had impregnated many, many women."

Alex asks questions about his illustrious 'relative' from the past and Garland knows the answers. Alex, by chance, asks if he heard of Minsa. Garland beamed that indeed he knew her very well. "... and so did Alexander... perhaps too well... Well, perhaps I knew her too well as well (he laughs). Is Madame Minsa alive and well?"

Alex tells him of her demise and that they were close friends for years. That Minsa had suffered a stroke and could not speak and could barely move in her last years. Garland wondered about who took care of her. Alex said he did. "To the end?" Alex nods. Garland touches Alex lightly on the arm and says, "Come with me." He leads Alex to a huge atrium. The walls are filled with framed posters of magicians from the 1920s. Many are of Alexander. There are several of Minsa and others. In front of a huge Alexander poster, Garland comments, "Alexander's personal artist was the best of all. Kid Jones. Kid would head an advance team into a town where Alexander was scheduled to appear and pepper the town with his powerful posters two weeks before the show. Kid hung out over at La Push as well. Over here is a stack of Minsa posters I just bought in an estate sale in Seattle. Not quite as punchy but…"

Alex recognizes them as the ones that were on Minsa's wall and says, "These were Minsa's."

Garland counters, "Don't worry, they have a good home." They stop in front of an Alexander poster announcing a "Ladies Matinee."

"Alexander was the master of the ladies matinee… he would cater to their every whim. When he gave a lady his undivided attention they would swoon (he coughs)… ah, well, back to business…" He then informs Alex that he must do him a favor for an old friend, "…a mutual friend." (Alex looks at him questioningly) "Bring a family of Chinese nationals into the United States undetected." He explains that Alex will be amply rewarded by the person who has requested this favor. Alex replies that he really doesn't know how to do it. They discussed it a while longer and it was decided that the safest way to bring the Chinese in was with cargo. Alex mentioned that the captain of the ship was in charge and would have to give his say-so. He states that he is only along to learn about Alexander. Garland laughs and says, " that's not quite right, my boy… he may be the captain but you are in charge… here is the plan, (he spreads out a map) explain to your captain that he is to wait off Oak Bay here. A small craft will meet you and transfer the cargo and passengers onto your boat. My crew are professionals so don't worry, my boy…" Alex is wary.

Alex exits the Bentley, and as at Port Townsend, the car waits until he boards the Illahee. Inside, Alex explains the plan. James is angry for losing control of the operation but has to go along. Alex assures him that he is the captain. When James realizes that he has to pick up the Chinese illegals, he becomes furious. The rendezvous is made, but James refuses to take the Chinese aboard. Alex demands that he take them and James hits him in the gut, knocking the wind out of him. James yells, "I'm the Captain." They proceed across the Straits to the Olympic Peninsula and their drop point, the little township of Gardiner on Discovery Bay.

On the journey, few words are exchanged. The relationship heals somewhat when James asks if Alex feels better and tells him that he didn't get the instructions to pick up illegals at Port Townsend so wasn't taking any chances. Clara breaks more ice and points to the map and asks if the John Wayne Marina was named after the actor. Alex looks at the map saying it can't be. James argues that it was. Clara laughs nervously, saying that Wayne was on the football team that Clara Bow diddled. "…least that's what my papa told me…"

Alex argues, "…it's just a myth."

"Well, papa said he read it in a book." Later, Clara is studying the back section of the book that features 'Doctor Q' explaining his magic tricks. Alex is practicing holding a crystal ball, using the 'boule' ball. Clara says, "Hey, you're getting good." They surmise that Doctor Q is really Alexander. James demands that the two take over the helm as he prepares the drugs for delivery.

Below decks, James opens the package and extracts a bit of the coke and replaces it with sugar, then wraps the package up again.

Later, in the darkness, approaching the treacherous entrance into Discovery Bay, James takes over the wheel and has the experienced Clara as lookout, stationed at the bow. Alex sneaks below decks, finds the coke packet in a gym bag and puts the heavy crystal ball in, and zips it up.

At the Gardiner dock, James orders Alex to pass over the gym bag as Clara mans the wheel and James now is steadying the boat at the old dock with a pag pole. The whole situation is very 'rickety' especially in the dark and Alex "slips" and falls over with the package when he attempts to hand it to outstretched hands. In the confusion he swims away before the area is flooded with light from flashlights. The men at the dock are furious. James demands his money and the men at the dock direct James to go to Port Townsend. One wielding a gun jumps aboard. The Illahee moves on back to Port Townsend.

As the boat leaves, deeper in, at the head of the bay, Alex swims ashore and tries to get away but is found by the Backer's oriental gang. They go back to the old dock where the drop off was to take place. The men dive down until they retrieve the package. The group silently gets in the car. Alex is handled gently but is obviously a prisoner.

The car trip from Gardiner passes the fantastic ranch (with all the statues), where the Backer's Mercedes meets them in the moonlight. Alex is transferred over along with the wet package that held the coke. The Backer feels the package and states, "Alex, you dropped this on purpose."

Alex answers curtly, "No, I slipped, but I don't like drugs."

"It's not your investment at stake here."

Alex snaps back, "I don't like drugs."

The Backer looks at Alex in a bemused sort of way and calls him a "hypocrite," then looks down at his watch. "Best be getting back to 'Townsend. (he turns to Alex) You're going to go back to Victoria and bring the Chinese family across." His portable phone rings and he answers in rapid Chinese, then snaps his fingers at the driver. As they drive hurriedly, the Backer talks of Alexander's past. The Backer is very reserved and a bit formal but reveals his own past as an entertainer's agent. He states that he knew all the famous celebrities of the 40s and 50s. He says things changed during the 50s, "...after that filthy Brando," so he retired to 'operate' behind the scenes. The Backer is as flamboyant as a stage performer and gestures grandly. "...creative ones need fuel... I dedicated my retirement to providing them with the fuel of their choice."

Alex is confused. The baleful side of Alex seeps out and he blurts out, "But I'm not creative." The Backer laughs fully, "nonsense, my boy, nonsense... you're just honest... more innocent perhaps than honest. We shall see."

He shows Alex $25,000. "This will be yours for delivering the Chinese." The Backer puts the money back in his pocket and changes his attitude and coolly tells Alex to go back and pick up the Chinese. "Then the money is yours." Alex tells the Backer that the money is James's, that James is the smuggler, that he is only along for the ride. As dawn rises, the car stops in front of Ted's Café. Ted is at the window, wiping a dish... The Backer ushers Alex out with a nudge to the back. "...Just like Alexander, always kidding. Alex, if you get those Chinese into the U.S. safely, you will be the toast of Hollywood; that I can guarantee. Make haste, boy... the Gods are waiting. And the Gods cannot be shorted." He winks. Alex is confused. "Young man, Alexander influenced millions because he believed in himself totally. (The early morning sun starts to shimmer over the mountains behind them.) Look behind you, Alex, those are the Olympic Mountains, named after the home of the Gods... Make haste!"

Entering Ted's Café, Alex becomes increasingly agitated as he realizes he has become more than a willing hostage 'riding shotgun' to find out about his namesake magician. He has been drawn into illicit activity perhaps started by Alexander at the turn of the century.

Over hot coffee, Alex notices the Illahee arrive. Alex climbs aboard as the oriental guard departs. Alex tells James the new orders that they must immediately return to Oak Bay and pick up the Chinese family and bring them directly to Port Townsend. James goes ballistic. They have a fight but Clara breaks it up. The two need each other. James takes a walk and calls Clara's father and tells him to hurry to Port Townsend, that he will pay the father to get rid of Alex. Upon returning, James tells Alex that the boat's engine is not ready so their departure can't be until early next morning. James is hoping that the father will arrive in time. During the wait, Alex, sensing a moment when he can escape, jumps to the dock but freezes when he sees Ted watching from the café. Ted is on the phone.

At Lake Crescent, Clara's father is driving fast in the rain and hits a doe. He stops, appraises the damage, shoots the wounded doe, guts it and places the carcass in the truck. This delays him. *(the focus of the scene is on the doe's eyes like it was on Minsa's eyes at the beginning of the story.)*

Later, at Port Townsend, a Mercedes stops and two stocky oriental men step out and approach the Illahee. James comes out to confront them but they silently untie the boat and fling the rope gently onto the deck, pushing the boat away from the dock. One of the men draws his gun and jumps aboard and utters to James in perfect Queen's English, "Get this boat under way now."

James gets the message and starts the motor, then backs out of the harbor. Alex and Clara watch from the rear of the cabin. Clara doesn't see the old rusted blue Ford pickup turn down toward the docks. It's her father's truck. Along the back window gleams a rack of high-powered rifles. The Mercedes moves on, its occupants unaware of the new arrival. The father gets out and in the moonlight aims his rifle at the departing boat. Alex is staring out the window when he sees a little pinpoint of light run across the window. It is the telescope's aiming laser beam from the rifle searching for his head. Clara sees it too and understands what it is. As it crosses Alex's face, she pushes him down to the deck. A shot rings out and a window is shattered. Clara has saved Alex's life. The Backer's guard gets on his portable phone and speaks urgently in Chinese as James pulls the throttle wide open. James's anger deepens as Clara attends to some minor cuts on Alex's face caused by the shattered glass. James goes to a drawer under his bunk and pulls out a fifth of Southern Comfort and takes a swig. Back at the dock, the Mercedes returns and follows the truck as it roars away from the harbor.

At Oak Bay, lights are flashed and the Chinese come aboard. One is a young lady that the drinking James takes a shine to. James is becoming more reckless as the night wears on. Returning across the Straits, James abruptly changes course. Alarmed, Alex asks him what he is doing. James looks at him hatefully. "We're going to La Push."

Alex repeats what the plans are. James rages out, "<u>I'm</u> the captain; you want to mutiny, you pay the price."

The guard gets on his phone and James finds his moment and slams the whiskey bottle down on his head and pushes him over the side. Alex, in the corner with Clara, rushes over and tries to grab the guard but James trips him and tries to push him over the side as well. Alex hangs on and James starts to laugh. In the other corner, the three Chinese crouch as James asserts himself more and more under the influence of the bottle. He rages, "I'll kill the lot of you!" He goes over to the Chinese girl and starts fondling her. He points to the cabin with a leer on his face. Alex confronts James again, spinning him around and hitting him hard. James falls, hitting the back of his head, momentarily stunning him. Alex takes the helm as the boat rounds Tattoosh Island. The island's lighthouse beam rakes the Illahee. James recovers and hits Alex from behind, knocking him out. James grabs ahold of him and slides him to the side of the boat, drunkenly struggling to get him over the side. Clara attacks James, drawing blood with her fingernails. He grabs her and slams her below decks with roundhouse wild swings. She crumples sobbing into the cabin. James now shoves the Chinese in the cabin with her and locks it with a pin in the latch.

Back on deck, he starts to dump Alex over the side when his radio squawks. It's the Coast Guard asking him to identify himself. James stops and rushes over and opens the throttle wide. On the ocean side of Tattoosh Island lies a thick fog bank. Behind him speeds a small Coast Guard craft in pursuit. Over the radio, the Coast Guard again demands that he shut down his boat and prepare for boarding. James, in his rage, steers into the fog bank. Next, he goes out and works the small rubber lifeboat free off its clamps atop the cabin and bounces it down on the deck. He lurches to his locker and retrieves the hunk of coke he had pilfered from the shipment, climbs topside, and throws it into the raft. A chopping is heard as a Coast Guard helicopter arrives above the boat hidden by the fog. A voice over a loudspeaker bellows out for the boat to stop. James rushes into the engine room and opens the sea cocks and seawater quickly rushes in.

As James readies the raft, Alex wakes up and sees what he is doing. He body slams James, who stumbles over the side into the churning cold water. James is clinging to the side of the raft and reaches out to Alex who is just out of reach. Alex grabs for his magic trick ropes and throws it to the grasping hand. The hand clutches the rope but the show rope breaks from the tension. Alex then tries to grab him by his hand but James disappears. Alex sees the water rapidly rising in the boat. Above, in the fog, the loudspeaker bellows, "Stop your engines!" The cutter, hidden in the fog, fires a warning shot just in front of the Illahee. He sees the cabin door shut and held fast by a pin. He pulls the pin and the door is pushed open. Alex leads the four to the rubber raft. Another shot is heard. The rotorblades of the unseen helicopter buffet the boat with a crazy wind. He sees the end of a Jacob's ladder fluttering from out of the fog as unseen officers aboard the helicopter prepare to descend. Alex yells loudly, ventriloquizing – directing his voice starboard. "Help! We're over here!" He watches the rope ladder jerk crazily to the right. The boat is almost sunk as Alex plops the rubber raft over the side. The five jump in. He sets the raft free and they fall rapidly behind the Illahee and her tormentors. Silence envelops them as they drift. Shortly, in the distance, they hear a 'humming.' Clara recognizes it as the wail of the Strawberry Siren. They paddle in that direction. Out of the mist, a large wave explodes around them and they pass close by the huge monolithic, but hollow, Strawberry Rock, standing like a silent sentinel guarding the sacred Macah Bay of the tribe of the same name. Clara knows where she is and directs them through the rock outcroppings. Another wave capsizes the raft and the group tumble to the beach. They find each other under the sacred rock at Rock Reef.

As they gather themselves in a huddle the fog slowly rises. They make their way to a vacant beach cabin belonging to a friend of Clara, carrying the life raft with them. On the way, the tribe's herd of Appaloosa gallops by in total silence as the sand muffles the weight of their gallop. (We looked closely at the horses... and their eyes are Minsa's.)

At the cabin, Alex calls the Backer in Port Townsend and explains where they are. Clara makes a fire in the cabin and they dry out and wait. The Chinese have some herbal tea, which the mother prepares. The cabin is similar to the one at La Push with intricate Indian carvings in the wood.

The Backer in the Mercedes comes up the road and stops. Out of the rear door steps a well-dressed older Chinese man. The Chinese woman rushes over and they embrace. She tells him what has happened in rapid Chinese, and the man comes over and hugs Alex and then Clara. They enter the cabin. Alex and the Backer huddle in front of the Mercedes. The Backer thanks Alex, explaining that honor in these sorts of endeavors is a life-and-death sort of thing, "...all the way up, and all the way down the ladder..." Alex asks him what he is getting at. The Backer turns to the Chinese and hands him pilfered coke.

Alex looks at him with hate in his eyes. "The ball in the gym bag belongs to the library. Will you see that it gets back to them!"

The Backer smiles. "Sure."

The group climbs into the Mercedes and heads out. At Lake Crescent, where Clara's father had killed the deer, the Backer asks her if she wants to be taken to La Push. She says no, that she wants to stay with Alex. The Backer brings out a newspaper and tells Clara that her father was killed by assailants last evening. As the paper reported, he had killed a deer. They found his truck on the side of the road by Lake Crescent. He had been shot. The deer, his rifles and valuables were missing. Somebody must have robbed him. Clara changes her mind and says she will pick up her truck at Port Townsend and return to La Push. Clara grabs Alex's arm and shivers. The Backer asks if she wants to call her mother immediately. Clara explains that she never knew her mother. They drive on through the fog in silence.

The Backer turns to the front page and shows the headlines to Alex. "FISHING BOAT ILLAHEE SINKS – NO SURVIVORS!" "The owner, James Duchin, cannot be found. It is presumed he and his crew went down with his boat. The boat was last seen in the Port Townsend harbor with a crew of three people on board. Mr. Duchin has been suspected of drug activity in the recent past, and it looks like he ran into trouble." Clara vacantly tells Alex that James was named after James Island at La Push.

The Backer tells Alex he would gladly put him up but it's best that he go to Seattle immediately with the Chinese family. Alex agrees. The group shares a silent moment, then the Backer says, "James told me you were a drifter. A descendant of Alexander shouldn't be drifting for very long." The Backer hands Alex an envelope with $50,000 in it. Alex refuses to take it. He admits that he was only along to research Alexander's life and that he didn't earn it.

The Backer laughs. "Alex, my boy, you did your job. You did what was asked of you."

Alex admits that he is not related to Alexander; that he was only playing a role. "I'm just a hack magician," he confesses. Clara overhears this. "You mean you're not related to Alexander?"

Alex just stares at her. Clara sees Alex as if for the first time. His (baleful) eyes are filled with strength and character – like Alexander's. The Backer mollifies, "Just like Alexander would have wanted it. Illusion or reality? What counts is how well you play the role."

The Backer turns to Clara and continues, "Alex played his role as well as anybody would have." He turns back to Alex. "The money is more for bringing the Chinese safely into the country. Garland informed me that you took care of Minsa in her final days. ...These people are descendants of hers. You did what she asked you to do... considerate it your inheritance."

Alex is dumbfounded. Clara jabs him in the ribs and Alex reluctantly takes the envelope. They ride in silence through the fog and stop at Clara's truck parked at Ted's Café. Clara kisses Alex and promises to meet him in Seattle in a week. She starts to leave but turns back, rummaging in her purse, then hands Alex his wallet and Beethoven tape. "You'll need these now." She turns and leaves.

The Backer and Alex drive on. The car moves up the hill and Alex coolly asks, "Well, what about your smuggling, now that James is gone?"

Sensing Alex's emerging power, the Backer says, "Sir, we didn't want him. We just wanted to meet you, the pretender to the Wizard's throne. Our system is in place."

At the mansion, the Backer gets out of the car and Alex stops him and whispers, "Was Alexander a smuggler?"

The Backer is guarded. "Truthfully? No, but truth will not alter legend. It's been embellished by two or three generations... it's got a life of its own now."

Alex fires back, "A legend that justifies your smuggling ring? You didn't know Alexander, did you? ...These Chinese aren't related to Minsa."

The Backer smiles curtly: "Legend has it that she was born in Katmandu; rumor has it she was born in Kansas. Alexander was from the Dakotas... so what? The point is, they made their reality work for them. What are you going to do with yours?"

Alex presses: "Did he kill Chinese illegals?"

The Backer looks at him with a blank, unfriendly gaze. "No son." He looks back at the family of Chinese and shakes the man's hand, then raises his clenched fist. He gets out and leans in and tersely tells Alex that he is a good magician, "...but you're not as good as Alexander, nobody was and nobody will be. In the envelope is a letter to an old friend of mine who lives in Benedict Canyon. It's a letter of introduction. This chap's an old codger, older than I, about as old as Garland, but he can open some mighty big doors. He loved Minsa even more than we did... Minsa Mahatma... did she ever stop smoking that old-fashioned opium?"

Alex reddens slightly, checks himself, and answers truthfully, "no."

"That's what you were giving her... dope?"

"She was in pain."

The Backer adds: "We are all in our own way in pain." He relaxes and straightens from leaning into the car's window. "You better hurry down to Hollywood; we old-timers are moving into the real spirit world pretty quickly these days." He waves and turns back, "Alex, in a couple of years, come back. I'll show you my collection of Alexander's magic tricks. They are quite elaborate. For now, keep it simple. Learn. One step at a time. Goodbye and keep in touch." He turns and formally walks away. The Mercedes leaves for Seattle.

Later that week, Alex and Clara enter the Magic Shop. They're dressed to the nines in Victorian-style clothes. Daniel looks at them appraisingly and asks, "Well, well, well, I guess you want your job back?"

Alex looks at him squarely, then laughs, "I came to pay you for the book I borrowed... the Alexander book." He gives Daniel $200.00. "That's $150.00 plus interest.

Daniel is surprised. "Well, a mystery solved, well, well, well. Thanks, Alex.

"Oh, my name is not Alex anymore... it's Q, as in 'Doctor Q'... and this is my soon-to-be wife and assistant, Suzie Q." Clara smiles, "Nice to meet you, Daniel." She turns to Alex. "We best be off or we will miss our flight to Burbank."

"Daniel, I'll have my crystal ball, please." Daniel, without questioning, gently lifts it out of a display cabinet. "I could've sold it for a lot of money... this old English codger swore it was Minsa Mahatma's... of course, if I'd sold it I would've given you your percentage." He smiles. Alex takes it and holds it up with authority. He looks at Daniel briefly, then turns and looks deeply into the ball. After a bit, he turns and tells Daniel that he will have an excellent sales day.

Daniel whistles, "Not bad, not bad at all Q, I mean Doctor Q."

~ ~ ~

Once upon a time…

VII
Niburu Child

Shey's bungalow rests on pilings far below the bluffs of Seattle's Magnolia district. Inside, Beth and Shey make passionate love in front of the bay window filled with highrise shimmering in the morning sun. The room is covered with memorabilia of Shey's exploits as an athlete. Football trophies, a golf set, magazines featuring sports, a stack of *Playboys*, a certificate denoting first place in a sharpshooters contest shares a frame with a picture of him holding his rifle. Three employment forms are piled on his desk, partially filled out.

The lovers have expended themselves…

High above the beach on a mansion's balcony, Pepe is peering through his telescope. He scans from the highrise down to the water's edge and focuses on the bungalow as Beth emerges.

Beth gets in her blue Beetle and heads towards the center of the city.

Pepe scans the city to come upon a departing ferry headed for Bainbridge Island. Through his arc of vision, the Olympic Mountain range slides into view.

*

Nic is hunched over a coffee in his studio. Around him are piles of books about ancient history. He is writing and talking to himself about Bonobo apes. An open book about the perpetually horny apes is on the table. His face is contorted in thought as he tries to find the word groupings to express himself. He mumbles of genetics, Atlantis and the Old Testament, trying to bring his thoughts out coherently.

He holds one of Zachariah Stitchen's books. "You have unlocked the door to the past thus the future." His gaze rests on his paintings. "We will help you open it further."

*

The ferry toots. Beth's car emerges and moves up the ramp, passing a sign announcing "Bainbridge Island."

At a vast field filled with old cars in stages of decomposition, Beth parks and gets out. She is carrying a brown bag full of food with the logo of the Pike Place Market on it. The Olympics are in the background.

She walks through the maze of rusting cars to come to a pathway into darkness. She enters and walks through to a door with a cow's skull attached to it. A name on the door reads "Katal Nickolis."

She enters his dingy abode and moves through the "pig's sty" to the fridge and stuffs the contents of the brown bag into it. Then she walks to a back door, out and into a little court with a bicycle leaning against the wall, and enters Nic's studio. It is a converted trailer garage.

The high walls are hung with Nic's artwork in various stages of completion. They are life-size drawings of Beth in various postures. Some realistic, some surreal – all nudes.

Nic gets up and moves to his easel as Beth enters. She calmly goes over to the sofa and undresses. Her body is poised and powerful and she is totally in control of herself. No words are spoken between the two until Beth breaks the silence with a tiny fart.

Nic sighs, "Good morning." The ensuing conversation is short and curt. Nic puts on some jazz and Beth starts to pose. She moves very slowly. She smiles at Nic and tries to get him to respond. Nic answers with a brief smile as he stays intent on his work. He mumbles, "Try to get that etheric thing going." She looks at him, confused. He smiles. "No. Don't try, just be yourself."

*

Later, at Shey's, Beth and Shey are arguing about his lack of money. He is demanding to borrow one hundred bucks from her and she is refusing, telling him he must find a job. He explains that his deal is coming through and that he will be a millionaire and pay her back. They wrestle, then make out. She gets serious as she digs into her purse. "Nic's such a turn-on when he doesn't respond; it's the same strange feeling that I get from Pepe." She nonchalantly hands him some cash.

*

That night, Beth arrives home. Pepe is sitting in an imposing evening chair having a brandy. They talk about the day's events. Beth of course tells him nothing about Shey or the modeling job. She tells him about shopping

82

and the little store at the market. She asks him about etheric. He explains that it has something to do with a layer of energy that wraps the body. "A very old word, from ethereal I would imagine. Madame Blatavski's disciples used the term from time to time."

*

Beth goes up to her study and opens the encyclopedia and reads up on the word. Later that evening, she climbs into bed with Pepe who is already fast asleep. She tickles him a bit and he grunts, then she snuggles up close to him.

*

That night, Nic is meditating under a huge cedar tree, talking to the tree, then to the stars. He points to the Orion cluster and asks questions of the stars: "We came from, we return to... dust? No way. We are eternal, indestructible electrical energy." Nic walks back to his shack amongst the maze of junk cars talking to himself and formulating his ideas of the past. He sits in a gutted Hudson, a white cat appears to listen, then moves on. "Present, future, past, it's a question of focus. Bring the past into focus it becomes the present. Think, dream of the future and the future instantly becomes the present.' He rubs the dash of the derelict car. "Would you, Hudson, have given me as much pleasure and enlightenment then, as you do now?"

*

He goes to his studio and up to a six-foot, life-size drawing of Beth. He talks to the image, then checks himself laughing, reassuring himself that "you are only my drawing." He studies it for a long time. "Are you alive? Tell me, are you real or just living in my imagination? A slow-moving trick of animation. A fluke. Are you real, Sady? That's what I will call you – Sady."

*

The next day at the session, Beth asks him about what he meant by etheric. Nic gets embarrassed trying to explain his rough theory on The Shining Ones: "A lost race briefly mentioned in the early records, the "old" testaments... and... mythology. I call them Nibruans. I think they were made to appear as gods of some sort that live in or on another plane and didn't have a body but needed one so took over humans and used theirs."

"Why?"

Nic laughs. "For procreation most likely since I sense they are like, well, a thick woven pile of electrical impulses in a plasmic state invisible to those who do not know how to see them. Some people tried to explain their visions and called their glow 'etheric doubles.' Most humans would go mad if they realized they are alive unto themselves. Not ghosts. Not even aliens anymore, they've been our partners so long. Almost as long as we have been around for that matter. They're very real and the memory of them in our consciousness comes out convoluted because of the wrath of Yahweh, of God, the... the Biblical flood, triggered by superheated magnetic storms, the wrath of God burned mankind's brain back into unconsciousness – into neolithicness. Not until Zeus through Marduk did we begin to rekindle consciousness. The Nibruans remained, even when their human died, but were trapped on their etheric plain, waiting for humans to regain consciousness, thus the ability to communicate with them again. We are all eternal, etched in electrical impulse entwined like a ball of string.... All Gilgamesh had to do was believe he was eternal. He would have passed through physical death into eternity held by the hand of a Nibruan. With each generation, the Nibruans' ability to function on the physical plane diminishes. They make themselves available to humans who are not afraid to "sense" them. But, like sensing a ghost, most are afraid.

"What do I have to do with it?"

"Everything. They were sexless and you are oversexed, so they need you. To communicate to me."

"Why you?"

"I don't know – I haven't separated my facts from my imagination yet."

"You wouldn't know sex if it was thrown in your face." She undulates to him and around him. Nic works fervently, ignoring her advances. In frustration, she spits out, "You're the one who's etheric."

"We shall see, we shall see." He holds up the recently finished drawing and it is indeed more a drawing of her aura than her physicality. She looks at it wide-eyed.

"Who is that? It's me. But..." The drawing is stark but filled with a life force.

"It came out of you... I'll call it Apoolonia."

"It?"

"Shall we ask what sex it is or wishes to be assigned to?"

"I don't understand."

"It's an image of a Nibruan. I sense she is a she."

"What ? How?"

Nic smiling at the image, "Well, for one thing, she came through you, didn't you, Apoolonia?"

*

That night Beth tells Shey about the story of the Nibruans. "But it was so real, so vivid, like two of the other images he gave names to. I came early once and caught him talking to them, asking them questions about Atlantis and something called Nan Madhol."

"Does he make any money from his paintings?

"He ought to, they're damn good. But he doesn't ever sign them. Not one."

"I guess they never leave his studio?"

"Yup."

"Do his friends help him?"

"He doesn't have friends, just the images he pulls out of me. I don't think he says ten words to me in the two hours I pose for him."

Shey is scheming and changes the subject. "Two hours with you nude and he doesn't want to screw you?"

They embrace.

*

Later that night at home, Beth reveals to Pepe, "I've been modeling."

"Really."

"Nothing fazes you."

"I've understood that you have been modeling for a while now. You are exceptionally beautiful, young, so it stands to reason you would want to model. But if it bothers you why continue?"

"What do you mean?"

"Well, you announce it to me like you're confessing. You have nothing to be ashamed of with me, dear Beth. You do satisfy yourself, I would hope. One question: why did you want to know about the word *etheric*?"

"Nic, the artist I model for, pulls the most Fantastic images out of me while I pose."

"I'm sure he does."

"Not that. I mean, people, actual kind of peoplelike, but not with features, but fluidlike… with exaggerated arms and things. They kind of shine in their weird way. He calls them Nibruans that live on an etheric plane. I see me in the stuff but I also see energy, force of life. Life Force. Kind of scary, especially when he talks to them… It's kind of like he's not all there."

"Nuts?"

"No, he's more than sane. Totally professional. Above board. But it's weird, he's totally intense when he talks to the images."

"How big does he paint?"

"Big."

"Life size?"

"How did you know?"

"It figures."

"Have you been following me?"

He nonchalantly closes the conversation with a dismissive "No."

*

The next day, Beth drives aboard the ferry. As the ferry readies to depart, Shey scooters aboard.

*

At Bainbridge Island Beth departs and Shey follows her as she turns down the lane to the car graveyard. Beth parks and walks in. Shey hurriedly follows. He loses her and gets lost in the graveyard. After some wandering, he finds Nic's shack. He sees that there is no smoke from the chimney so he looks in, tries the door and it opens. He quietly enters.

His nose wrinkles as he fights off gagging at the smell of the place. He shuffles to the next doorway to enter the living room, finds the back door. It's ajar and he goes through it. He hears some jazz wafting across the patio. By the bicycle he slips down and peeks through the translucent windows. He sees Beth slowly moving to the jazz tune as Nic intently works at his easel.

He looks around the room as best he can and sees many life-size drawings of Beth, some as tall as six feet. They all radiate a shimmering, alive quality.

The music stops and Beth looks at her watch. She takes a drink of wine and dresses. Shey hides as she prepares to leave. "Same time?" Nic nods as he continues to work. She leaves.

*

Much later that evening, Shey slips into the studio, grabs three drawings, rolls them up, and takes them with him.

*

That night, when he returns home, he sees a note left by Beth that reads, "I miss you. Love you."

*

Shey scooters to Pike Place Market with the three drawings of Nic's that he has signed. He parks and moves into the crowd working his way to an art gallery. The owner is a small, shifty guy who is sitting behind a huge table that serves as his desk. Shey unrolls the work. The owner smiles and offers Shey $100 each. Shey feigns outrage and they settle on $200 each.

The gallery owner wants more work. He wants to visit Shey's studio to prepare for a major exhibition. Shey then realizes a 'motherload' but must not only get rid of Nic and take his paintings, he must also take over his studio. He also realizes he must get rid of Beth as well.

*

Nic tries to explain his thoughts to Beth. He is drawing a horizontal pose of Beth. She moves seductively to music. As he works, an idea takes shape in his mind and he uses the drawing to help express it. "The wave of knowledge spread like this, like Chaktras in reverse, because the knowledge came back down from the heavens. That's where they went during the flood to satellites tethered to Earth by cables. The memory of this is manifested in the children's story 'Jack and the Beanstalk.' These satellites were like what is happening today. Star Wars, only tethered like barrage balloons during World War II. The old tethered satellites protected Earth from asteroids. These tethers were set at energy points. Ley line junctures, as they call them in England. This also was part of the knowledge base trying to come out of our unconsciousness but as crystal versions of each, medieval mechanical contraptions representing the solar system, were closer now with Star Wars. The Shining Ones, the Gods (he starts to draw from over the head in the image) Chaktras of our consciousness, our plane of existence, our reality flows. Resonance points that are physical and spiritual and eventually evolve as cultural centers; they started here at Lake Titicaca, then the South Pacific, Nan Madhol or Burma, then to China Number 5, then over to India, to 3, the Sumer culture, then on to the Nile Delta and finally waking the Kundalini of Africa."

"Just seven Chaktras?"

"Chaktras in the universe are endless. They resonate at each juncture point – strings of energy. Juncture points can be so heavy that they become black stars imploding so powerfully that mass is created. Stars, then their backwash the planets. It's like how the ancients numbered the planets from outside in. It was in the third awakening that was the most complete at Sumer – a large group of many different specialists washed ashore at Mount Arratt and the first balanced human community was re-created – you see, all educated people were specialists back then. At other Chaktras only small groups of specialists of a certain type survived, like astronomers in Middle America – the Maya or more accurately their forefathers rebuilt the culture but from their unique knowledge base.

The Egyptian group of survivors must have been doctors who worked in genetics. The history survived but was reinterpreted by the different slant on the mother language and – like now – professional fields evolved into almost their own language that in just a few generations created a world girding Tower of Babble of their own making. Several of these cultural centers suffered a stiltedness that sterile technology can bring, becoming no more than elaborate cargo cults sinking deeper into the mud of unconsciousness with each passing generation. Some, like Egyptian culture, became incredibly stultifying, lasting thousands of years in a somnambulant state. When the Pharoah Akhenaten tried to wake Egypt out of her unconscious mind-numbing religion, he was destroyed." Nic points, "That's a bust of his wife Nefertiti.

"Several of these rebirth centers succumbed to natural calamities; particularly unstable is the South Pacific, eternally destabilized when the original 'crossing' occurred. The crossing of the water planet Tiamat and Niburu that occurred on the other side of the globe. Where Nibruan gravity ripped Tiamat's wafer-thin mantle inward, a ring of fire was created, pushing the mantel opposite out of the water. The plan worked and Earth was born. The creation of a planet of both water and landmass for the biology to grow and evolve in was perfect for the Nibruans – they were now ready to find a way to become physical. All-important was allowing the biology to grow on land; in perhaps 10 Nibruan years all the work came to a head as man was created. You see, one of their years equals 28,000 earth years. So, in 280,000 years, man was created from Bonopo ape and the rest is now our recorded history."

*

Shey has been successful at selling Nic's drawings at $1,000 apiece. He puts money down and buys a PT Cruiser where he stows his rifle.

*

On his third burglary, he inadvertently steals Nic's favorite, Apoolonia. When Nic discovers the painting is gone, he goes deeper into his 'mindset' and takes her disappearance as a sign to "follow her."

He takes out his notes and starts to study, opening several books to help in clues as to where she went. His calculations tell him to go to Mount Shasta.

He rushes out of his studio and gets on his cycle as Beth arrives. Nic tells her what he is doing. She doesn't comprehend at first but fears for him. She tries to stop him physically. "I'm to blame for your madness – these things came out of me. I gave birth to them. I'll take you there."

*

They cross the Sound, arriving in Seattle where her car is spotted by Shey who is in the ferry line waiting to go to Bainbridge Island to kill Nic.

Leaving the ferry dock, Beth explains that she has to stop home and tell her husband and get some things for the trip. Nic argues her out of this. "No time, no time!"

*

Shey follows Beth. He has a distant look in his eyes.

On the trip down I-5, Nic explains other aspects of his theory. The Mother culture and the floods and the survivors. At Portland, a thought flashes across his mind: "Turn Left and Head East. We're going to the Valley of the Gods."

*

Shortly, Nic, who hasn't driven in years, takes over the driving as Beth gets tired. Nic explains he has to be there at the right time to fulfill his destiny.

"What destiny?"

"Well, I don't know. I think to meet the Gods." He laughs. "I shouldn't be doing this; I don't have a license – not even a wallet! Well, you only live once."

At Moab, they stop at a gas station owned by Jesse Suck, who asks them where they are headed. When they tell him, he laughs and tells them to be very careful because the Beetle is so low. "Got lots of Beetle parts in case you need some service."

Behind the weasel-looking Jesse, his sidekick Scud sits on the running board of an antique tow truck, nursing a Bud. He smirks. "Down the highway about ten miles take a right at the sign…less potholes, more scenery."

Shey sees them leave the gas station and goes in himself. Jesse gives him the same advice: Take a right, etc… As Shey leaves, Jesse turns to Scud. "Well, Scud, me boy, it looks like we're going to be busy this afternoon. Did you see how low that PT was?" Jesse fires up the old tow truck.

*

Entering the Valley of the Gods, Nic sees the stone towers as archetypes. He points out the similarity of their shapes to man's creations, such as the Maya pyramids, the massive statues of Ramses, and the Roman Colosseum.

"No Giza pyramid?"

"The Pyramid is different. It was conceived in remote antiquity, built much later by deeply imprinted minds. It marks the exact epicenter of earth's landmass after the Crossing. It also serves as a time machine to measure our growing knowledge base. It may be a marker if and when the Nibruans return. But here must have been a center of the mother culture a hundred thousand years ago."

He surmises that the survivors of the floods found this place through interpreting their legends and myths just as we are doing, and decided that it was here that it all began. We call the mother city Atlantis. "But I know Atlantis was a whole world culture – our mother culture.

*

The road becomes impassable. Nic parks and they walk towards one of the towers hand in hand. The heat of the day is rising.

Shey sees the blue Beetle in the distance. This distracts him and the car rams a jagged edge of a rock, creating a slow leak unnoticed by Shey. He parks, gets out, and takes the gun with him, marching up the roadway towards the Beetle. At a point halfway there he leaves the road for a narrow pathway that leads up the side of an adjoining edifice. The trail ends, so Shey has to climb around rock and gravel to reach his destination – a ridge still about 100 feet higher.

*

Below, about a thousand feet away, Nic and Beth study the stones in silence. Nic looks at Beth as if it was the first time, kisses her, then removes her clothes and strips himself. They make love, and just as he is about to climax, he rises and a bullet tears through him and Beth. Both are covered with blood. Another gunshot erupts and the bullet again hits them.

*

Above, Shey starts to climb down back to his car but stumbles and twists his ankle. The sun rises. He tries to get up but cannot, so he starts to crawl amongst the sharp boulders towards his car, 2,000 feet away.

In the distance, Jesse and Scud's tow truck lumbers up the road. Jesse points to the PT Cruiser. "Number one."

END

Once upon a time…

VIII
Pike Place Market Musings

A comparison of Istanbul and Seattle's Public Markets

Nico, originally from Turkey, presently a clerk at DeLaurenti's at Pike Place Market, introduced me to Istanbul. His suggestions were basic and invaluable: Get a small hotel in the center of the city and walk. He urged me to be careful, as one would in any city. What he didn't prepare me for was Istanbul's day market, which stretched perhaps three kilometers and must have included over ten thousand street stalls in this city of fifteen – going on twenty – million inhabitants.

I arrived at night in an irritable mood from Thessalonika via a turboprop-powered plane with very small seats. (A strike in Athens had forced me to this mode of travel.) I set out early in the morning, my grumpiness lessened by the sweet, sonorous Islamic muezzins broadcasting from the hundreds of minarets in this thoroughly Moslem city. Post-Ramadan-related celebrations were still going on in the Islamic world, so the Grand Bazaar was closed, but this didn't stop the street vendors from setting up outside. My plan was to get an overview of market activity, so, as Nico suggested, I walked. On and on, down the hill, past stall after stall filled with things to buy. Down to the vegetable stalls sandwiched behind the perfume market (closed), then across the Galata Bridge. The fleet of ferry boats were preparing for their schedules, chugging up the Golden

Horn. Up the Bosphorus to the Black Sea and down to the Dardenelles. Watching them made me just a wee bit homesick.

At Karakoy, on the other side of the bridge, a slight, furtive man was selling Russian eggs from a tired, wooden veggie box set on end. The painted eggs were exquisite: eight, each looking slightly different, nested one inside another, all the way down to a tiny one no bigger than the tip of my little finger. He introduced himself in English as Pablo Sikorsky (Catalan mom, Muscovite dad). No, he assured me, he didn't sell helicopters, just painted Russian eggs. He hastily added, with a hiss, that he would inquire about helicopters if I wanted to buy one. I said no, but the eggs matched my mood and a million lira an egg was cheap, so I bought one without haggling. I waved and continued walking up streets festooned with overlapped canvas coverings. The cords holding them taut created intricate free-form string compositions that only a drunken spider could emulate. I began to feel disoriented and tired from all the walking and gawking, and mumbled to myself, "Helicopters?" Then I looked up, pointed at the cords and shouted, "'aha, the true origin of the String Theory of the Universe.

Revived by my outburst, I finally arrived at the Balik Pazar Fish Market bordering Taksim, the "posh" section of the city. I could see that this incredible, loose-knit system of street vendors apparently went on forever. This fish market was the center of yet another octopoidal labyrinth of streets filled with vendors selling every type of edible imaginable. Realizing I was finished for the day, I grabbed a kabob and a tea from a kiosk, sat, and gave my feet a rest.

The old question of what constitutes an in-city public market (which we have grappled with at Pike Place over the years) came to mind. Market management has taken the stand that the Historic District is the real Market. I have always argued that the Market spreads beyond the District: down to Union, up to Lenora, and across Western and First Avenue.

In Istanbul, the 'official' markets make up just a small percentage of the street vendor economy. Young, mid-sized Seattle and giant, ancient Istanbul have many similarities as waterborne crossroads cities. In particular, in their historic cores both attract and encourage talent and enterprise from all walks of life. Unfortunately, in Seattle we are losing ground in this area because current Pike Place Market management rarely emphasizes grassroots participation in the Market economy. They should lighten up and guide the Market to "free-wheel" and expand. This would rekindle the energy, diversity and entrepreneurial spirit that brought about the Seattle Market's dynamic rebirth in the early 1970s.

In a lofty daze I returned to my hotel. Later, over several potent rakis, the manager suggested that perhaps I should hire a guide. I did so.

He called himself Erol, "like Errol Flynn," he says. He wore a deep impish grin, a beret, black suit and turtleneck. His English was 'interesting.' I informed him that "I've misplaced my key," to which he responded, "You need to take a pee?" It was also colorful. Since I was traveling alone, he said, "May I suggest a visit to LE HOT?" This, he explained, was a Turkish bath "weeeth all theee trimmings." He suggested dinner at a fish restaurant on a side street of Kumkapi, the fishing boat district (Ballard with serious patina – Ballard, Seattle's fishing district, has its own claim to fame as homeport to the world's largest fishing fleet). On cue, a young lady suddenly plopped herself on my table and arranged herself around my steaming grilled lüfor (bluefish). I sensed Erol smiling in the shadows. But still I wondered: Would this delightful damsel, with her deep, dark eyes, later perform a belly dance for me? Every pair of eyes in this city, it seems, are deep and dark and twinkling.

Erol, like his city, was a man of the world. He proudly told me, as he flexed his muscles, that Istanbul was decidedly male, "a perfect partner to the beautiful Roma. We took over the world from her when Emperor Constantine (the first Christian Roman Emperor) made us his capital and called us Constantinople (330 AD–1453 AD). We were the capital of Byzantium before Alexander the Great, then the Romans (653 BC–330 AD). The Islamic Ottomans ruled their empire from us [a vast area, from Morocco to Hungary to Iran], for over 400 years, right up to just after the first World War [1453-1922]. They changed our name to Istanbul and gave us Islam."

With this heritage in his blood, it was no wonder Erol acted like a Roman Istanbulian– he was above the politics of the moment. For instance, he talked about the threat to Iraq and sympathized with them, but he also understood the mind of a Saddam Hussein and why he must be contained. (In fact, I never sensed a threat to me as an American in this Islamic city; Istanbul is thoroughly international.)

Erol's world was completely Byzantine (a word which evolved from Istanbul's first moniker). He was constantly asking, "'Who are you really are?" Ah, delicious Bosphorian intrigue. Through this gentleman I experienced the Istanbul of history, of life's theater at center stage. Of sultans and their immense wealth. He kept his political views couched in a wry sense of humor. (For example, on a side tour of Topkapi Palace, he told me that "the Harem has long been dormant, not active like your Clinton White House was.")

On the final evening of my stay, we discussed the next morning's itinerary. The Grand Bazaar would finally be open. He suggested that we be there a half hour early.

The next morning, with a cup of fresh orange juice in hand (dispensed from a colorfully dressed street vendor from a traditional urn on his back), we walked up to the Bazaar and turned left behind the adjacent mosque and down a narrow street that was dug up for repairs. (Piles of three-inch-square rock slabs were awaiting the stone placer. This type of street material can be found throughout the Med, from Lisbon to Cairo.) It was raining so we had to step over streams and puddles, but we found our "secret" gate and entered the silent maze of four thousand shops shut by iron gratings.

The original Bazaar, some seven hundred years old, is still defined by its brick-arched ceiling, which is similar in style to the ceilings of the vast kitchens of Topkapi Palace (less than a kilometer to the east). This original structure today is reserved for the sale of modern tourist-oriented sportswear, like Shaquille O'Neal tee shirts! We moved on into the covered streets that we identify today as the Grand Bazaar: white stucco arcades with elaborate mosaics on the walls and archways. (In a more recent expansion, on the fringe of the bazaar, some of the streets have wood roofs.)

In silence we wandered from arcade to arcade. The Grand Bazaar is like Cairo's Khan-al-Khalili – somewhat sectionalized, with leather coat vendors favoring one section and the porcelain people another. Ditto carpets, silver, gold, ceramics, etc. There are dry goods shops and cafés, even a tiny mosque, but I didn't see any produce or flower stalls because this is basically a tourist market.

Suddenly the gates opened and a flood of serious shopkeepers and their clerks hurried in. The rat-a-tat sound of thousands of iron grills rolling up echoed through the Bazaar like machine guns at full fire. A horde of shoppers poured in, led by a stout, purposeful-looking woman of northern European stock, brandishing her furled umbrella. The lights came on, revealing racks of ceramics, heaps of leather coats, piles of gloves, lace underwear and hankies, cans of soup piled high, all on display cases that were hastily carried or wheeled out in front of their shops. More than anything, this "spilling out" of products made the Bazaar come alive. The Grand Bazaar was open for business. (The cluster of lower-level Pike Place Market businesses would increase their business tenfold if they were allowed to do the same.)

After hours spent exploring the maze of arcades dominated by rude hustlers of tourist dollars, I could see that the Grand Bazaar is the economic heart of the whole system. But its soul is the intricate network of freewheeling markets that spill out and down into the city.

Later, Erol accompanied me to the airport. On the way, he mentioned that each year an estimated 500,000 people come to Istanbul to live. Many of these "foreigners'" first job is selling in the street markets. Their wares are either assigned to them by a wholesaler – watches, lighters, carrots, stolen goods, you name it – or they just sell the clothes out of their suitcases. (Hm-m, maybe Pablo didn't carve his Russian eggs after all.)

It's funny – like Seattle, the term 'foreigner' just doesn't seem to apply. I sense, as I do when in Roma, that these two ancient imperial cities are for all people.

Istanbul's markets reflect its history as a crossroads where Europe and Asia have always met. Even so, Pike Place is much more international. Could a person from Istanbul find an American "Nico" who would spend the time to introduce Seattle's Market? Perhaps. I suspect that in Istanbul everything is possible.

The driver stopped at the hospital. Erol got out, "for a checkup," he explained, "and, by the way, who are you really are?"

"Just a guy from Seattle," I said, tightly clutching my Russian egg. I stared at the fleet of bobbing ships anchored in the Sea of Marmara.

He winked, put up his collar, barely masking his deep-set eyes, and said "Boeing, Boeing." I winked back and pulled my West Seattle Stetson tighter over my eyes as my driver snapped his stingy brim once and slowly elbowed out into the Caddesi Kennedy (JFK Highway), and into the notorious Istanbul traffic.

[NOTE]

Like Rome, Istanbul is layered with history. Today, Istanbul has a much larger population than Rome. But whereas Rome is the capital of Italy, Istanbul is no longer the formal political center of Turkey. The two cities dominated their epochs and are chockfull of history within a few square kilometers of their civic heart. To visit this world of a market, I suggest you stay at a small hotel in Sultanahmet, which puts you right in the center of the ancient quarter. From there, the modern center across the Galata Bridge is also within easy walking distance. Enjoy.

Three Thumbnail Profiles of Market People

Charlie Chong

"Ho'opono" is a Hawaiian term that means "to do what is right."

This term is on a plaque sitting on Charlie Chong's desk in Seattle City Council chambers. He says the philosophy is in the heart and soul of all native Hawaiians.

Charlie was born in 1926 in Hawaii, raised by his father, Libert (of Chinese ancestry) and his mother, Hannah (a pure Hawaiian). He grew up on the island of Maui, did a stint in the Army, then enrolled in Georgetown University's School of Foreign Service. He joined the Air Force for two and a half more years, serving in Intelligence. After his duty, he returned to Washington, D.C. where for the next five years he did research on international law and public finance. Then, it was on to Minnesota for five more years, working for a small cannery as the number two executive. Next, he took a breather to return to Hawaii and his family.

Charlie returned to D.C. in 1964 where he joined the Anti-Poverty Program because a friend of his had been appointed director of the Vista program. After a few months working as a volunteer, he was put on the payroll and served almost 20 years. Over the length of his career, he became one of only 13 special technical assistants who usually worked alone as problem-solvers in different field locations around the nation. Vista was designed to help all disenfranchised people; Charlie worked in Arkansas organizing and training poor people. Next, he went to Pasco, Washington; then Alaska, ending his service in Seattle.

It was the policies of Ronald Reagan that cut short his unique career in 1983. As Charlie put it, "I was forcibly retired." It was rather tragic, for Vista and the Anti-Poverty Program provided an official structure to help people, just as our Pike Place Market does today. (Little did Charlie know that his vast experience would serve him well deep into his retirement as he became the most popular elected official in memory when he won his seat on the City Council with a landslide 57 percent of the vote.)

After settling in West Seattle with his longtime partner, Mary, in 1984 they wrote and published a book of poetry about Saint Joseph. Three years later, Charlie got involved with the Market's day-stall community and their fight against unfair rent hikes. (The rents were eventually raised, but I remember the spirited and noble fight.)

Then, it was back to gardening, until word got out in Charlie's neighborhood that a developer was planning to develop the ravine behind their houses. The ensuing fight was won by the neighborhood coalition, led by Mrs. Lee Van Antwerp. Charlie became the spokesperson because Lee wanted to stay in the background. Later, Lee helped Charlie get elected president of the Admiral Community Council. Seattle officials began recognizing Charlie's civic worth; the Parks Department got him to sit on the Seattle Open Spaces Committee.

Time for gardening was getting more rare. He next served on SPIF (Shoreline Parks Committee) and sat on the committee that drafted the city's Environmentally Critical Areas Ordinance (1991-1992). In 1993, he served on a task force on comprehensive (city) planning, resigning a year later to fight the Urban Villages Plan. By now he was well known as a neighborhood rights leader. In West Seattle he was elected chair of the Neighborhood Rights Group and president of the West Seattle Defense Fund. In 1994, when the City Council adopted the Urban Villages concept, their [the neighborhood's] slogan became "We will remember in November." Charlie ran against Margaret Pageler and lost, but when Tom Weeks retired, Charlie won his seat by a landslide against another establishment-supported opponent. He did it without any major media endorsements. Talk about making a major political statement.

Today, this gentleman is dedicated to the principles of his upbringing: *Ho'opono* – to do what is right – for all. He has a special place in his heart for the Market and has stood up for our disenfranchised – and some say, abused – marginal income community.

We were sitting in Lowell's [restaurant] and Charlie had to move on to a meeting in Laurelhurst. He painfully stood up and explained why his back ached: Koa, his 12-year-old, 105-pound Bouvier, was sick and had to be carried about. I asked him what Koa meant and he said, "It's Hawaiian for brave."

He smiled, saluted Elizabeth, our waitress, and left. I looked out the inside window of Lowell's, and as I watched him walk slowly but deliberately up the Main Arcade, I had the answer to a most perplexing question.

Through his committee's civil rights hearings I had noticed that time stands still around Charlie. I now realized why – it's because Charlie Chong has patience.

If a person truly wants to help others less fortunate than oneself, patience is the single most important quality to have. I wish more than ever that the PDA officers would have attended Charlie's hearings. Perhaps it would have rekindled in their good minds what I believe is a missing link in managing our Market: the quality of Patience.

Charlie Chong is a brave man who lives by his principles – and his presence – in these most impatient times, and is inspiring the "system" to do likewise. I raised my cup of tea and silently saluted him. [Interviewed June 1997]

Nancy Covert

shopper

With my brown bag full, I grabbed a stool at the Tran Sisters for a cup of joe and a look-see at the throngs deep in the heart of the Market. A sharp looker with two full bags of very fresh produce was balanced on the stool next to me. She smiled and told me that Lowell's used to be a Manning's Cafeteria way back when. She was knowledgeable, warm and willing, and had that saucy Market twinkle in her eye. You know – that fresh Market look – real inviting. I promptly saddled up closer to her, scanned her firm, full brown bags, and asked her – with a touch of swagger – for an interview.

Nancy Covert smiled coyly and revealed that she had been a regular shopper at the Market for nearly 30 years. She looked around, then whispered that she was born in Pittsburgh and that her father was a railroad man. Sadness came over her when she told me he had died on a hunting trip. "They found a rabbit in his pocket," she said. She gripped my shoulder when she told me how much she loved him, and how he loved life and shared that with his four daughters. She removed her hand and rested it in her lap, then told me that her mother still runs an office in Pittsburgh at age 72.

Seattle was first graced by Nancy Covert's delightful presence in 1960 when her then-husband, Dave, was assigned to Fort Lewis. She gave birth to three children – Steve, Jenny, and Jeff. She said with a smile, "Steve was the first male born in our family in 21 years."

She explained that her life was dedicated to her kids, but in the late 60s her creative strings were being strummed by a fountain pen, just as the pen had done to her famous cousin, Mary Roberts Rinehart (a popular mystery writer whose novels include *The Bat* and *The Spiral Staircase*). Later, when Nancy and her family settled in at Moses Lake, Nancy entered Big Bend College and took up journalism with a vengeance, rapidly rising to the post of editor of the college newspaper. With a distant, wistful look in her eyes, she spoke of her years in eastern Washington. She must have blossomed like a desert rose for, after college, she became a features writer for the *Columbia Basin Herald*. Her assignments enabled her to meet a number of fascinating personalities, including a man named Sam Israel, who eventually became one of her close friends. She said Sam was already a top-notch photographer when she decided to take up photography as well. She recalled one time when she joined him on a photo shoot expedition of the desert near Soap Lake. It was on that trip that she discovered the beauty of Lake Lenora. I began to comment but she stopped me and said, with a slight blush, "Yes, I know, the lake is named after [Market barber] Viola Brown's mother. I read your profiles every month."

Gazing at the passing parade of Market shoppers, she spoke fondly of some day finding the time to write Sam's story. (She already has extensive notes for a book on the legendary Nell Shipman, the 1920s actress/director, who was the subject of the popular retrospective film showing at the Seattle Art Museum.

Nancy mentioned her divorce and then paused to search for the dial of her wristwatch. She said her time was up and that she had to leave. I tried to hurry, a big mistake with someone so freshly laden with sweet produce as Nancy was. She flicked a wisp of hair back from her forehead and said firmly that she was sorry, but it [the interview] was definitely over. I pressed on and got that she was leaving the city to get back to Olympia in time. "You see," she said, "I am the editor of the *Grange News.*"

She held out one last carrot of hope by revealing that she comes to the Market each week on the same day. She usually stops at the Tran Sisters for a Coke and a *hom bow* before returning to the capital. Maybe we would meet again, she suggested. Then she disappeared into the crowd as I paid the bill.

I had this sudden urge to find an ashtray. The strange thing was, I don't smoke. I haven't had a cigarette in 20 years. I guess Nancy had that kind of effect on me. That cookie was one smart shopper. [Interviewed May 1991]

Jim Dandy

Former shoeshine blues man

I decided to ask Jim Dandy to be our next profile when I absentmindedly started humming Laverne Baker's tune, "Jim Dandy to the Rescue" while crossing White Pass in the Cascades. A swatch of the tune went like this: "Jim Dandy on a mountain top…" Let me explain further: The seed for my decision had been planted in Yakima about an hour earlier. It was at Mel's Diner, in the late evening, over joe. I was flirting with a brown-eyed waitress named Stephanie. Behind her hung a long line of antique photographs. The one directly behind her was of the Market's Corner Market Building where today Jim Dandy's shoeshine stall is located. (It's built for comfort, with deep, relaxing seats.)

Steph loved music and the big city, so I had told her a bit about the building – to me, one of the most significant in Seattle. I mentioned that it was rich in history, having started out as a lowly horsemeat slaughterhouse, then housing a barber college that anchored several small stores such as the Three Sisters ice cream parlor. Next, the building gave birth to the first Tradewell supermarket. Today, it is a center of popular music and culture. On the top floor is one of the nation's best restaurants, Chez Shea. The basement houses Patti Summers' Jazz Club (by the Chinese market). On the main floor is the Pike Place Bar and Grill, where Diane Schuur performed at the beginning of her career. (For years, the Grill's house band was Little Bill and the Bluenotes!) Anchoring this incredible mosaic of human activity, sandwiched between the very English Crumpet Shop, the Kosher Delight, and Madam Lazanga's tattoo parlor, sits Jim Dandy's brand-new shoeshine stand. In fact, I told Stephanie that I understood Jim Dandy to be the "Keeper of the Key" – the personification of the history and the incredible "creative force" of the Corner Market Building. I explained that this tall, dignified and Stetson-adorned individual is the first person one meets when entering the building.

Jim agreed to the interview, but it was just a glimpse (for that is all I was allowed; he is a very private man); I realized that my description of him to Steph was accurate: Jim Dandy has a history as rich as the building itself.

His parents were Arkansas sharecroppers, and he and his four sisters and two brothers (all older) had to work the cotton fields from dawn to dusk. He told me that even if they were ahead in their work it meant nothing to the white landowners who wanted the family to work continuously.

On Sundays, the family sang in the neighborhood gospel choirs and eventually Jim became a well-known "minstrel" – a gospel and blues singer and dancer performing with polished groups from around the state. As a young man he started working for the railroad at Little Rock, not too far from where he was "country born." A weird, surreal – but all too real – incident led him north to St. Paul and to better social conditions. His southern white boss had hired a white person to direct Jim Dandy at a plumbing job, but the guy was ignorant about plumbing. So, because of the conventions of racism at the time, Jim had to tell the newcomer how to direct Jim at doing his job! That's when Jim abruptly headed north. He discovered that the civil working conditions in Minnesota were very refreshing.

Over the years, Jim sang a lot and moved around the country. In the 40s, in Memphis, he associated a bit with B.B. King. Later, in L.A., he became noted for – as he quietly says – his "fancy dancing." I asked him to elaborate, but he wouldn't. He talked of many of the great blues men he had known, like Muddywaters and Howling Wolf, two artists who eventually moved to Chicago and world fame. He says he appreciates Memphis-bred Elvis Presley's talent, but qualified his appreciation intensely by saying that Elvis was singing songs from the black culture and he thought that, if anybody, Chuck Berry should be considered "the King." He spoke fondly of Beale Street, the area of Memphis famous for jazz – especially the compositions of W.C. Handy. He mentions that B.B. King has just opened a club on "The Street." He talked about Bo Diddley, another Chicago musician whom he liked. We discussed Bo's distinctive rhythms, which he said were "shoeshine rhythms" created by impromptu a cappella groups who hung out at big-city shoeshine stands. I remember this as a fad in Seattle too in the 50s. The "rhythms" had evolved as "hand jive," where, rather than slapping rags over shoes, you used your hand to slap your forearms and thighs to create the sound and rhythms. This was immortalized in a tune by L.A.'s Johnny Otis called "Willie and the Handjive."

Jim Dandy arrived in Seattle in 1969 and worked for Burlington Northern. Upon retiring from the railroad, he opened a shoeshine stand on First Avenue between Pike and Union. In 1975, the building burned down and he went to work at Ben Paris Restaurant, deeper in the city. Next, he worked part-time for Charley, who first opened the stand at the Corner Market Building. After Charley died, Jim Dandy took over the lease on Martin Luther King Day in 1992, the same day we did this profile.

Jim Dandy is getting on in years and nowadays only performs occasionally for friends. I haven't heard him sing yet, but I hope I will soon.

I understand that, whether dealing with artists, spiritual people, or even brash business folks, some questions dealing with "facts" are out of line. But there were so many questions to ask that perhaps will never be answered. Like: When was a minstrel player considered a "Jim Dandy"? Was our Jim Dandy an "authentic" Jim Dandy? – a distinctive name given to song and dance men who brought joy and love into people's hearts during sad times. Could he have been the inspiration for the Jim Dandy tune Laverne Baker made famous? Minstrel acts were both black and white (whites performed in black-face). The most famous I know of was Al Jolson, star of the first talking picture, *The Jazz Singer*. But was he considered a "Jim Dandy"? Who was the inspiration for the (much younger than our Jim) 1950s white blues singer who billed himself as "Jim Dandy" and played with the Black Oak Arkansas band? Apparently, this Arkansas "Jim Dandy," following in the footsteps of our Jim Dandy, greatly influenced one of the country's top rock stars, David Lee Roth. Well, that's the trouble when you try to deal with "facts." The Market is supposed to be an oasis from the constraints of the "factual" world, so I think our Corner Market's creative spirits are in good hands with an original Jim Dandy holding the "key."

The interview was short, as befits a working day, and like all the Market folks we have profiled, volumes could be written about Jim Dandy's life experiences. I find it doubly amusing that this profile actually started in Yakima with a young, eager lady whose eyes told me to stay, but the pending blizzard demanded that I leave quickly. For foxy lady Steph herself made me reflect on what was far and away the best girl-watching place in the big city. It was looking in at the customers sitting at the raised bar with high stools in the front window of the Corner Market Building's Crumpet Shop! The legs... Well, okay – the truth is, I'm married to a very lovely lady, so... Ah, well, as Laverne would say, "Jim Dandy to the rescue!" [Interviewed February 1992]

Once upon a time…

The Five Pipsqueaks
(performed at a "Sherlockian" evening)

…Inside Holmes's cozy study.

Watson is reading the papers and comments on an article about a project in Wales where the Gulf Stream warms the coastline: "M-m-m… developers want to re-create a Mediterranean scene… in Wales, no less."

The butler announces the arrival of Mr. Vann. Mr. Vann enters in a rush, wearing his heavy overcoat and holding his hat.

Holmes, perturbed from being interrupted, gives Vann a cursory once-over and states:

"Why come directly to me from the north coast of Spain via the Bay of Biscay?" Before Vann can answer, Holmes continues, "…It is because you entered the country with your contraband small dog, asleep, draped around your neck as if it was a fur collar…. Your Mexican hairless is lost; it must have a name tag still on it so you now interrupt my time to ask me to help you retrieve it before the authorities find it."

Vann is speechless as he takes out his card and mumbles:

"But how did you know about Bubbles? How?" He takes out his card and holds it tightly. He completes his story: "Yes, it is true, I made it through customs but by the time I got home at Cornwall Gardens, my Bubbles was not around my neck. I'm in the import/export business and if the authorities find out about Bubbles… well, the quarantine is six months for bringing an animal into England so I… I just couldn't let Bubbles go through that."

"Where did you lose her?"

"I'm sure in a cab; I thought someone of your stature making discreet inquiries, for a fitting sum I might add, would resolve the problem post-haste." Still quite unsure of himself, he backs towards the door and places his card on the edge of the table and says, "It's such a small thing in your world but if you would... here is my card and 100 pounds is yours upon delivery of Bubbles."

Vann has left and Watson turns and asks Holmes, "How in the world did you deduce all that?"

"His fresh suntan, new Spanish-cut boots made of Valencian leather, the smell of sea air, the mat on his collar was squashed, yet no hairs of an animal. All this told me that he came directly from the dock to here worrying about something that had just happened."

Later, after Watson recovers, he returns to his newspaper as Holmes fills his pipe. Holmes says, "Indeed! Interrupting my day with such a trivial request..."

The butler enters and announces, "Miss Maidenhead is here, sir." Miss Maidenhead, a cool, sexy midget, enters. The eyes of Holmes burn with fury.

Miss Maidenhead gives Holmes a letter; he reads aloud: "M-m-m, from Lestrade." He opens it and reads: "Dear Mr. Holmes: According to the bearer of this letter, this morning 5,000 oranges were stolen from a Can Can dancer, Miss Tilly. She was struck down in the incident and died. Miss Maidenhead, who discovered her, assures me that this is true. I cannot fathom this and have referred her to you. Obviously, she is not a murder suspect because Miss Tilly was done in by a heavy blow to the head. Miss Tilly herself is a midget. Perhaps you can get Miss Maidenhead to speak things other than gibberish about 5,000 oranges... she's dehydrated or worse; apparently the troupe hadn't had a thing to eat in days. Get her to tell us where the dancers' agent – an American named Dino – is hiding out. He ran from the foyer upon my arrival." Holmes shakes his head. "For some idiot who lost his dog and now a murder of a starving midget who lost 5,000 oranges?"

"Miss Maidenhead, were you and the deceased in the same Can Can troupe?"

"Yes, we were... the whole troupe, all five of us, were to go to the eastern seaboard of the U.S. to be discovered. It was all arranged by our agent, Dino Leery of New York City."

"What was Tilly doing with 5,000 oranges? Did you see them?"

"Oh, yes sir, they were in the foyer in two clearly marked boxes. Tilly was so excited because we were very broke and needed nourishment so I ran up to fetch Dino. We returned to find the oranges gone and Miss Tilly dead in their place."

[She starts to cry.]

"Where is Dino?"

Miss Maidenhead is hesitant. "I don't know... he seems to have disappeared just before the detective came."

"Disappeared?"

"Well, he sort of ran away."

"How much time elapsed before you and Dino returned?"

"No more than five, six minutes... I fetched him from the fourth floor and he came immediately down to the foyer."

"What is the name of your dance troupe?"

"The Five Pipsqueaks, sir."

"How big were the boxes, Miss Maidenhead?"

"Oh, they were over my head... two of them there were."

"Go home, Miss Maidenhead. I know who murdered Miss Tilly."

Miss Maidenhead leaves and Watson turns to Holmes. "Egad, Holmes, who is it?"

"Let's go down to Covent Garden, Watson..." Later, at the Garden, Holmes leads Watson to the seedy side of the vast public market, then down a hall to stop at Grogan's, a butcher long noted for being suspected of dressing pets. Above the serving block hangs a row of small dressed animals, some looking suspiciously like a cat or a dog. Holmes walks down the row to stop at the runtiest and then peers closely at the carcass. Grogan approaches them, wiping his knife suggestively. "What it be, mates... you buying or selling?"

"Pay you double for the little one if you give me its collar back."

Grogan looks as innocent as a lamb, but greed gets the better of him. "You the Yard?"

"Absolutely not! Here is the money, take it or leave it."

Grogan looks at the money, shrugs his shoulders, "The dog was dead when the girl brought it in..." He goes to the trash bin to pick out several collars. He brings them over. Holmes looks at them and selects his. The carcass is wrapped and Holmes and Watson depart.

Grogan hisses after Holmes, "You should give your little girl an allowance; all she got for the dog was a half-pence." Holmes and Watson leave as Grogan yells, "At least you could feed her properly!"

Away from the wretched stall, Watson looks at Holmes and asks, "But how did you know?"

"Elementary, my dear Watson. You forget my keen sense of anatomy." He flicks the dog tag with the name Bubbles prominently displayed on it.

Watson laughs. "Well, at least you made 100 pounds for your efforts."

"Not quite so, Watson, not quite so."

Back at the house, the butler enters to announce the arrival of Detective Lestrade, who saunters in with a gleam in his eye. "Did a Miss Maidenhead come to you with a cock and bull story about some oranges this afternoon?"

Holmes admits, "Yes, she did. Sultry little thing."

Lestrade brags, "Well, I don't know what she said to you but she wouldn't tell us where her agent was hiding... but we found him and have booked him on murder of Miss Tilly, his lead dancer (he winks knowingly)... seems that he and she were lovers in a tiff and she began to ignore him. He just hit her and she died... the orange crates were a figment of Miss Maidenhead's fertile imagination fueled by almost being starved to death. Besides, how would she have got rid of them? Those dancers hadn't had a thing to eat in days. By the way, Holmes, why did you call me over here on this late, stormy evening anyway?"

"Why Detective, I..." Sherlock is interrupted by the main who announces the arrival of Mr. Vann.

Mr. Vann enters the room, looking expectantly at Mr. Holmes.

Mr. Holmes announces, "We have found your dog, sir. Place the reward on the table and you may have her."

Vann does as he is told and waits anxiously.

"Sir, I am sorry to say that Bubbles is dead. She is wrapped in this packet. Here is her collar." The deeply saddened Mr. Vann takes the collar and acknowledges that it is Bubbles'. He picks up the package and murmurs, "She feels so cold."

"I advise you not to open the package. But to trust me that indeed what is inside is the remains of your dog. There is one other problem you may wish to focus on. You killed Miss Tilly Lane."

Detective Lestrade laughs out loud. "My dear Mr. Holmes, please..." Mr. Vann laughs as well and looks at the detective. "Indeed, sir – who is this Miss Tilly Lane?"

"Your shipment of imports was hand delivered to Miss Tilly by mistake. She lives in Glouster Gardens just across from you. You read your copy of the Bill of Lading and, being a clever sort, clever enough to have draped your dog around your neck to bring her into the country, you figured out the sloppy handwriting done in the rain. You rushed over there, found your packages with Miss Tilly greedily trying to open one of them, you struck her and left with your packages."

Mr. Vann looked blankly at Watson, then back at Holmes.

Holmes continues, "I checked with your shipping agency and indeed they deal in perishables like oranges."

Watson comes over and whispers into Holmes's ear: "But Holmes, I beg of you to rethink your theory. Surely Mr. Vann could not have moved 5,000 oranges in the short space of time between when Miss Maidenhead left to find Dino and when they returned."

Holmes looks straight at Mr. Vann. "Your boxes were filled with 5,000 orange pipps to be transshipped to Wales for seeding in a Mediterranean setting. You were reading about the experiment this morning, Watson."

Holmes continues: "...The boxes only appeared large to a midget but were easily transportable by a man as large as you... You dropped your sleeping dog who was still draped around your shoulders in the foyer when you moved the boxes."

The detective breaks in, "but surely Holmes..." Holmes cuts him off by asking him if it was true that Miss Maidenhead was hungry when he questioned her. "She was ravished, but what has that to do with this..."

He [Holmes] takes out his fiddle and tunes a string, then turns to Mr. Vann and says, "She sold your dog for a half-pence, and fed herself before she came here... she had found your dog still asleep in the foyer." He turns to Watson, "Miss Maidenhead could easily have been mistaken for a young girl by Grogan, right Mr. Watson?"

Mr. Vann falls down on his knees clutching the butcher paper-wrapped package and cries, "BUBBLES!"

Holmes announces, "Take him away, Lestrade... take him far away."

They leave and Watson, after a long silence, notices the 100-pound note and says, "Well, sir, as I said, you at least made 100 pounds for the inconvenience."

"Not quite, Mr. Watson, after I deduct for my services I shall award the rest, about 93 pounds, I should guess, to Miss Maidenhead, for she found Bubbles, and perhaps the Five well now, Four Pipsqueaks can go to America and be discovered after all."

A Hydro Racer Cages His Morning Coffee
(a teleplay filmed in the Market)

EXT.   UNDER ALASKA WAY VIADUCT.   MORNING

(Sound effects) SFX theme song: "Ghost Riders in the Sky," sung by Gene Autry.

PAN from train tunnel to old VW van with California plates.

The door slides open as SOUTHERN CALIFORNIA MIKE falls out. He's big but agile and dressed like a longshoreman.

SC Mike slides the door shut, pats his hair, presses the wing window closed, puts on his watchman's cap, and leaves.

EXT.   FRONT OF CHOCOLATE FACTORY. MORNING

A late-model Rabbit convertible with New Jersey plates parks and ALMOST MANHATTAN MARK steps out. Mark is neatly dressed in levis and a sweater adorned with several hydroplane buttons pinned across the chest. It's obvious he's a hydro fan.

He picks up *THE WEEKLY* tabloid from a stand, glances at the cover as a WORKER puts up a ladder behind him.

Overhead, an old, huge sign of an overly cute boy slurping an ice cream cone has come loose. The WORKER is being directed by CLAIRE, the waitress.

Mark holds the door for Claire, then walks into the café after her.

INT.   MARKET ARCADE.   MORNING

SC Mike walks between rows of fish vendors and veggie stalls filled with fresh fruit and veggies. He walks full into camera CU (close up) and stops to stare at the floor in front, shiftily looks around, and flicks his little fingers...

CU of his POV (Point of View) – a fat bunch of carrots has fallen from a stall; his hat quickly covers them.

TITLE: GREAT EXPECTATIONS #10

A HYDRO RACER CAGES HIS MORNING COFFEE.

SFX theme song fades out.

(COMMERCIAL BREAK)

INT.   CHOCOLATE FACTORY.   MORNING

MS (Master Shot) with Mark sitting in the foreground watching TV as yuppie types JEFF and BRENDA walk in.

(JEFF snapping fingers) We want a table and snappy...

CLAIRE rushes over.

Certainly... how about this one (trying to please), or here...

Jeff and Brenda sit as Claire comes over to Mark and takes a few flowers out of his vase and puts them in another.

CLAIRE (to MARK)

Share and share alike... (Mark smiles pleasantly as she carries the vase over to Jeff's table.)

JEFF

We want eggs, bacon...

BRENDA (breaking in)

...crisp.

JEFF

Several hotcakes and apple pie...

BRENDA

... yeah and oatmeal, and toast; don't forget the raisins in the oatmeal...

JEFF

Wheat toast, heels of wheat... we like the heels...

CLAIRE (taking the order)

Yes sir...

BRENDA

Like, we're hungry, we just came from a all-night party where a girl gave birth to a baby and we had to deliver it on the spot.

CLAIRE (concerned)

I'm sorry...

JEFF (nonchalant)

Coffee to start... Hey, not to worry. I'm a doctor, happens all the time... and she (he winks) is my little nursey.

CLAIRE (rather confused, stumbling backwards)

Coffee to start... (she passes Mark's table)

MARK (reading *THE WEEKLY*)

Say, do you mind switching channels? Says here there's going to be some hydro recaps this morning.

CLAIRE gets up on a chair and switches channels until the screen is filled with thunderboats. She adjusts the volume.

CU on TV screen as announcer relates the history of hydroplanes.

CU on Mark as his face registers enjoyment.

Pull back to MS as SC MIKE enters behind MARK.

VO (Voice Over)TV ANNOUNCER (over sounds of blasting hydros)

Yes, there have been so many sponsors – from the Miss 7/11 to Miss Thriftway...

SC Mike looks over the café as he did when he spotted the carrots. His gaze rests on Mark and he walks over to plop down into the empty chair at

Mark's table. Behind him, through the café's large front windows, the legs of the Worker are clearly visible on the ladder.

SC MIKE (making himself comfortable)

Hey, hey, hi...Gary.

MARK (turns, a bit put off)

Well, my name's not Gary, it's Mark...and I

SC MIKE

Well, how do you like that... coulda swore you were Gary, you got the same back... well, what's in a name anyhow, right? I mean movie stars change their names, so do reporters... I mean, sure you look like a Mark... I mean more than you look like a Gary... (looks at buttons and nods knowingly)... so you're a hydro man too... well, well, well.

CLAIRE (giving SC a wary look while holding a pot of coffee and a menu)

Breakfast?

SC MIKE

Just coffee, thanks, I'll have breakfast later... a health food breakfast if you will... (Claire pours) Oh yes, cream and sugar... no, wait, (he retrieves a packet of sugar from a pocket) I have my own sugar...

CLAIRE (a bit amused)

So, you brought your own... hm-m. (She finishes pouring and leaves)

VO. TV ANNOUNCER

...and the Miss Thriftway ran in Miami...

Mark gets engrossed with the TV show.

SC MIKE (tapping Mark's shoulder)

I'm a hydro man myself.

MARK (not looking away from the TV)

Really?

SC MIKE (grabs Mark's shoulder, then puts out his hand to shake)

Name's Southern California Mike hydro rider U.S.A.; been all over the States riding hydros, up in Seattle to catch a ride...

MARK (slowly takes his hand)

You race hydroplanes, huh?... (realizes what SC has said and gets excited) You are a hydroplane racer, sir?

SC MIKE

The best... absolutely! (points to TV) Even raced the old Miss Safeway...

MARK (thinking)

I never heard of Miss Safeway... the Miss Thriftway yes...

SC MIKE

The Safeway could beat the Thriftway by miles of knots. Hell, one time at Hartford on the Delaware I was a-headin for the finish line and almost beat her, the Albertson, Miss Tradewell and the 7/11...

MARK

Huh, I didn't know there was a race up the Delaware...

SC MIKE

Down the Delaware, Mark... would've beat them all if I hadn't run out of gas... had to turn around and head for home. It was my first big-time race, so I didn't feel so bad, just a mite embarrassed. It was called the Grocery Chain Regatta.

MARK

Never heard of it or of you for that matter... (points to TV) why aren't you there now in the pits revving up?

SC MIKE

That's TV, Mark, I'm the real thing. Hey, you want to see the pits, heck, I'll take you... I know the pits like I know myself... any time you want, old SC will show you what the pits are really like...

MARK (wary)

Huh?

SC MIKE

I was really in the pits in Mobile...

MARK (a bit unsure)

Alabama

SC MIKE

Yeah, during the Mobile River regatta... I learned a lot about bricklaying between laps...

MARK (suspicious)

Bricklaying?

SC MIKE

It was the reason why I missed the race...

MARK

Bricklaying?

SC MIKE

By the way, I set the fastest lap that was ever run at Mobile; still stands today, I believe...

MARK

Why did bricklaying cause you to miss the race?

SC MIKE

I was staying with Susy in a riverboat. She had a ton of bricks she was trying to sell... luckily her boyfriend had left a suit and tie with her so I could be properly dressed for the part. You don't get paid for hydro riding till after you're hired so I had to do it... unfortunately the bricks didn't belong to her so I ended up on a work release program laying bricks for a new square down by the docks.

MARK (shaking his head)

I didn't think Mobile sponsored a hydro race...

SC MIKE

That was several years ago, Mark...

MARK (to himself)

Maybe Miami...

SC MIKE

Details... you're just getting particular again, Mark... I mean, what's in a name anyhow... I mean, if you really want to get philosophical, then every city should sponsor a hydro race, then us superstars like me can have equal opportunity employment... I mean, it's no fun chasing around the country for hydro rides buddy.

MARK (irritated)

I'm for equal opportunity employment... but what happened to the bricklaying job – was that part of a jail sentence?

SC MIKE

It was just a few days. I suspect they wanted this square finished and needed workers, you see. I had eye contact with George Wallace there.

MARK

Eye contact? You mean you looked somebody in the eye...

SC MIKE (indignant)

Mark, in L.A. eye contacting is the highest form of relations between consenting adults... ever since sex has been relegated to disease carriers...

MARK

All right, all right...

SC MIKE

Here I was, on my hands and knees laying bricks, when I hear this authoritative wheeze, to look up and straight into the eyes of Governor George C. Wallace a-glidin' by in his wheelchair. Must've held eye contact for a full six seconds, that was until I saw Fats Domino a-racin' over behind his shoulder...

MARK

Fats Domino... the singer...

SC MIKE (wistfully)

They were dedicating the square to jazz... how did I know I was wearing his suit and tie.

MARK (remembering)
Susy in the riverboat... her boyfriend was Fats?
SC MIKE
Yup... Ever try to lay bricks in a suit ten times larger than your size? If you think that's hard, try racing a hydro in one... we became friends after about a block of him chasing me... he was wheezing and puffing, and after I told him about my hydro riding, how I was a star, he let me keep his clothes... even called me brother... (pulls out a hanky) He gave me this hanky.
MARK
Those initials read A.L.
SC MIKE
Was you there, Mark?... He gave it to me... anyway, me and Susy got married...
MARK
Is she with you now?
SC MIKE (freezes, looks around all tense)
I think she's still busted like... (he takes out the carrots from his cap and bites into the bunch)... Want a bite, Mark?
MARK (confused)
No... no thanks... what do you mean, busted?
SC MIKE (chewing)
She's on a farm in Redding milking cows for California last time I heard of her.
MARK (to himself)
Work release program.
VO. TV ANNOUNCER
Below the Blue Angels roars the Miss Madison in the 1967 Gold Cup...
MARK (continuing)
What did she do?
SC MIKE
Oh, nothing much... she was delivering the Miss Madison to Lake Havasu City when we innocently took a wrong freeway to Palmdale to end up in one of the paramilitary camps under Mount Shasta where they grow all that maryuanna... Well, we were ringed with 60 guards toting 50-caliber submachine guns... they thought the big hydro to be some sort of weapon... one guy yelled out "it's here"... something about a second-hand missile they were waiting for. Well, after about three days they sorted it out and let us go... well, the race was already run at Lake Havasu and the next one was to be in the Northwest somewhere so we headed up over the

Oregon border... where we stopped at a gas station and I started to call the owners only to look back at the truck and trailer now surrounded by cops.

MARK

Did you go back to help her... to explain?

SC MIKE

Oh, no... I had my career to think of...

MARK

You selfish crud! You let her take the rap!!

SC MIKE

I was only along for the ride, I didn't drive... I ride hydros, not trucks. Anyway, she was never charged with stealing a hydro once it was all explained; hell, my movie career was just starting. I had to get back to my body movement classes.

MARK

One thing at a time... what was she charged with?

SC MIKE

Well, when they took her back over the California border, she was carrying an apple in her purse. They don't take kindly with that kind of stuff... they came down hard on her... I warned her but she still did it... the hardheaded...

MARK

All right, all right... what was this movie stuff you were talking about?

SC MIKE

...Well, when I was last in L.A. I got a job as a grip on a movie about the Blue Angels of West Hollywood...

MARK

They're not from West Hollywood... they fly jets at hydro races.

SC MIKE

Judging from the script, they did a whole lot of things... as a group they can keep perfect pitch...

MARK (angry)

They fly jet planes!

SC MIKE

Big deal! We all do from time to time... look, don't worry about the details, Mark. Get the big picture, get an overview... get hep! (snaps his fingers)

VO. TV ANNOUNCER

The Miss Bardahl ran for many years – one of the most popular boats in her time.

MARK (uneasy, looks at the TV)

The Miss Bardahl, one of my favorite boats...

SC MIKE (yelling)

Waitress, oh waitress, can we have a refill?

MARK (turning to SC unwillingly)

Why do you have to be so rude? Why can't you wait till she comes over?

SC MIKE

Hey, she's a woman. Got to treat 'em tough, give 'em direction... (looks leeringly at Brenda) Bet there's a lot of pink under them clothes...

Brenda looks over and gives SC Mike an ugly look, then sticks her tongue out at him.

SC MIKE (continuing)

She loves me.

CLAIRE (approaches their table)

Are those your carrots?

SC MIKE

Huh?

CLAIRE

You can't eat them here... put them away. (she refills their cups) You said you're a hydro rider; by the way you smell, the only thing you ever rode was a sewer pipe. (she walks away)

SC MIKE (confident)

She doesn't know one exotic fuel smell from another, eh Mark? (to Claire) Why don't you button up!

MARK (questioning)

Are you a kook? You don't really ride hydroplanes, do you? You don't even know who Stan Sayres is.

SC MIKE

Stan was my father's best friend... that's how I got involved in racing in the first place.

MARK

I don't believe you.

SC MIKE

Were you there, Mark?... in Buffalo on the Buffalo Lake so many years ago...

MARK (breaking in)

Oh, now...

SC MIKE

...Oh, yes, I forgot a few of the names; all right, nobody's perfect. It was one hell of a race... we were neck and neck, only Stan and me. He made the turn but I went straight ahead right past the turn marshal and slammed into a manure scow. Lost the Miss Texaco on that turn… lost a rudder doing 100 miles per when I hit her… the scow, that is.

MARK (coy)

So you rode the legendary Miss Texaco, huh?

SC MIKE

Rode her all the way into the ground, buddy… she was one tough boat. But old

Stan what's-his-name won the race overall, had to settle for second place.

MARK

There was no Miss Texaco, and Stan Sayres is one of the most famous legendary men of the sport. He owned the record-shattering Slo Mo 4 and 5…he…

SC MIKE (breaking in)

What about Slo Mo 1,2 and 3… they were a pretty bunch… I used to race the Slo Mo 3 in the Beverly Hills Regatta! On the Beverly Hills River… two can play the name-dropping game, Mark!

MARK

Beverly Hills River? There's no such thing!

SC MIKE

Ever been to Beverly Hills, Mark?

MARK (seething)

No.

SC MIKE

The river winds its way down Sunset Boulevard where it meets the Santa Monica River under the Ventura Freeway to enter the sea at Malibu where all the starlets live… Like Hedy Lamar… and, yes I had eye contact with Hedy!

MARK (looking around the café for help)

What does Hedy Lamar have to do with racing hydroplanes?

SC MIKE

She was the announcer… and she had a far better voice than this character does (gestures toward TV) and she was so beautiful…. Did you see her in…

MARK (breaking in)

How old are you?

SC MIKE

Twenty-seven.

MARK

Twenty-seven?

SC MIKE

That's what I said, twenty-seven.

MARK

Maybe about twenty years ago.

SC MIKE

Hey, that's the age range my agents put me in – twenty-seven – talk to my agent if you don't believe me…

MARK (steering the course)

Hedy Lamar must be old enough to be your mother in real life… maybe even your grandmother!

SC MIKE (shaking his head)

You moderns, we think we lick racism, then up comes sexism. We think we get a handle on that and now it's ageism… look you got something against senior citizens looking good?… I know how good-looking she was. I gave her a ride in the Slo Mo 1 at Beverly Hills.

MARK

You told me you rode the Slo Mo 3.

SC MIKE

Minor detail.

MARK

You told me you rode the Miss Texaco… it doesn't exist!

SC MIKE

Details…

MARK

The Beverly Hills River doesn't exist!

SC MIKE (matter-of-factly)

Everything exists in Beverly Hills, Mark.

CLAIRE (comes over with a pot of coffee)

How are my charges doing; want a refill?

MARK (somewhat defeated)

No… I think I gotta be going… (takes a fiver out of his pocket)

SC MIKE (slips into his carrot-snitching pose)

Let me spring for the refills, Mark; you'll miss the hydro recaps… (gestures toward the TV)

CLAIRE (points to the "refill free" sign by the coffee bar) The refills are free, big guy, in case you didn't know. (She places his bill firmly in front of his eyes) You can pay for your coffee… try a little eye contact on your bill.

SC MIKE (takes out broken glasses)

He… what's, shit! Thirty-six cents for a cup of coffee! Why, (outraged) I… (his jaw freezes shut)

SC Mike gasps for breath as Claire and Mark try to separate it. His mouth disappears between his moustache and beard.

CLAIRE (purposeful)

Where the hell did that mouth go?

JEFF (rushes over)

Let me help; I'm a doctor… (they wrestle with SC MIKE)

PULL IN and CU on TV

VO. JEFF

Brenda, punch him in the gut gently… (fade)

Commercial

PULL BACK from TV to MS of café with SC MIKE being slapped on the back by the doctor.

SC MIKE (breathing deeply)

Thanks, Doc. (Jeff and Brenda go back to their table)

The worker, who had come in holding a hammer and a crowbar, goes back outside.

VO. TV ANNOUNCER

The Bluebird Special held the world record briefly in the fifties.

MARK

Are you all right?

SC MIKE

Yeah, nerve reaction to a hydro accident I had riding a hydro up the Amazon a ways back.

MARK (dazed and still holding the fiver)

I never knew they held a race on the Amazon… I thought only piranhas and crocodiles lived there.

SC MIKE (yelling to Claire)

Sorry, we'll make up for any disturbance we may have caused. (to Mark) Won't we, Mark? Like leaving a big tip. (claps Mark's arm) You're my buddy… you're all right…

CLAIRE

I'd prefer it if you just take a big trip, like ride your hydros right out of town.

SC MIKE (to Mark)

Don't worry about her, she loves me… you can tell.

MARK (absentmindedly)

You know her?

SC MIKE

I know her type; they all fall head-over-heels in love with me.

MARK (drumming his fingers on the table)

What hydro were you racing up the Amazon?

SC MIKE

<u>Down</u> the Amazon, Mark, it was the... ah, you'll only say you never heard of her.

MARK

Why does that make any difference now – never heard of any of the boats, rivers, regattas – none of the places you talk about. I mean, you gotta be putting me on... I'm not that out of touch... I mean,(fondles a button) I got one of the most complete collections of hydro buttons that exists...

SC MIKE (concerned)

I'm not putting you on, I hardly know you... and why would I do it in the first place? (eyes the fiver in Mark's hand) Where you from, Mark?

MARK

New Jersey.

SC MIKE

Could've sworn you were from New York City...

MARK

Never been there... saw it a lot of times from the Cliffs though...

SC MIKE

You're from New York City, admit it...

MARK (refocusing)

No... I've never been to Manhattan.... I'm from Englewood Cliffs, New Jersey.

SC MIKE

But that's just across the river from the City, the GW Bridge! Hell, I raced under the GW Bridge.

MARK (not accepting the bait)

Nope, never been there. (gaining strength, becomes impish, the fiver slips back into his pocket)

SC MIKE (reacts with panic to the fiver disappearing)

But you're so Manhattanish, your eyes, your voice, you, your, your...!

MARK (taking control)

Ever been to Manhattan SC? I mean you were there, SC, right? Don't put me on...

SC MIKE (grasping)

Hey, man... hey. Almost-Manhattan Mark... those... those are my lines!

MARK

What's all this garbage about you being a hydro driver... you couldn't ride an electric lawn mower without running over your own cord...

SC MIKE (self-righteous and stern)

I demonstrated lawn mowers for SEARS ROEBUCK... I endorsed three models... John Wayne was my co-endorser!

MARK (getting caught in SC's spiel)

When was that, before or after the Amazon race?... before or after your movie career...?

SC MIKE

It was when I had a strong session of eye contact with John Wayne.

MARK (trying to pull out of the conversation) John Wayne died years ago.

SC MIKE

Details!

MARK (flabbergasted)

How could you have had your so-called eye contact with a dead man?

SC MIKE (matter-of-factly)

He was as healthy as an ox when I saw him a coupla years ago.

MARK (firm)

Two years ago?

SC MIKE

Yes... it was...

MARK (cutting him off)

(Opens newspaper) Look, it says right here he died in 1978. How could you have seen him two years ago?

SC MIKE

You cut me off. I'm trying to tell you... it was in *She Wore a Yellow Ribbon*... man, he was great in that film.

MARK (staggered)

You had eye contact with him in a movie!!!

SC MIKE

In one of his greats. Right at the beginning of the film... he looked straight into the camera, something only the truly greatest can get away with without distorting reality... It may have been for only a tiny bit of a second but man, in those heavy eye contacting situations, those moments can seem like a lifetime.... Like a race driver experiences when he's traveling at 250 miles per hour...

MARK (convinced)

You really are a kook!

SC MIKE (above it all)

No… no, Mark, I am not a kook… I'm just a humble soul from Southern California… who relates to the gods and rides hydroplanes.

MARK

Now John Wayne is a god.

SC MIKE (reverent)

You said it, not me.

MARK (jaw dropping)

I don't believe this…

SC MIKE

Nobody's asking you to… (gets ready to leave)… Just have a little fun, I gotta start thinking about getting down to the pits…

MARK

The pits?

SC MIKE

Gotta audition for a ride…

MARK

You going out there now?

SC MIKE (stands up, hesitates)

Yeah, gotta go. (arranges watchman's cap heroically) Want to come along?… Wait a minute, I can't let you go unless I've left the deposit down for you so they can check their computers… they have a thing against undesirables. (he sits down expectantly)

MARK

How much is the deposit?

SC MIKE

Ten dollars.

MARK

Shucks, I only have eight dollars on me.

SC MIKE

Tell you what, spring for our coffees and I'll get you in for five.

MARK

All right. (gets ready to pay for the coffee when he is distracted by the TV announcer)

VO. TV ANNOUNCER

…one of the most exciting duels in the history of the sport took place at the Apple Cup where the Bud and Miller went neck and neck…

CU to TV screen as we see this exciting race.

VO. TV ANNOUNCER

…and the winner is the Budweiser.

MS CAFÉ

MARK (happy)

Man, I've seen that ending a thousand times...

SC MIKE

Let's go.

MARK

Wait, why am I trusting you? I hardly know you...

SC MIKE (frustrated)

I don't believe this... Look, I know my limitations, fella... I don't cheat or con my friends, especially my friends... I may be guilty of something, everybody is, including your mother...

MARK

Leave my mother out of this!

SC MIKE (moody)

I'm only trying to make a point.

MARK (remembering)

What was this Amazon race you were going to tell me about?

SC MIKE

Your mother was not involved with that race if that's what you're wondering...

MARK (yelling)

What!

JEFF (shouting from his table)

Be quiet over there.

CLAIRE (rushes over)

Sir, you're going to have to be more quiet!

MARK (looking at her dumbly)

But I'm usually quiet... sorry...

JEFF

Please... you're disturbing my nurse. (she sulks)

WORKER (comes in front door dragging in the huge, bizarre sign)

Well, we got it off, Claire... where do you want it?

CLAIRE (pointing)

Over there. Want a coke?

WORKER (sliding the sign behind SC Mike and Mark)

No thanks, got to get back on the roof; the other sign is just hanging there. (exits)

SC MIKE

Mark, the Amazon race was just like that sign back there – big, bright and flashy.

MARK

What hydro were you racing?

SC MIKE

The Blueplate Special, rocket-powered monster, speeds over 300 miles an hour...

MARK

No hydro has ever done those speeds in a race.

SC MIKE

It's about time to let you in on a big secret, Mark... to inform you that nothing's impossible. This race was held in secret to test the most advanced hydros in the world. The Bluetip was one of them. Not the fastest... just the second-fastest... the Miss Wesson Oil was the fastest.

MARK (throwing up his hands)

The Blueplate, the Bluetip, the Wesson Oil. I suppose a Wingless Jumbo Jet was tried as well...

SC MIKE

So you did hear about this race!

MARK

I don't believe this!

SC MIKE

Well, in case you forgot the outcome because it was all top secret wartime tests to adapt hydros to helping in the river wars of Vietnam... I remember how accurate they were at target practice shooting bull's-eyes out of water buffaloes half submerged at 200 miles per hour... I remember them screaming along at the same speed to retrieve parachute packages by snagging their payload of fuel, medical supplies, and jeeps with perfect precision just as they were ten feet from the water...

MARK (angry)

What? You can't tell me that...

SC MIKE

Why not?...

MARK

If they tried snagging a parachute at 200 miles per hour the hydro would suffer tremendous damage from the open parachutes' hitting the wind.

SC MIKE

Was you there, Mark? Look, regulation issue for each hydro was several pairs of very long and sharp scissors... part of the crew's duty was to keep them very sharp. Off duty you could see them sharpening away as if they were whittling. The glint on the shiny scissors started a whole new cult amongst the natives.

MARK

This is just one of your crazy stories...

SC MIKE

Nope, it's true... they even gave the cult a name – the Thunderboat Appreciation Club of the Amazon.

MARK

Whatever you say, SC... you mention crews – how big were these so-called hydros?

SC MIKE

Varied. Average 150 feet, crew of 15...

MARK (disgusted)

SC... what in God's name have you been smoking?

SC MIKE

Pall Mall filters.

MARK

What!

SC MIKE

I smoked Pall Mall filters up to about three months ago... I gave up smoking.

MARK

I don't believe this.

SC MIKE

Hey, it's easy once you put your mind to it; besides, hydro owners don't like their drivers to smoke on the job.

MARK (tense)

...Go ahead and tell me...

SC MIKE

No, I didn't win the Amazon race.

MARK

You came in second... didn't you...

SC MIKE

After a fashion...

MARK (alarmed)

Fashion?

SC MIKE

Yes, you see I hit a pregnant crocodile at full speed... 300 miles per hour... destroyed her and all her kids. She was big, almost as big as the Blueplate Special... lost the hydro and the crew and was attacked by a school of piranhas. Just then her boyfriend... must have been the father of her now-dead young because he came on so ferocious... well, I had to think quickly. By the way, all the other craft had DNF'd except Miss Wesson Oil who won the race... Well, I wrestled that croc around and exposed its soft underbelly to the piranhas who promptly ate their fill – the whole school, after hearing the recess bell, raced back to class leaving me holding the bag, so to speak – a crocodile skin bag. That's what was left of him. And those kinds of bags will always be in fashion, Mark.

MARK (going berserk)

Stop! Stop!... Stop!

Everyone in the café comes over to their table.

MARK (continuing)

How big was this crocodile?

SC MIKE

The crocodile's 160 feet long.

MARK

You're lying... I tell you.

CLAIRE (hands SC his bill)

Pay up and leave; you're disturbing my customers.

SC MIKE

He's paying. (points at Mark) He said he would...

MARK (singing)

Get me to the pits on time.

CLAIRE (firmly shoves the bill at SC)

Pay up.

SC MIKE (takes the bill and gets out his reading glasses as before; looks at it)

But 36 cents for a cup of coffee... (he has one of his seizures where his mouth slams shut)

CLAIRE

Oh... good!

JEFF

Let us through, we'll get it open...

MARK

Keep that mouth shut!

CLAIRE

Yeah, keep it shut this time!

BRENDA (grabbing SC)

He'll choke!

A battle starts between Mark and Claire against Jeff and Brenda, over whether to keep the mouth shut or open. The Worker comes in holding the crowbar.

JEFF

Get that crowbar over here; we need it.

A delivery girl with a box of apples comes in.

DELIVERY GIRL

Here's your apples you ordered.

She stumbles over the sign, sending apples every which way. She crawls on her hands and knees retrieving them as the sign almost topples over the group fighting over SC Mike's mouth.

TITLES over fight scene and PAN to TV.

VO. TV ANNOUNCER

Well, will SC MIKE ever get the use of his mouth back. Does he for once end up having to pay for his coffee…? Stay tuned to the next episode of GREAT EXPECTATIONS. Meanwhile, enjoy the race season.

SFX. "Ghost Riders in the Sky" by Gene Autry.

END

A Single Sweet Script

Once upon a time…

IX
Mio Campo
Spring 1956.

…in a suburb of Corrientes, Argentina.

Hitler, Goebbels, Goering, Eva Braun try to stage a comeback.

Hitler still has his "visions" but his sense of a "comeback" is distorted through time. His will and hypnotic talents are as powerful as ever, thus the group follows him without question.

Hitler would be approximately 65-68 years of age in 1956.

1   FLASHBACK TO 1941

Two airplanes: A U.S. B-17 and a German Heinkel towing a glider fly by.

The Heinkel's Luftwaffe insignia is painted out and U.S.A.F, markings are crudely painted on.

BEAT

VO. (VOICEOVER)   JOSÉ/HITLER

Hermann, ten years have passed since my valiant escape… ten years we have waited, the world has waited for my return, remember how my people worshipped me… ten years… I am not appreciated anymore… for what I am. (sniff)

DISSOLVE/FADE IN (Present Day 1956)

<u>2. INT. (INTERIOR)   A DILAPIDATED HANGAR.   NIGHT</u>

The same B-17, Heinkel and glider are sitting forlornly in the background. Piles of paintings are stacked about. The paintings are stolen booty from the Third Reich era. They consist of many famous paintings, collectively worth billions of dollars.

VO. JORGE/GOERING

Mein Führer, all is going as planned. Cells of SS are now established in virtually every country of the free world, and Russia...

JOSÉ, JORGE AND JOSÉ DOS – "The GROUP." They wear Argentina peasant garb and metal-shod rope shoes and are, respectively, Hitler, Goering, and Goebbels. They sit at a table. EVA (Eva Braun) is serving them wine from a carafe. They have aged well, a bit heavier, but otherwise very healthy. A handbill is tacked to the wall announcing a revue entitled *Mio Campo.*

JOSÉ DOS (tense, slamming fist)

They send your speeches back spliced! Your beautiful prose deleted...

JOSÉ (sad)

They don't want me anymore. Dosey, they only want my art. (He nods toward the stacks of masterpieces).

JORGE (explaining)

That's what's paying their way. (apologetically)   They wouldn't survive one minute if you didn't contribute a painting or two a month, my Führer...

JOSÉ DOS

They're getting old, no punch, only paunch. They're only running up the flagpole with other countries' flags. You're right. They don't want you anymore, José; they only want your art. But we shall persevere; the Reich shall rise again.

JOSÉ (picks up a letter and reads)

Claudio has the answer. This Hubbles is willing to negotiate with us. We auction off a bunch of paintings and buy a missile from Werner. With the missile we blackmail the SS cells, who in turn blackmail the world and we take over. Call Werner... Werner will save us!

The three snap to a Nazi salute, clipping their metal-shod rope shoes smartly.

JOSÉ (salutes)

Heil Hitler! We shall return!

THE GROUP

Heil Hitler!

JOSÉ DOS
We shall return!
JORGE (airily)
That's been said before, Dosey.
They crisply walk out.

3. EXT. (EXTERIOR) ARGENTINA VILLAGE STREET. NIGHT.
Some peasants stop the GROUP and ask them to autograph two
HANDBILLS announcing the *MIO CAMPO REVUE.* On the face of the
handbill is a poor reproduction of four transvestites who are THE GROUP
in drag.

VO. JOSÉ DOS (eager)
Do you think Claudio will break a leg tomorrow night?
ZOOM back as group moves on.
JORGE (bored with JOSÉ DOS' use of clichés)
Yes. His plane returns in the morning. He will perform with us.
PEASANTS (waving signed handbills)
Gracias… Gracias, Amigos…
FADE OUT.

4. INT. VILLAGE POLICE STATION. NIGHT
A dilapidated room with a huge, slowly revolving fan affixed to the
ceiling.

PEPE, a bored cop, is slouched in a wicker chair. THE GROUP are
huddled around the ancient telephone; the only one in the village.

JOSÉ DOS (urgent, into phone)
I vant to talk to VERNER!
VO. TELEPHONE OPERATOR (efficiently)
I'm sorry, sir. I can't understand you…
JOSÉ (grabbing the telephone)
Ve vant to talk to Verner, the rocket expert. Verner Von Braun…
VO. OPERATOR (impatient)
I'm sorry, sir, Mr. Braun is out to lunch; if you would like to leave a
message…
JOSÉ DOS (tense, thinking out loud)
A couple of Vermeers and a Van Gogh should get us a missile. Hey,
offer them to the Smithsonian Institution, and maybe…
JOSÉ (shouting)
Achtung! Operator! Operator! I was cut off!
EVA (kissing JOSÉ)
Never mind, dear, you can ring him tomorrow night.
JOSÉ gets embarrassed as he puts the receiver down…
FADE OUT.

5. EXT.   VILLAGE TRAIN STATION.   DAY

A train comes to a steamy, huffing stop. New Yorker SIDNEY STEINMETZ, short and fat, and Londoner CHESTER SMITH-HERBERT, tall and stooped, step off the train and look for a porter. Train toots, luggage is dropped down, and the train chugs away.

CHESTER (yelling)

Porter!

BEAT, SILENCE; THEN

The chirp of a bird, slowly a faint calypso is heard through the station's open window. SID walks up to the window and looks in. JOSH, a tall Jamaican, is practicing dancing under a low pole set between two chairs.

JOSH

Run, run, run, Missouri, run water down here, sweat, sweat, sweat me, baby, bend your little finer...

SIDNEY (coughs, then claps)

Porter (through the windows), that's great, really great, but could you kindly help us with our luggage; we're new here, you could get a tip.

CUT to reverse footage of JOSH starting his Limbo

JOSH (reversing on "tip")

Now, suh, that'd be fine by me. I'm only practicing. Hard to stop in the middle (he gets up, humming, and comes outside; picks up the luggage easily. Where too's?

CHESTER

To the Hotel Grande, where else?

EXT.   VILLAGE STREET.   DAY

SIDNEY (looking at his watch)

That train ride took ten hours.

CHESTER

Now, Sidney, you came along to relax, stop looking at your watch; that's the third time you looked at it in the last five minutes.

SIDNEY (tense)

I can't help it, on Broadway every minute is a thousand dollars, ten hours times sixty minutes is six hundred thousand dollars wasted (shaking his head); that's too big a loss, Chester.

CHESTER

You're on vacation, Sidney, you aren't supposed to be thinking about money. (subtle, baiting) Let me think about it. If this eccentric art lover has half the paintings his agent says he has, I'll certainly be in the chips.

SIDNEY

I still think you're chasing moonbeams; this is the most back backwater place I've ever seen.

CHESTER (looking at JOSH swinging with the luggage)
Why don't you develop him?
SIDNEY (Bored)
Interesting, but they're a dime a dozen in New York.
JOSH (singing)
Hotel, hotel, come a little closer, let my feet roll over and over... over and over...
FADE OUT
6.   INT.   LARGE ROOM, JOSÉS OFFICE.   MORNING
The room is plain, functional, save for the priceless masterpieces on the wall. Drinks are served by JOSÉ DOS. CLAUDIO, JOSÉ and CHESTER are discussing the paintings deal.
CHESTER (dazzled)
Señor José (saluting with his drink), it is indeed an honor to meet you. (looking around). A man of your eclectically impeccable taste.
JOSÉ (smiling)
Oh, these, I have them changed each week. Haven't had the same grouping on the wall in ten years.
CHESTER (coughing)
Surely, sir, they are not all done by such well-known artists. (looking) Degas, Constable, Renoir... I mean right here (awed) the value must be over two million pounds alone.
JOSÉ DOS (confiding)
If I may say so, sir, my master has the most complete collection of early Picasso drawings in the world.
CHESTER (dazzled)
Very well, I think, I, I, well, I have the authority to accept works for our auction house. But with such a priceless collection... ah. Which one do you wish us to auction off first?
JOSÉ (offhandedly)
What you see on the walls, plus the Picasso collection. (He snaps his fingers. JOSÉ DOS goes to another room and brings out a large portfolio, places it on the table and opens it. The work is exquisite Picasso.)
CHESTER (his glasses falling off)
I've never seen such a collection... Gentlemen, I must consult with my directors. They wouldn't believe me if I told them.
JOSÉ (matter-of-factly)
Certainly. Dosey, make the arrangements; I must prepare for tonight.
JOSÉ DOS (gathering up the Picasso portfolio)
Yes, sir.

7. EXT. VILLAGE STREET. EVENING

JOSH is talking to PEPE, MARIA and GARBANZO in front of the Police Station.

PEPE (to JOSH)

Are you sure one of them is not called Verner?

JOSH

I'm not sure of anything boss – one sounds American, the other English, and they are cheap, very small tip. José would never be a friend of a cheap mon...

MARIA

Josh is right. Maybe they're here to buy those old planes.

PEPE (to JOSH)

Was one of them named Führer?

JOSH

Don't think so. If they were family, why would they stay at the hotel?

MARIA

You're right.

GARBANZO

I hope they don't take Don José away. What would happen to our village, no show, no train, no nothing.

MARIO (taxi driver joins them)

No cab fares.

PEPE (sad)

No phone calls. No nothing.

MARIA (brightening)

Don't worry, they won't go, they like it here. They are our "Mio Campo."

8. INT. HOTEL ROOM. EVENING

CHESTER (excited)

Sidney, the place was full of masterpieces. Absolutely full! There must have been three million pounds hanging on the wall, plus a portfolio of Picasso prints that would sell like a stack of English muffins. You wouldn't have believed it, Sid.

SIDNEY (intent, studying a handbill; shaking his head)

It's Fantastic what you find in these out-of-the-way places. (showing the handbill) Look what I found on the lobby table. The ticket price is right; I figured it out, it comes to ten cents per person. For a live show that would certainly be a steal on Broadway. Humph! A live show would cost you a thousand times that, Chester. What do you say? Shall we go?

CHESTER (tired, wary)

I want a good stiff drink first, Sid; these amateur performances can be tiring. I just don't know where I've seen this art collector before?...where did he get this incredible collection?

SIDNEY (thinking, philosophical. Still studying the MIO CAMPO handbill)

One should never ask why, where and who when it comes to making a whole lot of money, Chester.

CHESTER (dismissing)

You're right... got to relax. (rationalizing) He was a high-strung sort, so better not rock the boat or he might take his collection to Dain Masters.

SIDNEY (smiling)

Now you're talking, Chester, let's head out for dinner, then take in the show, what say old trooper? (Looks at his watch, fans himself. Looking out the window sees MARCO's taxi) Taxi! Taxi!

CUT TO SID'S POV

MARCO's taxi stops

MARCO

No, amigo, this cab is reserved for the MIO CAMPO. (He drives off.)

VO. SID

Let's go, Chester. Might as well walk.

VO. CHESTER

OK. Sure is hot down here.

9.   EXT.   HITLER'S HACIENDA.   EVENING

JOSÉ, JOSÉ DOS, JORGE and CLAUDIO are sitting down.

JOSÉ

Si, si. You handled yourself well on that one, Dosey. Next week I make you a Colonel, si? His eyes sure popped out. He'll be back.

JOSÉ DOS (rubbing his hands together)

The money should start rolling in. (taking charge, mimicking JOSÉ) Should we ask for an advance? Who is going to pay the shipping? These things have to be sorted out.

JOSÉ (expansive, winking at JORGE)

You got yourself a job, Herman, you're the art expert. Start making up groupings for sale. Not too flashy now. It might attract attention.

JORGE (boisterous)

Hell, no one thinks when money is being made, Mein Führer. No one!

JOSÉ DOS

Herman, he is not talking about those people, but about the public. The world's not our oyster anymore, you know!

JORGE (laughing)

The public be damned; they only think what people want them to think.

JOSÉ DOS (looking analytical)

I know that, but we don't have control over the press like we used to. Remember that, Herman, we must be humble...

JOSÉ (in charge; to CLAUDIO)

Claudio, you are to maintain total control over delivery and sales. And be sure to ignore graciously any questions about me.

CLAUDIO (snapping his metal-shod shoes)

Heil Hitler!

They all leap up "Heil Hitlering" each other.

JOSÉ (with false humility)

Quiet! Quiet! Now we must prepare for this evening.

JOSÉ DOS (eager)

What can I do?

JOSÉ (surprised)

Do?

JORGE (handling nylons, discovers a run in them)

You can darn these nylons.

JOSÉ DOS (angry)

I only take orders from my Führer!

JOSÉ (nervous, tired)

I hope it goes well tonight.

JOSÉ DOS (comforting, holding the nylons)

Don't worry, my Führer, it will be a long run.

JOSÉ (grabbing the nylons from JORGE, clutching them)

A long run. (looks at nylons) Dosey! Prepare these socks for a long run. Now!

JOSÉ DOS

Yes, sir.

JORGE

Now, now, don't be nervous, Adolf. Soon you will be back in the limelight, you will see. The world will worship you again... and again... and again.

JOSÉ (breaks down)

Why? Why? My Reich is stagnating. They want to take, take, take, give nothing in return, just want me to support worthy causes, SS girls camp, youth marches; they don't want me for me...

JOSÉ DOS (counseling)

Mein Führer, you wait. When we get the missile with the H-bomb from Verner, they will listen, you bet your life.... Verner will save us. When we get through with them, they will be too popped to poop!

JORGE (exasperated at JOSÉ DOS clichés)

Gott in Himmel. What an airhead.

MARCO toots his taxi's horn. It sounds like a bugle. The group gets in formation and snaps to attention. JOSÉ DOS, at the head of the file, salutes JOSÉ.

Heil Hitler!

THE GROUP Heil Hitlers, then marches out. We follow them out the door and into MARCO's cab. MARCO salutes smartly.

CUT to the taxi leaving. Taxi winds its way through the streets to behind the theater.

CUT to GROUP entering theater.

CUT to GROUP entering dressing room.

JOSÉ

Attention! (They stand at attention)

JOSÉ

At ease. Prepare for the theater.

FADE OUT

10. INT.   BACKSTAGE OF THEATER.   EVENING

They are busy at the dressing tables preparing themselves for the performance; at the rear is a door with a large star on it. JORGE takes off his pants and peasant shirt, and starts putting on tights and a skirt. CLAUDIO is putting on a set of falsies. JOSÉ DOS is putting on nylons.

JORGE

Corporal, if you would put on a little weight, you wouldn't have to wear them.

CLAUDIO (put off)

We're not all perfect, Herman.

They dress as women, putting on makeup, etc. CU of them working. They change before our eyes from men to women. As they finish, the star door opens and JOSÉ emerges looking stunning in his high heels and tight-fitting short dress.

JOSÉ (all military)

Attention!

They all stand at attention in a file.

JOSÉ

Prepare for inspection! (He walks stiffly down the file and inspects their costumes as if he is a drill sergeant. BEAT. He stops in front of JORGE) Tuck it in tighter.

JORGE

Yes, sir! (JORGE arranges his over-large genitals so they don't stick out so much.)

JOSÉ (swaggering and strutting up and down the file)

Very well, men. Let's go out and knock 'em dead. Tonight is a big night, like all nights are big ones for the Reich. I want you to give it your all... look sharp! (He slugs JORGE in the gut.) You, you must lose your paunch. You must exercise, be fit to lead our armies, Jorge. Do you understand?

JORGE (petulant)

Yes, Mein Führer.

JOSÉ (firm)

Silence!... Very well, my comrades, let's go out and knock 'em dead. Right face...hup, hup, hup. (They march out onstage)

SOUND. VO. Scratchy record music of "In the Mood."

11. INT. THEATER. NIGHT

SOUND. VO. "In the Mood" continues.

CHESTER and SIDNEY walk down the dilapidated aisle wearing evening dress in stark contrast to the other theatergoers: peasants in peasant garb.

The peasants' loud laughter turns to inquisitive silence as CHESTER and SIDNEY take their seats.

A chicken squawks and runs down the aisle to land in Sidney's lap. He shoos it away.

A firecracker explodes; laughter returns.

VO.   CROWD MEMBER (in Spanish, warning)

Hola, Gringos!

SOUND   VO. MUSIC "In the Mood" and Glenn Miller's "Little Brown Jug" are played. Loud applause and cheers from the audience as the curtain opens.

PAN to stage.

The drawn curtain exposes JOSÉ, JOSÉ DOS, JORGE, and CLAUDIO vigorously dancing a "Charleston/Goosestep" to the Miller tune.

CUT TO the stage.

The four are very good dancers.

CLOSE UP. JOSÉ winks at JOSÉ DOS.

CLOSE UP   JOSÉ DOS winks at JORGE.

CLOSE UP   JORGE winks at CLAUDIO.

CLOSE UP.   CLAUDIO, eyes closed, is dancing intently.

THE GROUP stops with military precision and gives the Nazi salute.

VO GROUP   "HAH!"

Background sound.   Applause and hoots of laughter from the audience.

CUT TO CLOSE UP. SIDNEY is impressed; he chews slowly on an unlit cigar.

PULL BACK. CHESTER is laughing his head off.   The music dissolves into "Si, Si."

CUT TO THE STAGE.

The group is in a line, high-kicking in mini-tights and mesh stockings.

Background sound: the crowd cheers wildly as the show ends.

CUT TO AUDIENCE AND STAGE.

The AUDIENCE runs up to the stage, offering chickens, fruit and vegetables to the group.

CUT TO THE STAGE.

A peasant holds a goat out to JOSÉ; JOSÉ accepts the offering. Another peasant offers his daughter to JORGE. JORGE declines.

The GROUP take their final bows and barely escape from their adoring fans to disappear backstage.

CUT TO CLOSE-UP OF SIDNEY'S FACE.

He casually chews his cigar in deep thought.

PULL BACK

SIDNEY puts his arm around the smiling CHESTER and winks.

SIDNEY (amazed)

The talent in this town. The potential!

VO. CHESTER

I never laughed so hard in my life. The fat one was built just like Churchill.

SIDNEY

You wait a moment, Chester, I'll be right back.

SIDNEY leaves.

12. INT.   BACKSTAGE DRESSING ROOM.   NIGHT

JOSÉ

Oh, Herman, did you see those fancy-dressed city slickers in the audience?

JORGE (nervous)

They looked like over-age OSS officers to me. (thinking) Do you think Interpol is onto us?

JOSÉ DOS (exultant)

Never. The audience loved us, as usual. I wish we could get a booking in Corrientes; then it's Rio, New York, London, and then…and then, Berlin!

JOSÉ (opening his door, sadly)

Holy Reich! I wish we could get a break… we gave it our all again.

A quiet knock on the door. It swings open on its own accord. SIDNEY stands there. He takes the cigar out of his mouth and looks sincerely at the four.

SIDNEY

You were great, kids, just great. I'm from Broadway. You may have heard of it in your travels. I'm a theatrical agent for aspiring performers. I saw your show tonight, and I thought it was great, just great. Look, if you guys want a break on Broadway, New York City, I'd like to give it to you. This is a poor country, so the trip will be at my expense. That's unusual, but seeing as your potential is so great… (looks at watch). Well, I will return with a backer, then I'll organize a press junket… Keep the faith, hombres… (starts to turn, putting his cigar in his mouth, hesitates, takes cigar out, turns back). It was great. One thing… your act could have some comedy skits added to it. You (points to JOSÉ DOS) look just like Hitler, and you (points to JORGE) look just like Churchill. Hitler and Churchill in drag. Think about it. Oh, the music was great, but try to get some two, three, four o'clock rock in there, OK? Great, just great. (He closes the door behind him.)

VO SIDNEY (through the door)

The talent in this town!

The GROUP are silent, then look at each other… JOSÉ DOS is angry, but the others break out in hoorays.

JOSÉ (doing his Paris jig)

Hooray!

JOSÉ DOS (intense)

He's Jewish. I knew it.

JORGE (patient)

This is 1956, Josef; and besides, he's going to make us famous. Why are you still so anti-Semitic? Can't you grow up? Some of our best friends are Jewish.

JOSÉ DOS (distant, to himself)

Have you ever done business with them? They are demanding, Jorge, demanding.

JORGE (clever)

Like you, Josef Goebbels, or should I say, half of you?

JOSÉ DOS (furious)

You speak Yiddish!

JOSÉ (excited)

mench…(starts singing) "he's all right for a mench.'

ALL singing and dancing.

Write this down, Josef. One, two, three o'clock, four o'clock, Mench. Five, six o'clock, Mench, seven o'clock, eight o'clock, Mench.

JOSÉ DOS (smoldering)

Yes, Mein Führer, but you're going to be sorry.

GROUP Sings (without the sulking José Dos)

Nine, ten, eleven o'clock, Mench…

JOSÉ (ordering)

You sing along, Josef!

JOSÉ DOS (deflated)

Yes, Mein Führer.

FADE OUT

13. INT.   SS HEADQUARTERS. DAY

A clean, bare room with a large window. Outside is an endless row of 'mothballed' ships. Several severely crewcut men are looking over the shoulder of HERR SHIZZER, Lt. Commander Waffen, SS, as he reads a letter.

CUT TO CLOSE-UP ON LETTER.

The letter reads:

Herr Shizzer: Greetings. I have found a quicker, more efficient way for funding your prolonged exercise. Instead of sending bulky paintings through the inefficient mail services, I will now send cash. The burden of responsibility of finding buyers will be mine, freeing you further to advance the cause of the Fourth Reich. Goodbye, Herr Shizzer. Keep up the good work. Heil Hitler!

CUT TO MASTER SHOT

SHIZZER and GROUP (rigid, at attention)

Heil Hitler!

SHIZZER (pissed off)

Send cash, huh? That crazy loon will upset all kinds of plans if we let him get away with this. He'll blow our whole cover. He'll swamp the art market and set every crazy Nazi headhunter on our trail.

GUNTER DALMATIAN, young, handsome, steps forward

GUNTER (saluting)

Sir, I volunteer to find the hideaway of our beloved Führer and talk sense to him.

SHIZZER (distant)

Gunter, my friend, you do not know the spells our Führer can put people under. He, in his old age, has hypnotic power that will blind you and convince you of the truth of his reckless acts. No, my friend... (whispering to GUNTER). Wait a minute. (He dismisses his men; they leave. GUNTER waits.)

SHIZZER closes the door and turns to GUNTER.

SHIZZER

Attention!... About face. (He knocks GUNTER out with the butt of his luger)

BREZIERS (one of the men in the GROUP) reenters

Very efficient, sir.

They both pick up GUNTER and place him on a couch. DOCTOR BREZIERS enters and prepares a syringe.

SHIZZER

Now we will have our path to Herr Hitler, Doctor. Administer the needle.

BREZIERS (injecting GUNTER in the arm)

Hitler has a weakness for Mona Lisa paintings. We will send him a letter and accept his terms with pleasure. Then in the letter we will send a copy of the Mona Lisa and say it was a poor starving SS corporal who works long hours painting signs in a dark Viennese cellar. We will perform some facial surgery on Herr Gunter and make him look a bit like Hitler. He can't help but be moved.

SHIZZER (holding handkerchief to his nose)

Brilliant, doctor. This potion will turn Gunter into a dog when he wakes up, a dog programmed to sniff out our Führer. (He picks up a pair of long underwear with a badge stitched on titled: "Führer, Third Reich, 1941.") He smothers Gunter with the long underwear, then turns to BREZIERS.

BREZIERS (wincing from the smell looks into GUNTER's eyes)

Good. He is ready for his instructions... (GUNTER starts to stir.)

GUNTER (prostrate under the long johns)

Woof, Woof. Wooooooooooo...

FADE OUT

14. INT.   HUBBLES, LONDON. DAY

A large executive room. CHESTER is reviewing his journey to Corrientes with the four-member board of directors.

CHESTER

Gentlemen, the walls were covered with authentic masterpieces. Renoirs, Degas, a complete portfolio of early Picasso prints was brought out. Authentic, absolutely authentic; if they are copies, I still suggest we accept them. They are absolutely authentic copies.

MR. JOHNS (a director)

But why would such a vast collection of masterpieces be collected in such a backwater as Corrientes, Argentina? Where the hell is it anyway?

CHESTER (unfolds a map of Argentina and points at it. They all look.)

My guess is Don José (Hitler) is a retired Rio millionaire who collected the paintings.

MR. JOHNS (fearful)

Or maybe this Don José is a retired Nazi? Did you think of that, Chester? This collection may be booty from World War Two.

CHESTER (firm)

Our business is the auctioning of the paintings and such. Our business is not to meddle in other people's business. If we did, ninety per cent of auction material would not see the auction block anywhere in the world.

MR SMITH (agreeing)

Exactly right, Mr. Smith-Herbert, exactly right. Let's not ask, we certainly can wonder, Mr. Johns, but when business is concerned, business for Hubbles, well then, I'm sending some experts and negotiators down and see for ourselves.

MR. JOHNS

I'm not so sure.

MR. SMITH

Hell, man, let's take a vote on it then. All in favor of sending a team to Corrientes, raise their hand.

They all raise their hands except MR. JOHNS (Beat) who shakes his head, then relents and raises his hand.

15. INT.   NEW YORK CITY OFFICE.   DAY

SIDNEY is talking to a large group of reporters.

SIDNEY (rolling his cigar)

Gentlemen, I promise you when you see this group and the originality of their revue, you'll be swept off your feet. They're bold and the music is fantastic. You will know what I'm talking about when you see them. Look, I'm expected back in a day or so to see how the act is going; then in a week I will bring you all with me – free of charge, I promise you that, but you must promise me some press coverage in return. OK? You know, a blurb here, a blurb there… (confiding) Have I ever let you down before?

Old Sid, ever let anybody down, especially an audience? Never. So, guys, believe me when I say it's a great show. It's great. (Looks at his watch) Gotta close, any questions?

REPORTER

What kind of music do they base their revue on?

SIDNEY

A cross between Glenn Miller and that new music – one a two a three o'clock rock. (He coolly blows smoke from his cigar as the crowd breaks out in applause.)

REPORTER

What kind of dance routine?

SIDNEY (blowing smoke from his cigar)

You won't believe this... a cross between a fat Fred Astaire, a fat Winston Churchill, a young Adolf Hitler with a bit of old Shirley Temple thrown in. All in brief but demure costumes.

REPORTER (excited)

Fantastic, what's it called? The revue, I mean.

SIDNEY

For now, Operation X. Truthfully, we haven't found a good name yet. It's called MIO CAMPO down there, but that's a bit too much.

REPORTER

MIO CAMPO. I like that. Means "My Camp" in English; I like that...

SIDNEY

"My Camp." I never realized. That's great. "My Camp." Mio Campo. Great!

REPORTER

So can we use Mio Campo?

SIDNEY

It's Spanish.

REPORTER

Pretty soon half of New York City will be Spanish.

SIDNEY (looking at his watch)

Well, OK, why not... yes, let's keep MIO CAMPO.

The REPORTERS leave, shaking SIDNEY's hand as they go. When they are gone, SIDNEY buzzes his secretary.

VO. SECRETARY

Yes, sir?

SIDNEY

Could you please pick up a copy of the latest Rock and Roll records, you know, one, two, three o'clock rock...

SECRETARY (surprised)

What! Yes, sir.

He puts the phone down and looks at Aerolineas flight schedules. The phone rings.

VO.   SECRETARY

Sir, it's Mr. Smith-Herbert in London.

SIDNEY (picks up the receiver)

Put him on... Chester, mio campo. How are you?

VO.   CHESTER

Fine, fine, Sidney. I want to ask you if you would like to go to Corrientes with me again. I'm returning with the art experts. I can meet you in Rio.

SIDNEY

Absolutely yes... Look, I'll bring Houndstooth with me.

VO.   CHESTER

The Producer...?

SIDNEY

He's interested in the Mio Campo Group.

VO.   CHESTER

He what... you mean the transvestites? What an interesting idea. For Broadway?

SIDNEY

That's right. Love you, Saturday... right... Ciao...

VO.   CHESTER

See you Saturday in Rio. Bye. Bye.

16. INT.   HITLER'S HACIENDA.   NIGHT

JOSÉ, JORGE AND JOSÉ DOS are reading a letter from CLAUDIO.

JOSÉ (reading)

"Dear Herr Don José: Sidney, the Broadway agent, is bringing a producer down to see the show. (to Group) Hot viener schnitzel! (reading) Traveling with him is Chester, who is bringing down a Hubbles team to negotiate the proposed auction; (to Group)... I will be there for the audition. The accompanying package I picked up at our Berne post box. Adios and Heil Hitler."

GROUP

Heil Hitler!

JOSÉ DOS

This is fantastic, we got to call Verner and tell him to reserve us a missile...

JOSÉ

Let me read the other letter, gentlemen. (reading) "My dear beloved Führer. Commander Shizzer, your eternal servant here. We accept your graciousness in freeing us from the burden of finding buyers for your artworks. A simple check (you are right, as always) will greatly facilitate our concentration on the building of the Fourth Reich. In closing, dear Führer, I wish to present (see photo) a young Viennese painter, frightfully in need of guidance. A copy of his work is attached. He is an utterly dedicated young man who has been reduced to sign painting. If you could find room for him on your staff, we will all appreciate it. Somehow, he looks like you, and we are all touched by this. Again, thank you sir. Heil Hitler!"

The GROUP looks at the photo, which looks strikingly like a young Hitler. The copy of the Mona Lisa is unrolled and passed around, and quickly discarded. JOSÉ picks it up, staring.

JOSÉ DOS (suspicious)

Looks too much like you, Adolf. It can't be.

JOSÉ (beaming mystically)

Anyway, we must help him out. We must. Herman, include this work in the first bundle of artwork.

JORGE (worried)

But my dear Führer, it's good, but not nearly the quality of the masters.

JOSÉ

I am aware of that, Herman, but the boy has genius, you must admit it. You must include it!

JOSÉ DOS (looking at the copy)

You must, Herman. It's good. (winking at JORGE)

JOSÉ

We shall ask full price for it and send it to this Gunter to help him, or better yet, for his plane fare here.

JOSÉ DOS (alarmed)

Not here, mein Führer, ah, ah, somewhere else...

JORGE (equally alarmed)

Mein Führer, think of it. Maybe it's a plot on your life.

JOSÉ (as if in a trance)

My life? Yes, I guess you're right. OK, he can't come here, but we owe the young servant of his Führer a chance. Include his work in the first collection. (Staring at the photo of the young man.)

JOSÉ DOS (looking at his watch)

Time to rehearse, gentlemen. Shall we?

They stop doing what they are doing and form a chorus line.

ALL

A one, a two, a three o'clock mench... A four, a five, a six o'clock mench.

17. EXT.   TOWN CAFÉ.   EVENING

The villagers are milling around GARBANZO, the old town gossip.

GARBANZO (excited)

I tell you, those gringos were from the big theaters up north. They plan to take away Don José and his group.

JOSH (the tall Jamaican limbo/porter)

Ain't that a shame. José said I could join them when I get just a little better. When I helped those gringos at the station, they seemed pleasant chaps.

CUT TO C.U.   JOSH's face

CUT TO C.U.   GARBANZO

GARBANZO

When I saw the little fat dejected one backstage, I thought something was fishy.   I didn't understand a word; they spoke that confounded ENGLISH!

CUT TO CU. MAYOR

MAYOR (tall, distinguished)

If they go, we won't have a chance of winning the Corrientes amateur theater contest.

CUT TO C.U. MARIA

MARIA

If they go, I'm out of my maid's job.

CUT TO C.U. MARCO

MARCO

If they go, who will I drive around in my taxi?

CUT TO C.U. GARBANZO

GARBANZO

They won't give me their spare cabbage; I make so much money on selling it in the market. We can't let them go. That's for sure.

PULL BACK

Hold on. Hold on. We are all plucking dead chickens. Give them the benefit of the doubt. They promised us they would represent us at the theater contest. Old Don José never goes against his word.

PACO (police chief)

If they go, who would make expensive long distance calls; keeping us hooked up to the national system?

MARIA

Let's wait and see…

TAXI DRIVER

I'll keep my ears open.

GARBANZO

I'll keep my eyes open.

18. EXT.   TRAIN STATION.   MORNING

The train stops.

SIDNEY, CHESTER, HOUNDSTOOTH and the two art experts, DERMOTH and SCRANTON jump off. (Scranton and Dermoth look and dress exactly alike in dark blue business suits. They will answer all questions addressed to themselves as if they are one.) JOSH dances up and takes their luggage, putting it on a cart.

JOSH (winking at SIDNEY)

My mon, good to see you again! What brings you south?

SIDNEY (noncommittal)

The weather. (aside to HOUNDSTOOTH) The local would-be star. Every town down here has one. Ignore him.

HOUNDSTOOTH (nose in air)

Harrumph!

CHESTER (looking at his watch)

Sidney, could you take care of our luggage; we are quite late for our appointment.

SIDNEY

Of course, Chester, of course; see you at the hotel.

CHESTER

Come along, Dermoth. Come along, Scranton.

DERMOTH and SCRANTON (perfunctly)

Yes, sir.

19. EXT.   STREET.   MORNING

GARBANZO (observing the newly arrived group across the street)

Look, look in Marco's taxi. Gringos.

VO.   MAYOR (squinting)

Now, who do you suppose they are? They sure look important.

VO.   GARBANZO

One was here before. They're heading for José's hacienda, I bet.

PAN TO THE TAXI STATION

The train disappears down the track.

GARBANZO

Look, two more gringos. We're being invaded.

VO.   MAYOR

Hmmmm, same one as before, the tall one looks important. They must be staying a long time with all that luggage.

FADE OUT

JOSH is dancing down the street towards the hotel. SIDNEY and HOUNDSTOOTH walk behind him, ignoring him.

20. INT.   JOSÉS HACIENDA.   MORNING

JOSÉ is sitting like Lord Jim in a large high-backed rattan chair. CLAUDIO is studying a paper. MARIE is in the background, quietly cleaning. The doorbell rings. CLAUDIO answers.

In walk CHESTER, DERMOTH and SCRANTON. They shake hands. CLAUDIO brings them over to JOSÉ.

CLAUDIO

Don José, may I present Mr. Smith-Herbert (they shake hands, but JOSÉ does not get out of his chair) and our art specialists, Mr. Dermoth and Mr. Scranton.

DERMOTH and SCRANTON (bowing low)

How do you do, sir?

JOSÉ

Very well, thank you. Shall we proceed? I believe Chester here explained to you what we want, and what we want is to put on your auction block the paintings you see on the walls here today, plus the portfolio there on the table. Please examine.

DERMOTH and SCRANTON (going to the paintings)

Yes, sir.

They start looking at a Degas. DERMOTH and SCRANTON grunt as they take out a jeweler's eye.

DERMOTH (noting in their book)

Fantastic.

They walk to another painting.

SCRANTON (in front of the Renoir)

Absolutely authentic!

DERMOTH (studying a Van Gogh)

Incredible. Chester, they thought this was lost twenty years ago. It's worth a fortune.

DERMOTH goes to another painting.

SCRANTON

This Da Vinci drawing is invaluable, sir.

DERMOTH (in front of GUNTER's Mona Lisa, incensed)

I'm afraid we found a fake, Mr. Smith-Herbert.

CHESTER comes over.

CHESTER

A fake! (sees the crude copy, smiles)

Oh, some kind of joke. (wipes sweat off his face)

JOSÉ (standing)

A fake, never! This was drawn by a young genius! It is the epitome of the Romantic Era. It is a near-masterpiece, gentlemen. It is a painting of the artist's mother done with love and deep devotion. If you take any painting from here, you first must pay five thousand dollars for it. Cash!

CHESTER

My dear, Don José, it is a copy of the Mona Lisa.

JOSÉ

My demands will be met if you want the other work. Give the young master a break. He is reduced to painting signs in a cold basement in Vienna. Save him. In a few years, you will appreciate helping him.

DERMOTH and SCRANTON look at each other quizzically, then down at the portfolio of Picassos, then at Chester. They become engrossed in the portfolio.

CHESTER (relieved)

Okay. (takes out a checkbook and writes out a check)

May we take them with us now?

JOSÉ (sniffs)

Leave them here 'til morning. I wish to feel their presence 'til then. I will miss them.

CHESTER

Yes, sir. Well, let's go, gentlemen. Good day, sir.

JOSÉ

Good day.

21. INT.   HOTEL ROOM.   DAY

DERMOTH and SCRANTON (excited)

That's the most expensive private hanging we've ever seen. We just don't believe it, and then he goes and pulls that blather about that junk copy. Eccentric isn't the word! Did you hear him rant, like a man possessed. You have got to keep your wits about you when you're around him, Chester. That's for sure!

CHESTER (working with calculator)

Well, we did it. I figure ten million pounds for the lot. That's more than we make in an entire year.

SCRANTON and DERMOTH

That man is mad, mad...

SIDNEY knocks on the door, then enters. All stop talking.

SIDNEY (rolling his cigar out of his mouth)

I'm sorry to break in on your business meeting, but I came to tell you to please not miss tonight's performance; you will love it.

SCRANTON and DERMOTH (miffed)

I and my associate do not go in for pornography. We will not be there.

SIDNEY (shrugging his shoulders)

Suit yourself. It's free.

SCRANTON and DERMOTH

Free. Well...

22. INT.   THEATER.   EVENING

SOUND EFFECTS of loud peasant theatergoers

C.U. ON SCRANTON and DERMOTH's faces.

SCRANTON and DERMOTH are sitting self-consciously...

PULL BACK. They are sitting in the theater.

PULL BACK.

HOUNDSTOOTH, SIDNEY, and CHESTER are sitting in the seats behind. They wear suit and tie in contrast to the other theatergoers.

A huge round of applause. C.U. SCRANTON and DERMOTH cover their eyes. SCRANTON holds on to DERMOTH's arm as the finale tune is heard – "In the Mood" on record (scratchy).

22A   STAGE.

The performance is almost over.

The applause goes wild. The GROUP are high-stepping. At the finale, they kick very high and JORGE's genitals fall out.

SOUND A huge roar from the audience.

CUT TO

22B   Close up on SIDNEY and HOUNDSTOOTH.

A shock, then a satisfied glow on their faces. A terrible screech is heard.

PULL BACK

DERMOTH screams and SCRANTON screams, clutching each other.

ZOOM on SIDNEY nodding to his friend knowingly.

FADE OUT

VO.   Audience, wild applause

23. INT.   DRESSING ROOM.   NIGHT

JORGE is standing with his head bent down.

JORGE (shaking)

You idiot. You have ruined our chances.

151

JOSÉ DOS (taking charge)

We're finished.

JORGE (pleading)

I'm sorry, fellas, but I'm too big. I told you I couldn't hold them in.

JOSÉ DOS

If I had scissors, I'd snip it off quick enough. (looking) Where is a pair...

PAN JORGE runs behind CLAUDIO

The door swings open; SIDNEY stands there as before.

SIDNEY (taking the cigar out of his mouth, speaks slowly)

Great... just great, fellas. The last bit has got to stay in, you know, where your, ah, things pop out... don't worry, we'll fix it up with the censors, art and public demand and all. One thing, I think... and the producer.

VO.   GROUP (breaking in)

Gasp

SIDNEY

Yes, fellas, I brought down a producer, wants you all to let it all hang out at the end, like you did (pointing to JORGE). That was great, let me tell you. It was great... see you in a week or so because the press people want a sneak preview... show biz types (winks). Oh, one thing, we insist, only for cleanliness... don't get the wrong idea, but health laws and all. If you're not circumcised, like Jorge, you'll have to get a circumcision... (winks) nothing big, just a nip, that's all, not even painful... ciao, and thanks... you were great, just great... Oh (takes records out of a pouch)... Here are some latest releases; study them and try to include them in your act.

The door closes.

JOSÉ

What's a circumscription?

CLAUDIO

I don't know.

JOSÉ DOS (sweating)

I think I know. Oh no, it can't be. (looks around) Where's a dictionary?...

CLAUDIO (finds one on the makeup table and tries to spell it.)

C.E.R.

JOSÉ

No, no, circ...

CLAUDIO (reading carefully)

C.I.R.C.UMCISION…the Jewish rite of snipping off the foreskin.

BEAT

Silence and all but JOSÉ hold their crotches.

JOSÉ DOS (whimpering)

They can't mean it, they can't.

CLAUDIO (moaning)

This is too much, my mama always told me never to do business with a Jew. Oh! Oh! Oh!

JORGE faints. JOSÉ runs over and helps him.

JOSÉ (angry)

This has gone too far. We must call Werner. Werner will save us. We'll bomb Broadway.

CLAUDIO (desperate)

We got to run away.

JOSÉ (thinking)

All is not lost. We will find a way out of it. You wait and see. No one is going to take my men's wing wangs away. No one's going to spoil my chance to return!…

The GROUP leaves the theater and is confronted by a group of townspeople.

MARIA (wary)

Salute for a fine performance.

MARCO (breaking in)

"Por favor," please stay here. Here is all the money I have saved for my son's college. Please stay in Corrientes. (he hands JOSÉ a jar of money)

JOSÉ takes it uncomfortably.

MARIA (crying to JOSÉ)

We saw all those important people in the audience. We're sure you're going to leave us; please don't. Please. Here is a pig for you. (she hands JOSÉ a rope leading to the enormous pig)

JOSH (to JORGE, winking)

Boss, you gotta stay, what about our checker games at the police station?

PACO

They will take away the village telephone if we don't use it.

HOTEL OWNER

I'll have to close the hotel; the train won't stop here anymore… they'll close the village down. Please stay.

The townspeople hold on to the MIO CAMPO performers like groupies to rock stars. The GROUP breaks away and starts running; the townspeople chase them yelling. The four run off in different directions. We follow JORGE going into the train station and into the men's room.

JORGE goes into a pay booth and locks himself in.

JOSH (looking coyly at the three booths, looks down at the second one and sees JORGE's feet.) Gotcha, Boss!

JORGE

I ain't coming out of here till daylight! Leave me alone! I don't want to go to jail.

JOSH (rhythmically patting his belly)

Jorge, Porgy, Porgy. You said you would never leave me. You said I could join your group. They can't all be false promises (patting heavier, singing). White on black, white on black. Black. Black. Black on white...

JORGE (sweating)

Please, Josh. I love our times together, our checkers, especially when you jump me, but please leave me alone. We're not going anywhere... not as things stand...

JOSH (patting out a calypso tune)

Now, now Jorge Porgy (starts to dance a limbo, humming the tune)... Pudd'n Pie, Kissed the Boys and made them sigh...

26. INT.   INSIDE TOILET.   NIGHT

JORGE (holding his crotch)

Please go away. Oh, not tonight. I've had a painful experience, please...

JORGE sits down on the toilet, holding himself; we hear the rapidly breathing JOSH rhythmically tapping his tummy.

JORGE has a look of shock. CU. His POV. We see JOSH limboing under the toilet door.

JORGE jumps on the toilet seat.

JOSÉ (singing)

Doors, doors, doors can't keep me...me, me, me away from you, Oh You, Oh you, you, you... cha cha cha uuu Black, Black... Black on white...

JORGE (sweating, panting)

Oh, oh. (he falls over JOSH, knocking him flat and proceeds to go down on him.)

27. INT.   POLICE STATION.   NIGHT

CLAUDIO and JOSÉ DOS are behind bars. The jail is comfortable... filled with presents from the villagers – fruit, pillows, etc.

CLAUDIO (enraged)

You can't keep us here. It's against our rights!

MARCO (sorry)

It's for your own good. When all those gringos leave, you can come out.

JOSÉ is brought in.

JOSÉ (shouting in German)

Achtung! Achtung!

JOSÉ DOS (concerned, yells)

Where did they find you? Where's Jorge?

JOSÉ (angry, to MARCO)

This is an insult! An outrage! I will see you all in hell for this. Who do you think you are? I am the Führer. (he speaks in German; the townspeople do not understand) You cannot do this to me... I will have you all hanged from the palm trees. I will have guards destroy you, cut you up and eat you... I'll call Werner!

JOSÉ DOS (to COP)

Let me use the telephone.

COP

At this time of night?

JOSÉ DOS

It's to America.

COP (surprised)

America, for sure. That will be six thousand pesos. (hand goes out)

JOSÉ DOS

I don't care. Give me the phone.

(In the background, JOSÉ is screaming) "I want to call Werner!"

The COP hands JOSÉ DOS the phone.

JOSÉ (grabbing it out of his hand)

Hello, hello. I vant Verner. Yes, United States. Hello, hello, United States, yes. I know what time it is, yes...(yelling) for God's sake, get me Verner.

VO.   COP

Someone go back after Jorge.

28. INT.   HUBBLES' OFFICE, LONDON   DAY

They are looking at several headlines about the auction of the masterpieces. Two detectives from Interpol are questioning MR. JOHNS.

FIRST DETECTIVE LEVI

Mr. Johns, this is serious. Those paintings that you have up for auction are suspected as contraband from the Second World War. There is no proof, but you must tell me the owner's name.

MR. JOHNS (cool)

Mr. Levi, I am not at liberty to disclose this information.

LEVI

You must. If you go through with this auction, you will open up all kinds of wounds from the Nazi era.

MR. JOHNS (cool)

The ownership papers are in order. The works are authentic. There is nothing to hide. We only insist on discretion by all. The owner is beyond repute, but if he is revealed he could be subject to all kinds of pressures he doesn't deserve.

LEVI (confiding)

Our superiors feel that the only Nazi who could have amassed such a collection is none other than Herman Goering.

MR. JOHNS (laughing)

Goering! Ha, Ha, Goering was as fat as a pig. I'm sorry, gentlemen, but the owner is a very thin man, as thin as Hitler himself. You have got the wrong man.

LEVI

Nevertheless, it would be wise to come out in the open. Governments are pestering us. Israel thinks it's a line to hidden Nazis. Art galleries are calling from all over the world.

MR. JOHNS (matter-of-factly)

All I'm at liberty to say, gentlemen, is that your so-called suspect is a gentleman farmer with exquisite taste. He lives a sedate life. He's, well, a very wealthy, retiring gentleman.

29. INT.   SS HEADQUARTERS. DAY

COMMANDER SHIZZER and BREZIERS are reading the same headlines. Through the window we see the long line of mothballed ships. GUNTER is scratching himself in the corner.

SHIZZER (looking at headlines)

So this is your game, Herr Hitler.

BREZIERS

We're out on a limb.

SHIZZER

After this stink, if they dig just a little further, the press will find out everything. We're sunk. We've got to find Hitler. Time for Plan Two.

BREZIERS (looking at a list and map)

Let's see… Rhodesia is first, then Tasmania and Argentina…

SHIZZER (snapping fingers)

Sit, Gunter, sit. (GUNTER barks and sits dog-fashion, thinking) We have to find Hitler.

SHIZZER (takes three flags of the countries out of a drawer and puts them in front of the salivating GUNTER.)

Sniff, Boy, sniff (a telephone rings, he answers)

Ja, Ja

GUNTER sniffs SHIZZER's leg and lifts his leg, peeing on his pants.

SHIZZER

Achtung! You mongrel! Achtung! (grabs his swagger stick and starts whipping GUNTER repeatedly with the flag of Tasmania in his fist.)

GUNTER (snapping at the Tasmanian flag)

Ohwoo (starts pointing at the Argentine flag)

SHIZZER (into phone)

Notify our Tasmania Branch...

VO   GUNTER

Wooooo...

SHIZZER (to himself)

Darn, those potions are strong these days.

SHIZZER (into phone)

Get some men to cover the auction. See if you can find anything there. Hurry and make arrangements. Also, I want round-the-clock surveillance of their postbox in Berne. We must find him before he destroys us all. Move! (puts the receiver down and looks quizzically at GUNTER) Ah, Hah!

SHIZZER puts the list in front of Gunter's nose. Gunter sniffs, then picks up Argentine flag.

SHIZZER (whips Gunter with his swagger stick again)

Heel, Gunter, heel! (dials phone) Ah, Breziers, pack up. We're going to Argentina. Ja, ja...

30. INT.   SIDNEY'S NEW YORK OFFICE   DAY

SIDNEY is talking to a group of reporters.

SIDNEY

Fellas, I appreciate the buildup you've been giving MIO CAMPO. Now it's time for the payoff. Next Saturday you are all invited to join me in a sneak preview in Corrientes, with the compliments of Mr. Houndstooth, the producer, and myself. The U.S Government, owing to my Brigadier General, retired status, will lend us a fully equipped C97 Stratocruiser, all in the name of art and private enterprise. We will fly down on Friday, and see the show and be back in time for your Sunday deadline. The local hotel has been hired to prepare a fiesta and a feast in your honor. It will be an event none of you should miss. The plane will leave La Guardia at ten a.m. sharp. All those going must be there by nine...

31. INT.   JOSÉ'S HACIENDA   DAY

JOSÉ, JOSÉ DOS, JORGE and CLAUDIO are reading three-day-old headlines from Rio, New York City, and London about the art auction.

CLAUDIO (concerned)

I didn't expect such a quick reply from the press.

JOSÉ (flippant)

It will all blow over. It's nothing to worry about.

JOSÉ DOS (concerned)

You may be right, mein Führer, but I think we should be prepared for any eventuality. Like escape, for instance.

JORGE (alarmed)

The way the townspeople want us to stay ...

JOSÉ (angry, to JORGE)

I know about you and Josh! It's common knowledge that you are having an affair with him.

JORGE (shit-eating grin on his face)

Mein Hitler, it's not like I'm polluting the genes. We can't have babies...

JOSÉ (shouting)

Soon you will have to choose between him and me, Herman! Josh is a porter; I'm a Führer.

JOSÉ DOS (placating)

Stop! Please! We are faced with the possibility of being exposed. Our jigs will be up!

CLAUDIO (concerned)

I don't like Commander Shizzer asking us to take on this Dalmatian fellow. It sounds like a plot. Why was he being so kind after we took control of his money supply?

JORGE (thinking)

Look at these headlines. I hope to Hitler we can trust these Hubbles people. (reading) "Interpol to conduct an investigation." "The Israelis are going to look into it." Here's a list of suspect countries with Argentina second to the top of the list... I don't like it.

JOSÉ (mystical)

The townspeople, my beloved townspeople, who have stuck by us through thick or thin. They turned on us and made us prisoners. We can't even make the break to Broadway.

JOSÉ DOS (alarmed)

Broadway! We can't go there even if we get away. They want to lob our wieners off!

JOSÉ (alarmed)

Prepare the escape plan!

JOSÉ DOS

Where will we escape to?

JORGE

If only we could get through to Verner.

JOSÉ

That's it! We will fly to Verner. Look in your collection of *TIME* magazines... Dosey, remember something about Miami Beach?

JOSÉ DOS (searches)

Here, Mein Führer.

JOSÉ (grabbing the *TIME*, turns the pages rapidly)

Here, here it is. Look in the people section. (Reads.) "Werner buys a home on Miami Beach. Where's the map, Herman?"

JORGE

Western or Eastern Hemisphere?

JOSÉ

Western, you dolt! (takes the map and looks to find Miami Beach) Look, look, it's only up here. We have got to make that flight. Verner will save us.

<u>32. INT.   HANGAR.   DAY</u>

JORGE is trying to fire up the Heinkel, but the engines just cough and wheeze. CLAUDIO is below the fuselage looking up at the engine. He shakes his head.

CLAUDIO

Just isn't gonna make it, Jorge.

JORGE

We have got to use the Heinkel. It's German! We must take the carburetors apart and clean them.

FADE OUT   FADE IN

CU of hangar floor. It is strewn with carburetor parts.

JORGE

Dammit, it's hopeless! I'm not an expert on carburetors. We must call the Heinkel Works and see if they have a spare.

CLAUDIO

The B-17's carburetors are in a mess, too.

JORGE

If we can't get them from Germany, we can always try Boeing. We have to try, Claudio; we have to try.

32A.   INT.   VILLAGE POLICE STATION NIGHT

JORGE and CLAUDIO are on the phone.

JORGE

Ja, ja, ja, Heinkel, one second. (looks at papers) Heinkel model number one one one one two three four five, built in nineteen forty-two. What... impossible. Discontinued? Ja, ja, ja, adiós. (He puts down the phone. To CLAUDIO) They don't make the spares anymore. Factory burned down in an air raid in forty-five.

CLAUDIO

Well, try Boeing.

JORGE (slumps shoulders)

OK, but it's useless. (in phone) Operator, get me Boeing. No, no, it's not a city. (looks at papers), USA. Thank you. Hello, Boeing Aircraft. I would like to order a part for my B-17...What?...OK. (waits)

CLAUDIO

What happened?

JORGE

Sh-h, they are connecting me to their parts department. (in phone) Huh, yes, the B-17, A, B, C, D, E or F model? (looks at papers) Uh, the E model, yes, four carburetors, yes, ours are corroded. Yes, Western Union. Well, yes, we're at a suburb of Corrientes, Argentina; yes, there is a little clearing, a field on our property; (BEAT) yes, flown in, (BEAT) for sure... Thanks.

A plane is heard overhead, it circles and lands at JOSÉ's hacienda. CLAUDIO and JORGE look at each other and run over.

33. EXT.   JOSÉ'S HACIENDA.   BACK FIELD.   DAY

A large black Western Union MESSENGER hops out of the airplane with four tiny parcels. He comes over and salutes smartly.

MESSENGER

Your packages, sir; that will be thirty-five dollars and twenty-five cents, plus airfreight charges. Seattle to Corrientes, round trip, seven hundred and eighty-five dollars plus tax of four percent. Nice thou bill will round it out, that includes my tip, what say, Amigos?

JOSÉ nods to JORGE.

JORGE (reaching into his pocket)

Certainly. (brings out a handful of dollars and counts off the money.)

34. INT.   HANGAR.   NIGHT

CLAUDIO is waiting for JORGE. He is sitting there with the opened boxes of carburetors. We hear the Western Union plane start its engines.

CLAUDIO (holding a manual)

They enclosed a booklet on how to install them, so bloody efficient.

35. EXT.   TOWN SQUARE.   NIGHT

GARBANZO

A small plane landed on the field behind José's hacienda.

MARIA

I saw a large black man get out and go with Jorge to the back.

PACO

I don't like it. You know José still has those old planes; maybe he was a friend of Jorge's. Jorge was a pilot, I hear.

MARIA

He didn't come into the house.

PACO

He didn't meet José?

GARBANZO

No.

JOSH (listening all the while, getting angrier)

A black man, you say?

MARIA

Not as black as you, Josh.

PACO

I don't know what to make of it; tell Maria to watch and see what else develops.

36. INT.   HANGAR.   NIGHT

The sound of the B-17's engines is heard.

JOSÉ (beaming)

Ah, the B-17 is running well. Our safety is assured.

JOSÉ DOS hands a letter to JOSÉ.

JOSÉ (reads letter)

"Heil Hitler, wherever you are. We are dismayed by the turmoil the recent auction at Hubbles London has stirred up. We can only surmise that such a large amount of paintings can only come from your collection. We beg you, Führer, that in the future you be more discreet when you wish to auction off some more of your treasures. Our whole operation is at a standstill. The U.S. Government is sifting through all applicants who wish to buy Army surplus. Please, Mein Führer, for the good of the movement, please act more discreetly in the future. I am yours forever and ever.

(Signed) Commander Shizzer

P.S. Good Wafen SS Dalmatian wishes you well, and thanks you for the check and having his picture included in the auction."

CLAUDIO (disgruntled)
You made them buy it.
JOSÉ
Here's the worst part; read the paper clipping.
Newspaper clip reads:
"This farce of an auction took a turn for the absurd. It was found out today that the mysterious eccentric forced Hubbles to buy a worthless copy of the "Mona Lisa" as if it was a masterpiece. Public, arise to this outrage on the art world. Obviously this is World War II booty. How could such a collection suddenly surface? It must be the work of Herman Goering. And where is he? Spain? Switzerland? Russia? Argentina? A commie plot? Argentina has absorbed so many Nazis in the past. Why not Herman Goering? Why not Adolf Eichmann, Josef Goebbels, and Hitler himself? It was never proved conclusively that they are dead. I for one suggest that we start our search for the eccentric gentleman farmer in Argentina! Remember, all you sane folk of the free world. Seven million dollars was made yesterday, seven million dollars in the coffers of the Nazi elite. That elite perpetrated the holocaust of World War II!! SEARCH, SEARCH, SEARCH and destroy! To Argentina!"
CLAUDIO (sweating)
Phew, do you think they will start searching Argentina?
JOSÉ (sweating)
We have to move on, to Miami Beach… tomorrow.
CLAUDIO (faintly)
Tomorrow the men from the press come down to see our show.
JOSÉ (confused)
We haven't rehearsed. We haven't given our foreskin to the cause. (wide-eyed) What show? (sobbing) There won't be a show anymore.
VO   EVA (trying to help)
Darling, get some sleep, please come to bed and get some sleep.
CLAUDIO
Heil Hitler. Tomorrow we will load and be off to Miami Beach. Cheer up.
JOSÉ
Heil Hitler. (distant) He turns and goes up to his bedroom.
37. INT.   BEDROOM.   NIGHT
JOSÉ stands in the middle of the room and starts to take off his clothes. Then gets on his knees and prays.
38. INT.   JOSÉ'S HACIENDA.   MORNING
There is a knock at the door. CLAUDIO answers it. PACO stands in the doorway in uniform (the first time we see him wearing it).

PACO (stern, at attention)

Where is Don José?

CLAUDIO

Up in his bedroom; do you wish to make an appointment with him?

PACO (sternly)

I wish to see him immediatemente…

CLAUDIO

I, I cannot disturb him.

PAN

VO.   JOSÉ (coming down the stairs)

That's all right, Claudio, I'll see him now.

CLAUDIO

Yes, sir.

PACO (yelling)

We've been kind to you all these years, José. You owe us the chance to win the theater contest in Corrientes.

JOSÉ (soothing)

My dear Paco, how handsome you look in your new uniform. (takes PACO by the arm) Do come in and have a drink. (to CLAUDIO)
Pour the officer some coffee and rum.

CLAUDIO pours from an already-made pot, and hands it to PACO.

PACO

Gracias.

JOSÉ (soothing)

Don Paco, I would never in a thousand years think of leaving our beloved town and its beloved people. They have taken us in and treated us as their own. Of course, we will represent this barrio at the theater.

PACO (shy)

There is talk that you were visited by an airplane last night?

JOSÉ (explaining)

Jorge's old flying friend stopped for a coffee, just like you and me now. I didn't get to meet him.

PACO

Maria heard the motors of the old planes in the hangar.

JOSÉ

Jorge showing off again.

PACO

We haven't heard those motors for ten years.

JOSÉ (explaining)

A bet between him and his pilot friend. The pilot will be back in two weeks. He bet Jorge he couldn't get both planes started... (winks) He got one started. If Jorge keeps it up, he wins a case of Coca-Cola.

PACO (smiling)

Ah, <u>now</u> I understand. (relieved. Beat. thinking) Why are all those gringos down there? Talk is, they're from Broadway where all the theater lives. That they were taking you away against your will...

JOSÉ (angry)

Those Broadway gringos will never make us go. NEVER! We will fight them to the death if they try. (nervous) I admit, Paco, that we had illusions of grandeur. But the price a performer has to pay these days is too much. If I told you what they wanted from my men, you would faint! A peculiar rite of the extreme gringos on the far, far left, in league with the communists they are; blood is what they want. And I forbid my men to give even an inch! Rest assured, Paco, they will not lure us away for any amount of money, fame or fortune. Our hearts belong to Corrientes.

PACO (impressed with JOSÉ's sermon)

Thank you, Don José. Thank you for your assurances. I will pass them along to the townspeople; they will be relieved.

PACO puts the demitasse cup down and picks up his hat and fumbles for the door.

PACO

Gracias, Don José ... Gracias, Claudio, for the coffee. Adios... oh, one thing, tonight when you perform we will guard you from the gringos, OK?

JOSÉ (beaming)

You do that, Paco; you do that, Don Paco. Gracias.

PACO (out of the door, turns around)

No one has ever called me Don Paco before. (gushing)

The door closes on JOSÉ's forced smile, which quickly turns to desperation.

JOSÉ (to CLAUDIO)

How is Jorge doing? Has Eva packed? We cannot waste time, we must hurry.

Overhead we hear the arrival of the U.S.A.F. Stratocruiser. It lands on the hacienda's field.

JORGE (rushing in)

They're landing a huge airplane on our field.

JOSÉ (shaking)

Who is?

JOSÉ DOS (rushing in)

What's going on? Are we leaving? I hear the plane's motors.

JORGE rushes out and looks at the plane as it stops. Its markings are USAF.

JORGE (excited)

Gentlemen, gentlemen, you won't believe it, it's Verner! Verner has arrived just in the nick of time, just like in the movies.

JOSÉ DOS (rushes over and sees SIDNEY step out as the door is opened)

Oh, no, it's that pecker snitcher! (watching) Oh, my God, he's brought an army with him. (They all rush over and see SIDNEY, cigar in mouth, directing about thirty gringos up the roadway. SIDNEY approaches the hacienda. (The GROUP panics.)

JORGE

Oh, my God, what are we to do?

JOSÉ DOS

This is terrible.

JOSÉ

It's the end!

JOSÉ DOS

He's coming over here. How does he know where we live? He doesn't. He doesn't know; he's coming over to ask if the plane can land, that 's all. Eva, come here. Eva, please answer the door and take care of them.

SIDNEY knocks; the door falls open of its own accord, the GROUP stands as if caught.

SIDNEY (looks at his watch)

Good morning. Well, look at that, it's almost twelve. Lady, gentlemen, may I be so humble and ask if I may use that flat expanse behind your hacienda as a landing field for our little plane? You see, we were to land in Corrientes when the pilot saw such an expanse and we thought it would be more convenient for all if we landed here. Strange, from the sky we did not see your hacienda or hangars. It would be great, just great if you gave us landing privileges. Oh, we're willing to pay the going rate for landing privileges, two hundred and twenty dollars at New York City, does that suit you gentlemen? I mean, we don't need fuel nor service. We have enough of both. That's a US Air Force plane! We're proud of her. (hands EVA the check) Well, I expect we'll see you at the show tonight. Good night and thanks. (he closes the door)

EVA (gushing)

Two hundred and twenty dollars just for landing! Gosh!

JOSÉ DOS (screaming at the closed door)

We will never perform for you! NEVER!

JORGE (yelling)

Yea, we're going to Miami Beach.

JOSÉ (looking out the window_

Hm-m, they parked on the far side; there's plenty of room for us to take off. Let's go.

JORGE (nervous)

I think we will have to wait till siesta time. The pilots are suspicious. Oh, oh, they're looking at the hangar. Oh, ooh, they're walking towards it. We have got to stop them. (JORGE runs outside in his pajamas and yells) Hi there, come over and have some coffee. My aide will go to the train depot and get a paper; come on in and relax.

The PILOTS come over smiling and waving.

JOSÉ

Eva, serve them all the cognac they can drink. I'll talk to them. Claudio, go to the train. Get some women and the newspapers. Quick!

JOSÉ (worried)

Do you think Sidney knew who we were?

JOSÉ DOS

No chance. He only saw us in drag. (looking out of the window) Those must be the newspaper people.

We see the group haggling with JOSH and the taxi driver. Loads of reporters are being shuttled off a few at a time. Another car is put into service. JOSH slices a wiggling figure through the group, as he helps with the luggage.

JOSÉ

Come on, let's load the planes.

They leave as the USAF PILOTS enter.

CLAUDIO (dressed)

Well, I'm off. (in the distance we hear the train whistle) Here comes the newspaper. Please entertain our guests while I'm away.

FIRST PILOT (smiling)

Sure is nice of you, ma'am, to be serving us coffee and cakes.

FLIGHT OFFICER (tasting the coffee)

M-m-m-m, cognac. (shakes head) Not in the morning, on duty.

CAPTAIN (shrugs)

We're not flying until tomorrow. (downs the coffee)

FLIGHT OFFICER

OK, sir. (drinks his)

JORGE immediately refreshes them.

CAPTAIN (salutes with his glass)

It was a long haul.

FLIGHT OFFICER

Yep. Say, what kind of cognac is this? Sure tastes good.

JORGE (smiling)

French, ten-year-old genuine cognac.

CAPTAIN (looking around)

Where do you get such good stuff in a hick place like this?

JORGE (smiling)

You would be surprised at what you find in backwaters.

CAPTAIN

May I have some more cognac, ma'am?

EVA (concerned)

Oh, you should have something to eat.

She comes back with a plate of thick bread. JORGE helps himself with a mean look at EVA. The PILOTS get what's left.

JORGE

Why don't you invite some of the other pilots over?

CAPTAIN

It's a good idea. If they're not sleeping; that is, if it won't put you out ma'am. (slurs)

EVA (gracious)

Why...

JORGE (cutting in)

Why, certainly.

FLIGHT OFFICER (sways out and waves at the plane. Heads appear, then the four crew members emerge and come over.)

The CREW enter and sit around the patio as EVA and JORGE serve them liberally with cognac, coffee and sweets. A party atmosphere prevails with CLAUDIO returns with the three-day-old paper and some of the town prostitutes, hastily collected from their beds. They are a bit angry and yawning. EVA gives them a cold look; then gives them coffee.

CLAUDIO (smiling)

Here's the latest newspaper from Rio, three days old, but if you can speak Spanish...

CAPTAIN (drunk)

Three days old? You forget, I come from New York City; this news is six days old, three to get to Rio and three to get here.

CAPTAIN picks up the paper and scans the headlines.

FLIGHT OFFICER (coming over, drunk)

Hey, I read Spanish. (takes the paper, announcing) "NAZI art collectors in Argentina! Hordes of priceless masterpieces in the back country, Corrientes – Herman Goering is said to be hiding.

CREW MEMBER

Ha, ha. If they saw this desolate area, they would laugh! How would it get here in he first place, by train? (kisses a girl)

ANOTHER

That's rich. All I hear in these parts are that there's a bunch of faggots planning to take over Broadway. Hey, ma'am, do you know the faggots?

EVA (placating)

Faggots?

CAPTAIN

You know, sexual deviates that wear women's clothes and cavort on the stage. Supposed to be a hot thing here.

EVA (looking at JORGE)

Well, I heard about them, but have never seen them.

JORGE (blushing)

Every town has their quota; just these seem better than other groups. In fact, the townspeople are downright proud of them.

CREW MEMBER (yawning)

Well, fellas, I'm heading back to the plane. After all that drink, I feel I could sleep for hours,

The other crew members, save the CAPTAIN, return to the plane after thanking EVA and JORGE.

CREW MEMBER 1

Thanks.

CREW MEMBER 2

Thanks.

CREW MEMBER 3

Thanks.

The CAPTAIN sits and stares out of the window at the hangar.

CAPTAIN

I just don't understand what a camouflaged hangar is doing in the middle of this backwater. Could you satisfy my curiosity, sir?

JORGE (offhand)

The original owner had it built. I guess it's been there for more than twenty years.

CAPTAIN (looking at the paper; then looking up puzzled)

It couldn't have, sir, they didn't make planes that big back then.

JORGE (offhandedly)

I don't know, never been inside. There used to be a large plantation here; maybe it was built for that. More cognac, Captain?

CAPTAIN (remembering)

No, no thanks, got to mosey on to the plane, get some sleep, sober up a bit. (He gets up and bends graciously to EVA, and salutes JORGE in a crisp military salute. JORGE instinctively gives him a Nazi salute.) I thought so! (CLAUDIO comes up behind him and slams him over the head, knocking him out.)

JORGE

Dammit! Quick, in here!

CLAUDIO and JORGE put the CAPTAIN in a guest bed and strap him down.

CLAUDIO (remembering)

A strange car with Oregon plates was seen in town this morning,

JORGE (surprised)

Oregon? Why that's headquarters for Commander Shizzer! They must've got wind of where we were.

CLAUDIO

They didn't get any information out of the townsfolk. They told them that no foreigners live here, and they left.

CLAUDIO (laughing)

They saw all those reporters and got nervous. Garbanzo says they will come back for the performance, though. But that 's ok, because we'll be gone by then...

JORGE

I hope so.

<u>39. INT.</u>   <u>HOTEL.</u>   <u>DAY</u>

CHESTER is talking to SIDNEY hurriedly.

CHESTER

When I phoned you and heard you came down here, I left immediately in a private plane. Taxi all the way over. Had to come and talk to the old man who auctioned off the paintings. Give him his check and tell him to beat it. He certainly touched off an international scandal.

SIDNEY (advising)

It'll blow over, I'm sure, Chester. Give it some time.

SIDNEY (serious)

I never felt more sure in my life as I do about this one. (smiling) What about you creating an international scandal right here also, ha ha. (thinking) Say, where was the Hacienda where you had your meeting? Just up the street? (pointing)

CHESTER

Yes, that's right.

SIDNEY (surprised)

It's them, it's them. I knew this morning, I knew those people from somewhere. It's them, no, no, it's confusing. What did they look like?

CHESTER

Well, there were two of them present. One, I think about sixty, I would say; the other could be his son, walked with a military bearing, and eager to please...

SIDNEY

That's one of them; the other, the sixty-year-old, did he look like one of the cast in MIO CAMPO? Think hard...

CHESTER

You know, Dermoth made a comparison with them both; yes, they could be brothers or sisters...or what?

SIDNEY (excited)

It's them. It's them.

CHESTER (confused)

What's them?

SIDNEY

They are the MIO CAMPO group. I should have known. Talent doesn't strike twice in the same breath. I'm sure of it. The MIO CAMPO group is the eccentric and his entourage.

CHESTER (surprised)

Jesus, you know you could be right. How many were there when you landed?

SIDNEY

Four men and a woman – a matronly type, German...This is getting too hairy for words...

CHESTER

What are you thinking?

SIDNEY

I'm thinking that your art collector, my MIO CAMPO group, and the Nazi hordes the press are screaming about, are tied together. Why would they have an airfield large enough to handle a Stratocruiser?

<u>40. EXT.   ROAD FROM CORRIENTES. DAY</u>

COMMANDER SHIZZER is driving. BREZIERS is at his side and GUNTER in a cage in the back of the "Woody."

SHIZZER (thinking)

It's all so puzzling: a huge U.S. Air Force plane lands with over thirty members of the world's press, art collectors, a transvestite dress rehearsal... it must mean something. Breziers. (Does a U-Turn with his car)

BREZIERS (thinking)

We will find out tonight at the theater in town.

GUNTER (barking very loud)

Woof, Woof, Woof!

SHIZZER

Maybe we're on to something. Gunter is getting excited.

BREZIERS

Step on it, Shizzer, and Heil Hitler.

SHIZZER

Heil Hitler.

41. INT.   HANGAR.   DAY

JOSÉ, JOSÉ DOS, JORGE, and CLAUDIO have just completed the loading of the B-17 and the glider. They are sweaty and tired.

JORGE

Well, I guess we'd better leave.

JOSH (emerging from the shadows with PACO and MARIA, all have guns) You cannot, you must perform tonight.

JOSÉ

What! Gott in himmel!

JOSH and his friends escort the FOUR to the house.

42. EXT.   JOSÉ'S HACIENDA   DAY

PACO (furious)

You said you would perform tonight, José, so you must keep your word.

JOSÉ (explaining)

Can't you see, Paco, that all those gringos want to take us away from you? Can't you see that?

PACO

We will defend you, get ready here. We will take you in the taxi.

JORGE (trying to explain)

But we are not ready; we haven't rehearsed; we will make fools of ourselves.

JOSH (laughing)

That's the whole charm of the show, handsome. (JOSH picks up JORGE's costume) Here, let me help you.

JORGE

God dammit, let's do it at the theater.

JOSÉ

No, let's do it here. Let me have my privacy, please. Let's do it here, then go knock 'em dead. Heil Hitler!

PACO

That's the spirit. We will sit here and keep watch.

43. INT.   POLICE STATION.   EVENING

SIDNEY (on phone)

I finally got through. Yes, look… I think your Nazis are here. I'm sure of it. You must hurry. (SHIZZER drives by; his severe bearing is a telltale sign of his militaryness). Jesus, I think I spotted another one. I'm getting spooked. Hurry… (Puts down the phone, pays, and goes out, down the street towards the hotel)

44. INT.   HOTEL   EVENING

SIDNEY enters the bar where a number of reporters are seated.

SIDNEY goes over where CHESTER is sitting by himself.

SIDNEY (whispering)

Chester, if we hurry, we can collect some art objects worth millions, far more than your commissions and my stake in this revue. Listen…I got an idea.

45. INT.   JOSÉ'S HACIENDA   EVENING

The GROUP are in drag, at attention and angry. PACO waits for JOSÉ to finish his inspection.

JOSÉ

At ease, gentlemen.

PACO

You all look so good. Shall we go?.

From the guest bedroom we hear noises. JOSH goes over and opens the door. We see the CAPTAIN tied up.

JORGE

He tried to take us away.

JOSÉ DOS

He's the captain of the big plane that arrived this morning.

PACO

Tie him tighter, Josh. (to the GROUP) Let's go, amigos.

GARBANZO (running in hastily)

The whole group is coming this way, all of them, waving cameras and guns, the gringos, with that fat little man with the cigar…

JOSÉ DOS (grabbing his crotch)

Oh, please don't let him get me.

PACO

What are we going to do?

JORGE (clever)

You got to protect us. They plan to take us away.

PACO starts shooting out of the window. The reporters start taking pictures, using flashbulbs that look like gunfire.

PACO

Get down, you guys, we'll take care of this.

The GROUP, in drag, duck down. JORGE winks, mouthing, "Follow me." He creeps along the floor and opens a trap door under the table. They all sneak through before they are missed.

46. INT.   BASEMENT   EVENING

They run through a dark passageway and stop at a lighted room. In it, JOSÉ picks up a stack of old 78 rpm records and carries them carefully.

JOSÉ DOS

Hurry!

JOSÉ (reverently)

This is my complete collection of Glenn Miller.

47. INT.   HANGAR.   EVENING

The GROUP emerges and immediately gets in to the B-17...JOSÉ takes the Miller records to the Glider and puts them in. Gunfire is heard from the Hacienda.

CLAUDIO opens the hangar door as JOSÉ DOS starts the engines; first one, then the other, until all four are roaring. The vibration is terrific; the whole hangar rattles. The plane moves slowly forward.

48. EXT.   HACIENDA   EVENING

SIDNEY

I hear an airplane. But... they couldn't have come so soon.

CHESTER

Who?

SIDNEY

The Jewish Nazi squad. I called them, but I thought we would have ample time.

CHESTER

Hey, the firing's stopped in the house. Something's up.

HOUNDSTOOTH

In the name of show biz, rush that Hacienda.

Cameras flash as he stands in his heroic stance. Camera flashbulbs go off everywhere.

49. INT.   JOSÉ'S HACIENDA   EVENING

PACO (looking for GROUP)

I don't know where they went.

GARBANZO (spies the trap door, now clearly visible by the pushed aside rug; he opens it.) Down here.

They all rush down.

BEAT.

The door slams open as cameramen flash their cameras at everything that moves. Aside from a few bullet holes, there is a sinister pounding noise heard from the guest bedroom. SIDNEY opens it.

SIDNEY

Captain! (He loosens the rag around his mouth)

CAPTAIN

Hurry, I hear their plane. It's a B-17 by the sound of it; hurry, untie me.

SIDNEY (to reporters)

To the airfield, to the airfield.

The REPORTERS and HOUNDSTOOTH run out of the house.

SIDNEY (to CAPTAIN)

Just a minute, Captain.

CAPTAIN (trying to free himself)

Untie me, you bastard! They're getting away. The Nazi swine is getting away!

CHESTER and SIDNEY (after giving the Captain a knife) rush out and search the now-empty house for art treasures. Nothing is found. Gunshots are heard outside; the howl of the B-17 is louder. In the last room, they spy – forgotten in a corner – three Picasso clown paintings. They smile at each other and run out of the house in the opposite direction to the action, carrying the paintings.

50. EXT.   AIRFIELD   NIGHT

The B-17 roars down the airfield, being eerily lit up by many flashes from cameras, an occasional small bore bullet enters the fuselage, but does no damage. It passes the Stratocruiser as the startled crew members stare at it gathering speed. Behind it, the CAPTAIN races to the Stratocruiser.

51. EXT.   TOWN STREET   EVENING

SHIZZER and BREZIERS are getting out of their car in front of the theater. The theater is open but empty. People are running down the street to JOSÉ's Hacienda. They hear gunfire and immediately follow the crowd. They take GUNTER out of the car and he immediately 'points' like a dog in the direction of the gunfire.

GUNTER (excited)

Woof! Woof! Woof!

52. EXT.   JOSÉ'S AIRFIELD.   EVENING

As the B-17 takes off, we see another plane about to land. It's a B-47 Stratojet. It roars out of the sky to land, just missing the B-17 and swerves to miss the Stratocruiser. The jet stops at the end of the field as SIDNEY, CHESTER and HOUNDSTOOTH, with their three paintings, are trying to avoid the crowd of peasants.

ISRAELI NAZI HUNTER (emerging from the B-47 jet)

HALT! In the name of international law.

SIDNEY (hiding behind the painting)

No, no, you have got the wrong ones. (Speaks in rapid Yiddish) They are in the B-17 that just left – Hitler, Goering and Goebbels. I swear!

ISRAELI (shocked)

Are you putting me on?

From around the bushes emerge SHIZZER and BREZIERS. They see only the clown paintings in the glare.

SHIZZER

Herr Hitler, is that you?

ISRAELI (surprised)

Hitler speaks Yiddish?

SIDNEY

Goddammit, put those bright lights off, so we can talk about it. You're losing valuable time!

ISRAELI (spying SHIZZER)

Commander Shizzer, at last we have found you. Come out with your hands up!

SHIZZER (pulls out his luger and shoots at the Israeli, but misses. The B-47's turret swivels and slams bullets into SHIZZER and BREZIERS as SIDNEY, HOUNDSTOOTH and CHESTER hide behind their artworks. The shooting stops.) As GUNTER leaps out onto the field, he attacks one of the B-47's wheels.

ISRAELI (to SIDNEY)

What the hell kind of dog is that?... why it's a Nazi dog!

The B-47 rolls forward, crushing GUNTER.

ISRAELI

All right now, come on out, you cowards. (The gun turret swivels menacingly towards them. SIDNEY, HOUNDSTOOTH, and CHESTER emerge) You sure don't look like Hitler... (squinting at SIDNEY) None of you do. (Scratches his head)

SIDNEY

If you would be so kind as to follow that B-17, you will find Hitler, Goering, Goebbels and company. (He speaks in Yiddish)

Behind them, the Stratocruiser is taxiing over. In front of them, the reporters are coming up and behind <u>them</u>, the townspeople are attacking.

SIDNEY

Really, officer, this is all very embarrassing.

ISRAELI

What the hell is going on? (He looks at the advancing reporters rushing to the

Stratocruiser. The B-47 gun turret swivels toward them menacingly. The townspeople chase them. SIDNEY, HOUNDSTOOTH and CHESTER hide behind their clown paintings and sneak off as the Israeli agents follow the movement of the townspeople and the photo-flashing cameramen.)

Hey, where did those three clowns go?

<u>53. EXT.   TOWN STREET   NIGHT</u>

THE THREE run down the street with their paintings, and spy the Oregon-plated Ford "Woody" station wagon.

SIDNEY

There, that's their car. Get in.

They get in and rush off with their booty.

<u>54. EXT.   JOSÉ'S AIRFIELD   EVENING</u>

The B-47 taxis over to the C –97, and they speak to each other via loudspeaker as the townspeople shoot at them ineffectually with their small-bore weapons.

B-47

A crazy little New Yorker says Hitler, Goebbels and Goering took off in the B-17 that's towing a glider.

C-97

It's true. You'd better intercept him. You're faster.

B-47

I can't believe it – after all these years.

C-97

I overheard that they were going to get a missile from Werner.

B-47

A missile from Werner… Werner Von Braun? Jesus H Christ, let's move!

C-97

I'll take a due north tack to Miami Beach where Werner lives. You head up the eastern seaboard.

B-47

Out, right on, follow me.

The B-47 taxis out, then roars off, followed by the C-97. On the ground, the TOWNSPEOPLE are dejected.

JOSH

I knew I should've joined the group when I had the chance.

PACO

They will take the phone away for sure...

MARIA

Where will I find work to support my ten kids...

JOSH (crying)

It seems all a dream, they're gone.

PACO

No more music, gaiety, laughter...no more telephone.

The Oregon-plated "Woody" pulls up, the door opens and SIDNEY steps out.

SIDNEY (takes cigar out of his mouth, blowing smoke)

Townspeople, ladies, gentlemen... let me tell you something. That was great, just great, the way you handled those guns, the way you destroyed those Nazis here (pointing down to SHIZZER and GUNTER). Let me tell you, it's just great... now look, if we all pull up our shoes and pitch in, we can turn this town into a paradise of a tourist resort. HITLER'S HACIENDA, starring JOSH, the rolling tourist guide. I can see it now... Oh, oh don't thank me, thank Houndstooth here, he thought of it. (HOUNDSTOOTH emerges; they all clap) Look, we'll be back to fill out the details....

PACO

It's all great, but we'd rather have the MIO CAMPO back.

SIDNEY

Sorry, sir, but by now they have probably been blasted out of the sky to the Great Unknown.

JOSH

Oh, my poor Jorge.

55. INT.   B-17.   NIGHT

JORGE (at controls, goggles over his mascaraed eyes, wig askew, yelling)

Give me a bearing, give me a bearing, Jo...

CUT TO CLAUDIO, checking a map, trying to work a sextant.

CLAUDIO (sweating)

Been years... Got a bearing seven degrees east...

CUT TO JOSÉ and JOSÉ DOS as he checks out the cable to the glider.

JOSÉ

That's our future hanging out there. (He pats the taut cable)

JOSÉ DOS (intense)

I hope Werner will be there. (picks up *TIME* report) It says the villa is located at the north end of Miami Beach.

EVA (coming up with hot coffee and another sandwich)

Why don't you guys take off all those women's clothes; you'll scare hell out of him when we get there. (Eating, looking out at the glider flying in the breeze) You know, when we get there I can get a whole new wardrobe. I hear the fashion in Miami Beach is fantastic, and all those hotels with famous entertainers – Sammy Davis Junior, I adore Sammy… and Frank Sinatra…

JOSÉ (staring past the glider)

What's that? (He points at the B-47 as it roars by)

Help, help! (in megaphone to JORGE) There is a huge airplane on our left. Pour on the steam; it's the one from Corrientes.

CUT TO JORGE

JORGE (accelerating the engines)

Full power coming up. If we didn't have that damn glider…

There is a loud snap as the B-17 lurches forward.

JORGE

Hey, what the hell.

VO.   HITLER (on phone)

The cable broke, the cable broke…

Cut to tail of the B-17. We see the glider slowly falling away from the B-17. JOSÉ DOS is leaning way out over the glass gun turret. JOSÉ DOS falls through the hold, but hangs on to a piece of metal as the B-47 shoots a warning shot at the old B-17, shattering the gun turret. JOSÉ and EVA grab his arm, trying to haul him up.

JOSÉ (over his shoulder)

Claudio, get a fix on where that glider lands.

CLAUDIO (over the mic)

Yes, sir.

56. EXT.   CARIBBEAN.   EARLY MORNING

The B-17 is flying high up, circling the glider as it gently glides to the ocean surface.

VO.   JOSÉ

It's landing, get a fix, get a fix, Claudio. It's floating.

57. INT.   B-17.   EARLY MORNING

EVA and JOSÉ hug each other, laughing, forgetting JOSÉ DOS for a moment, who falls.

58. EXT.   B-17.   EARLY MORNING

JOSÉ DOS falls with a scream, directly on top of the glider, instantly sinking it.

The B-47 roars by.

CAPTAIN OF B-47 VO. OVER INTERCOM

This is B-47, USAF. B-17 , you are under arrest. You must fly to the nearest airport and give yourself up [surrender].

VO.   JOSÉ

My art, oh where is my art? …

VO.   CLAUDIO (busy)

Here's the fix.

VO.   JORGE

Hey, what's going on? The instruments are going haywire. Everything's getting foggy…

VO.   CAPTAIN OF B-47   (confused)

Hey, where is all that fog coming from?

VO.   EVA

How sad… such fine art…

VO.   JOSÉ (raving)

We will get to Miami Beach, we will continue the struggle, we will retrieve the art…

VO.   JORGE

I don't understand it, the instruments are going wild. I can't see anything. Help!

VO.   CAPTAIN OF B-47

Gunners, they're fading; blast them! Must be a Nazi secret weapon.

VO.   CLAUDIO (confused)

Honest, sir, the last reading was just over Florida, due south of Bermuda…

VO.   JOSÉ

Turn the radio dial.

VO.   RADIO

(song) Bermuda, Bermuda, Bermuda shorts… (turns the radio dial) Another mysterious loss in the Bermuda Triangle…

VO.   CAPTAIN OF B-47

Where the hell did they go?

VO.   HITLER

Nothing will stop us…nothing.

VO.   RADIO

The song Glenn Miller's "Toast of Vienna"
FADE
FADE OUT

The End

Epilogue

At rainbows end lies a pot of Gold
Never reached so never soiled
Rainbows exist where dark cloud form
sheets of rain that blot out the sun.
That blot out the sun.

For some the storm is short, for others it is long
For me forever will I see the sun
will I see the sun.

Los Angeles 1967

Michael Yaeger was born in Washington, D.C. and presently lives in the Seattle area, a ferry boat ride away in Poulsbo. His studio is on Bainbridge Island.

Printed in the United States
30036LVS00005B/145-249

9 781418 491581